VICE

CALLIE HART

Formatting by Max Effect
www.formaxeffect.com

PROLOGUE
THEN

"**A**re you *kidding* me? You're the one up here, finger fucking some twenty-one-year-old, and you're giving *me* shit?"

These are not words I ever expected to hear coming out of my sister's mouth, and yet as I climb the stairs of the Aubertin mansion, on the hunt for her and my best friend, Jamie, these are the words I hear.

Jamie speaks, his voice thick with amusement. "What's wrong? You never been caught in flagrante before, Laura Preston? Never been caught with your panties down?"

Oh, boy. The ball Jamie's father is hosting downstairs is in full swing, his guests chattering and laughing loudly like the rich, over-fed, over-stuffed hyenas that they are, so they can't hear the conversation taking place in one of the guest rooms on the second floor. I can, though, and it sounds like the shit has just hit the fan. I creep along the hallway, hugging the wall, not making a sound as I approach the open bedroom door. Lore and Jamie stand on opposite ends of the room, Jamie's hair tousled all over the place, the top button of his shirt undone, Laura's cheeks bright red, her brow creased in anger.

"*No!*" she cries. I nearly burst out laughing when she stoops down, snatches one of her golden pumps from her feet and launches it across the room at Jamie's head. She misses the first time, so she yanks off her other shoe and hurls that, too. This time she hits the huge mirror hanging on the wall behind Jamie's head, and the thing shatters into a million pieces.

"What the fuck, Laura?" Jamie yells.

Jesus wept. I have no idea what they're fighting about, but they need to calm the fuck down. I should go in there. I should knock on the door or something so they know I'm here.

"*You*! I can't—" Laura covers her mouth with her hand, and even from here I can see her eyes are wet with tears. "I can't fucking believe you," she says softly.

Jamie's outrage at the smashed mirror melts away as concern overtakes his features. "Hey. *Hey*. I'm really fucking confused. Do you want to tell me what's going on, or should I go and get Cade?"

My sister looks like she's about to explode. "Don't you dare go and get fucking Cade. You and Cade, joined at the hip, twenty-four-fucking-seven. You and Cade, vanishing off to fucking Afghanistan, leaving me here on my own. I waited here for you for four goddamn years, Jamie. Four years of waking up in a cold sweat every single night, wondering which one of you was going to die first. And then you come home and hardly even...hardly even look at me, and..."

What? No. No way. I must be imagining things right now—the way Laura looks like her heart has just been crushed. The way she's looking at Jamie like it would all be okay if only he took her in his arms and kissed her. How did I not see this before? She has feelings for him? It seems impossible. My sister is many things: stubborn; self confident; beautiful; fiery as all hell. I never thought she was *stupid*, though. Falling in love with Jamie must be pretty similar to falling off the top of the Empire State Building. The whole way down, you're praying you're going to survive the experience, but in your head you know you're gonna be fucking destroyed by the impact. Jamie doesn't date girls. Jamie doesn't fall in love with them. He has sex with them, and then he leaves them. In fairness, it's not as if he ever lies to them. They know what to expect from him from the very beginning, he's honest to a fault. Laura's seen him screw so many girls and then never call them again, so why the fuck would she be dumb enough to develop feelings for the guy? Jamie looks pained, like he's pondering the same question.

"Laura..." He reaches out, trying to tuck a curl of her shockingly bright blonde hair back behind her ear, but she shies away from his touch.

"No. Don't! Fuck, Jamie, you just had your fingers inside some girl's vagina."

Ouch.

Jamie tenses, clearly not knowing what to do. "Lore, is there something you want to tell me?"

"Fuck you, Jamie. I shouldn't have to tell you. You should already know! Ahh! Men! Why are you all so fucking oblivious? How can you be that completely blind to what's been staring you in the face since we were kids, Jay? I just...I gotta get out of here."

Shit. I was about to knock, to put an end to this train wreck, but now it's too late. Laura's heading for the doorway, and I'm about to be busted eavesdropping. Quickly, I open the door next to me, slipping silently into another of Jamie's father's bland, soulless guest bedrooms, drawing the door almost closed behind me. Almost. I can still see into the hallway through the inch-wide crack. Laura storms into view, and the gold sequins from her dress cast fragments of golden light over the walls and the ceiling like scattering fireflies. Jamie's only a second behind her. He grabs her by the wrist, and her face is a mask of pure rage as she spins around and slaps him. Damn. That looked like it hurt. Jamie jerks back, releasing his hold on her.

"*Shit.*" Lore covers her face with her hands. "Shit, I'm so sorry. I just..."

Jamie shakes his head. "It's okay."

"I just can't—"

"*It's okay,*" Jamie repeats. "It's fine. We can talk about it tomorrow."

She's crying. Laura and I are always at each other's throats, but at the same time we're close. She's my sister. My only sister. Seeing her upset is like a knife in the gut. For a second, I want to knock Jamie the fuck out. It's not his fault, though. I know that. Laura's been hanging around with us since we were kids. He thinks of her as a sister, just as I think of him as a brother. Hitting him would be fucking pointless.

3

Laura nods. She wipes a tear away with the back of her hand and sniffs. "Tomorrow." She turns and hightails it, racing down the stairs before he can stop her. Jamie stands there, watching her go, his hands on his hips, frozen like he can't believe what's just happened. He bows his head, sighing, and then slowly goes down the stairs, leaving me staring at an empty hallway.

I find Laura around the back of the house, leaning against the crumbling brick wall of an old outhouse, where Jamie's grandfather used to store cattle feed back when the mansion wasn't just a mansion but the main house of a huge farming estate. Jamie and I always used to hide from her here when we were younger, climbing up into the rafters of the outhouse, lying as still as we possibly could while she shouted at us and called us names below. Now, she's smoking a cigarette, eyes still swollen from her tears, her mascara streaked halfway down her face.

"Your hands are shaking," I tell her.

She nearly jumps out of her skin. "Jesus, you nearly scared me half to death, Cade Preston."

I hold out my hand and she passes me the cigarette. Taking a deep drag, I close my eyes as my head starts to spin. Been years since I smoked. I didn't even smoke when I was deployed. Leaning back against the wall with her, I nudge her with my shoulder, passing back the Marlboro.

"Wanna talk about it?"

She glances at me out of the corner of her eye. "*No.*"

"Okay."

She takes another drag, and then another. We stand in silence, both looking up at the stars, listening to the soft strains of music over-flowing out of the back door. "All right, then," she says after a while. "I don't *like* feeling this way. I don't *want* to feel this way."

I put my arm around her, drawing her to my side. "I know."

"I mean, who would? No one in their right minds, that's for sure. He's Louis James Aubertin the third, for fuck's sake." She flicks the butt of her cigarette away, and the ember of the cherry flares in the darkness before it disappears into the long grass a few feet away.

"What does that mean?"

Laura lets out a frustrated sigh. "He's just...*more* than everyone else. He doesn't even know it, and yet he is. He can have any girl he wants. He *does* have any girl he wants. Regularly. He's an asshole."

"Then why are you out here, beating yourself up over him?"

"Because...I don't know. I always thought he was going to be *my* asshole, y'know. Ever since we were kids. It just seemed as though it was always going to be us, the three of us, together."

I don't know what to say to that. I suppose, in a way, I figured that in the back of my mind, too. Or maybe I just never really considered that Lore might end up getting married to some guy I don't know, and that Jamie would carry on being Jamie.

We're silent again. She gets another cigarette out of the pack in her purse, and we share the whole thing this time, passing it back and forth between us.

"It doesn't help that he looks the way he does," she says eventually.

I let out a bark of laughter. "I can mess his face up if you like."

"Yeah," she says, leaning her head against my shoulder. "That would actually be really great, thanks. If he looks like a hideous, disfigured monster, I won't be in love with him anymore."

It rattles me to hear her say that—that she *loves* him. I sigh sadly, planting a kiss on the top of her head. "You think so, huh?"

She answers almost immediately. "No. Not really. I think it wouldn't matter what the fuck he looked like. I'd be in love with him all the same."

I hug her, my heart aching for her. "You know that old saying?" I ask.

"If you tell me time is a great healer, I'm gonna kick you in the balls."

Laughing, I shake my head. "No, not that one."

"If you're going through hell, keep on going?"

"Oooh, Churchill. *Nice*. But, no. Not that one, either."

"What, then?"

I clear my throat, trying to give my words some gravitas. "*I hope you step on a Lego, you arrogant motherfucker.*"

She bursts into laughter, digging me in the side with her elbow. "Yeah, I *do* know that one."

"Well, you're my sister, and I love you. So I'll start putting Lego in his shoes for you. It's the least I can do."

"The *very* least," she agrees, nodding. And then, softly, "Thank you, Cade."

"You are more than welcome. You wanna go back inside?"

"No. I think I'm gonna go home. This party is fucking *terrible.*"

"God, I know. Isn't it?"

••••

Next morning, I go into Laura's room and her bed hasn't been slept in. Not even a wrinkle marks the sheets. Downstairs, Mom and Dad are at breakfast, silently hating each other from across the table, as is their custom. I sit down, helping myself to coffee. "I didn't know Laura left already. I thought she was going to hang around here for a couple of days before she headed back to the firm?" She's just been made partner at Dad's law practice. While her work ethic is intense, she did promise to stay home for a little while, though. We haven't seen each other in a long time, after all, since she's been away at college, and I've been on the other side of the world, dealing with insurgents.

My father looks up from his newspaper. "Her car's still in the garage. She must have gone out for a run or something."

I keep my doubts to myself. She wouldn't have made her bed if she'd gotten up to run so early. And Laura *hates* running.

Hours pass, and still there's no Laura.

I have a sick, sinking feeling in the pit of my stomach. I don't know why, but I can't get the feeling out of my head that something bad has happened. Something fucking awful. I never should have let her walk home on her own last night. You can see our place from the Aubertin mansion, though. It's literally a stone's throw. She's run across the back field and slipped through the small gate in our fence line a thousand times before without any trouble. Why should last night have been any different?

"If she doesn't hurry up and get back soon, I'm going to miss my bridge game over at the O'Brien's house," my mother complains. "She promised she'd drive me so I could have a glass of wine."

"Fuck, Mom. If a glass of Chardonnay is so important to you, I can drive you over there," I snap. "Damn it, I'm going out to look for her."

"You are being ridiculous," Mom says in a sing-song voice. She kisses me on the temple. "Thank you, though. I really would appreciate the ride."

I leave the house, slamming the door behind me. *Fucking unbelievable.* They really are callous bastards. I walk slowly through the gardens, my eyes sharp, looking for anything suspicious. My parents' place is nowhere near as big or grand as the Aubertin mansion, but the grounds are still considerable. It takes me fifteen minutes to reach the tiny, hidden gate at the perimeter of the property, and I still haven't seen anything that might give me an idea where Laura is.

Down the hill I go, over the massive back field Jamie and I used to run riot through as children. My cell phone buzzes in my pocket. I get it out, and the man himself is calling me, the name 'Duke' flashing up on the screen. He hated the nickname he was given by our unit back in Afghanistan. He used to tease the shit out of me over the fact that he was ranked higher than me, though, so storing him in my contacts as Duke was just fair turnaround.

"Hey, man," I answer, distracted, my eyes still scanning the land around me.

"Hey. I'm up on the roof. I can see you." Jamie's always loved hanging out on the roof outside his bedroom window. I look up, and sure enough there he is, a centimeter tall, sitting with his legs dangling over the guttering of the small, flat platform. "Listen. Shit, dude, I don't even know how to say this," he begins. "I have something to tell you. About Laura. I think I fucked up last night."

"I know. I saw the whole thing."

He groans. "Fuck. You did?"

"Yep. It was like watching the Apollo mission explode midair."

"Damn. Is she okay?"

"I don't know. I can't actually find her. She seemed all right when she left to go home last night, though."

Jamie goes quiet.

"Don't worry, man. I'm sure she'll get over it."

"Yeah, I hope so. Hey, stop a second."

"Sorry?"

"Stop walking. Check your three o'clock. There's something weird in the grass there. About fifteen feet away."

I pivot, turning to my right, scanning the tall grass. I can't see anything. Still holding the phone to the side of my head, I begin to walk. I see what he's talking about after a few long strides, and my stomach falls through the floor. I freeze, not wanting to go any further.

"What is it?" Jamie asks. "It's shiny. I can see something bright refracting the light over there."

"It's sequins," I answer numbly. "Gold sequins."

For a minute, it feels like the entire world is standing still. Jamie says something, but I don't hear him. I'm looking at the bundle of clothes wadded up in the grass. At the small patch of dark soil, that looks suspiciously like it's stained with blood. His words reach me finally, echoing inside my head.

"Don't move, Cade. Don't fucking move. I'll be right there."

The line goes dead.

I can't wait for him to find out what this is, though. I move slowly, dread sinking deep into my bones. It's not a body, thank fuck. Carefully using the toe of my sneaker to disturb the pile of material on the ground, panic shoots through me like a series of lightning bolts.

It's her dress.

It's her purse.

And worse...

It's her bra.

It's her panties.

And every single item of clothing looks as though it's been cut with a knife.

ONE

NOW
A JOURNEY

Dirt. Dirt everywhere. Dirt for days and motherfucking days, working its way into my helmet, getting in my eyes, into my ears, making my nostrils burn. Seriously. So much fucking dirt. The sound of my brand new Yamaha scrambler snarling as the tires eat up the road beneath me. The universal smell of Subway foot-longs, gas station toilets, and leaking oil filters as I pass through small town after small town, trying not to notice the gaunt, starved-looking locals and countless shot-up signs, riddled with bullet holes. The language starts in English, quickly turning to Spanish when I cross the border. The gun holes get bigger.

Three Rivers welcomes you!

You are now leaving Boles Acres.

Richardsville! Home of the King's Cubs football team.

Truth or Consequences, population 6246.

Bienvenido a Atascaderos

La ciudad jardín de Santa María de los pobres!

I don't even stop in these ghost towns to sleep. At night, I pull off the side of the road and disappear into the desert, until the only visible lights I can see are from the stars overhead. My tent is enough. I carry everything I need on my back. Occasionally, I'll stop and grab a six-pack from a liquor store before I head out into the back of the beyond for the night. I sip each bottle slowly, thinking over everything that's happened in the last seven years.

Life got real fucking weird, real fucking fast. It hits me sometimes, how strange things are now. I don't even recognize myself anymore. I was meant to become a lawyer. Instead, I've gone from being a respected twenty-six-year-old war veteran with a bachelor's degree to the vice president of a motorcycle club. It's even weirder still that my best friend, Jamie, or Rebel, as he's now called, is the president of the same club. Then again, maybe it's actually *not* that strange. Our fates have been joined for so long now, that I never even questioned if he would disappear down this rabbit hole with me, on my search for my missing sister.

Name a law, and we've broken it.

Name a moral line, and we've crossed it.

Name a country, and we've been there.

We never meant to start the club. The Widow Makers MC was an accident, a by-product of our search for Laura. We needed a hacker, so we found Danny. We needed someone who was good with ordnance and heavy machinery, so we found Keeler. We needed someone who could fly a plane, so we scraped Carnie out of the dirt and took him home with us. Twenty-three people, both men and women, joined us over time, and none of them ever left again. Motorcycles were quick and efficient for getting in and out of sticky situations, and the cops were suspicious of so many social outcasts and ex-cons with criminal records living in the middle of nowhere out in the desert of New Mexico, so we formed the club as a front. And then we actually became one. Our genesis story is a bizarre one, and we keep it to ourselves. It's better for us if the other clubs, cartel leaders and mafia bosses we run with think we're simply out to make money and hoard power as they are. But in truth, we're still looking for my sister. We haven't given up.

Every night, I stare at a photo on the screen of my cell phone until my eyes feel like they've been scrubbed with sandpaper.

Laura.

My sister, crying as she stares down the lens of a camera, a leather-gloved hand wrapped around her throat. I was half dead when Jamie showed me this image. Over seven years of searching and then, out of the blue, some asshole motherfucking cartel boss uses it as collateral in a hotel deal gone wrong. I wasn't there, I had had both my legs broken and was lying in a pool of my own blood, but Jamie told me everything he'd discovered: that Julio Perez, a Mexican cartel boss we're well acquainted with, knew where my sister was. That he possibly had something to do with her disappearance. It took me three months to heal and recover from my ass kicking well enough to ride a motorcycle, but now that I'm fit and able, I'm going to find my sister. Even if it fucking kills me, I am *going* to find her.

Perez has run for what he considers safe ground, back to Mexico with his tail between his legs. He thinks the Widow Makers won't follow him there, that it would be too dangerous for a group of twenty guys on motorcycles to go hunting for him. And he was right. It *is* too dangerous for the whole club to go chasing him across Mexico. Me, on the other hand? One guy on a scrambler, sticking to the back roads and keeping my head down? That's safe enough. I plan on finding the piece of shit and hurting him until he gives me the information I need. Hence the gruelling slog from New Mexico to El Cascarero. Hence the crick in my back and the ache in my poorly knitted together bones. Hence the cold, black, murderous urge in my heart, and the single point of focus on my mind.

After five days of riding non-stop, I finally draw close to my destination. El Cascarero is a small enough place; Julio's family live twenty or thirty miles out of the town, on a peach farm of all places. Turns out Perez peaches are quite famous around these parts. I see signs for them for hours before I eventually arrive at the mouth of the dusty, worn single-track road that leads to the farm itself. I squint into the distance, straining to make out the layout of the buildings beyond. Four trucks parked outside the main house—trucks so beaten, rusted, scraped and scratched up that it'll be a miracle if any of them run. Still. Four trucks. Could mean a lot of people. I lose my helmet. The scrambler is hardly inconspicuous, so I kill the engine and climb off it, wheeling it away from the road and laying it down flat to the ground beside a lone Ahuehuete tree. Looks like a swing used to hang from one of the sturdy, thick boughs overhead, but now a snapped and tattered length of rope is all that remains.

The long grass, sprouting almost to my knees, should hide the bike well enough. I shuck the bag from my back and dump it at my feet, opening the zip to check I have everything I'll be needing:

One roll of duct tape.

One pair of pliers.

One thick black garbage bag.

One meter length of fine chain.

One small handsaw.

One small container of lighter fluid.

One box of matches.

I hadn't been able to cross over into Mexico with the items I was scanning through, now. I had to buy them at a hardware store in Río Bailando, but that was easy enough. The weight of the gun I also procured down a seedy back alley in Juarez presses reassuringly into the small of my back. I don't need to check on that. It's fully locked and loaded—I already tested it out in the desert. It's good to have a weapon, but in this instance it's a last resort. I'll only draw the gun if every other tactic I plan on employing fails. By that point, Julio will be a bloody, broken mess, and I'll simply be putting him down. He won't die quickly, though. A shot in the stomach means he'll have plenty of time to reflect on his shitty, worthless life as he dies in agony over a period of days, and I'll be long gone. Hopefully with Laura on the back of my bike.

Tiny sand flies swirl up from the damp grass as I hunker down and run quickly toward what looks like the main building. I swat at them with my hand as I hurry. Takes a long time to reach the perimeter of the building, though I'm sure I am unnoticed. White paint peels from the window frames of the crumbling two-story building. Inside, the sound of a rowdy game show blasts from low quality speakers.

Laughter. Applause. Someone speaking in Spanish, in that game-show-host voice that seems to translate across any number of languages. I crouch down below an open window to the front of the house, listening. How many people are inside this damn room? If I had the time, I'd sit in the grass and watch the comings and goings of the people arriving and leaving the house, but time is something I've run out of. Or rather I've run out of patience. I've already had to wait three months. Holding off for another hour is unacceptable. Another minute. Another second. I just can't.

Inside the house, a chair leg scrapes on the floor, followed by someone coughing loudly, and then clearing their throat. A woman doesn't clear her throat like that. No way. So there's at least one male in the room. Loitering below the window, waiting to see how many people cough, sneeze or fart, will drive me crazy, though, so I do something reckless. Something we're trained never to do in the military. I edge up, standing just enough so that I can peer over the splintered, sun-worn windowsill, and I take a look.

Four men, all over the age of thirty, as far as I can tell. One of them's asleep, the back of his head resting against the sofa behind him, mouth hanging open as he snores lightly. Another of the guys is bent over a low coffee table, plastic card in his hand, finely chopping up what looks like an obscene amount of cocaine. The other two men are fixated on the television, watching the redundant antics of the show's host as he bounces around, shoving a microphone into a stunned woman's face.

None of them see me.

None of them are Julio Perez, either, which makes my life that little bit more difficult. Where the fuck is he? Kitchen? Is there a downstairs dining room? I haven't had time to assess the footprint of the building, but the place is pretty big. I wouldn't be surprised if there are bedrooms on the lower level of the house. Either that, or Julio's family is much, much bigger than I anticipated. The game show cuts to a commercial break, and one of the men groans as he heaves his ass of the couch.

¿Alguien quiere una cerveza? *Does anyone want a beer?* It's only eleven thirty in the morning. If these guys are relaxed enough to start their day drinking so early, then they must have grown complacent. They're not waiting for anybody to storm the building. They're just enjoying their downtime. Do any of them have guns? I can't see a single handgun or a rifle within arm's reach of these assholes, so it's unlikely that they're even armed. Things are never as they seem in these circumstances, though. I've been involved in enough sieges and attacks on people's property to know there's always *one* guy ready and willing to throw down. Always one dude with a gun jammed down the back of his pants, just like me, complete with itchy trigger finger.

I duck back down again, continuing around the side of the house, counting under my breath.

Eight, nine, ten, eleven, twelve...

I reach a much smaller open window on the western facing side of the property, and I do the same thing—squat low on my haunches, thumbs looped underneath the shoulder straps of my backpack, holding my breath. My pulse thumps in my ears, but it's slow and steady. I've been in this situation too many times to count over the past ten years. The fear wears off after a while, replaced with a strange, flat kind of calm that eventually becomes a part of you. I suppose it's an acceptance of fate. I might die in the next fifteen minutes. I might not. Either way, I won't be sorry that I did what I had to do.

¿Dónde está Javier?

No lo sé.

Encontrarlo. Tenemos que irnos pronto.

Two men inside, talking about finding a third, Javier. Talking about moving soon. I can't be sure if the guy throwing around orders was Julio or not, but it could have been. I risk a quick peek into the room, but when I look over the sill, the small kitchen inside is empty, the door slowly swinging closed behind someone who has already left.

"*Fuck.*" I keep going around the house. The next few windows are all closed, blinds pulled down. I move round to the back of the property, and a low, rumbling snarl stops me in my tracks. A brindle pit bull, jowls pulled back, baring his teeth, is staring straight at me.

He's chained, but from the links of steel pooled at his feet it looks like he's been given a lot of leeway. He can definitely reach me, only four feet away from him. I lock eyes with him, clenching my jaw, pressing my lips together. Sometimes simply refusing to back down from a dog is enough to make them submit. Even as I attempt to stare him down, I already know this isn't that kind of dog, though. He snarls louder, taking a step forward, and I slowly reach into the pocket of my leather jacket, groping with my fingers until I find what I'm looking for—a small, four inch balisong butterfly knife. Cold hard steel, sharper than sharp and ready for action. I yank it from my pocket just in time. He leaps, and I flick the knife open, the blade snaking out and landing with a sickening wet sound, sliding past the dog's ribcage, puncturing his lung. He barks madly, hackles raised, claws tearing into the hard packed dirt beneath us as he lunges for me again. The wound only seems to have riled him up even more.

Someone slams a door inside the farmhouse, swearing loudly, but no one comes outside to see what's going on. Lucky. Really fucking lucky.

The dog's jaws close around my forearm, and he begins to jerk his head from side to side, growling furiously. Pain rips into me. My forearm feels like it's going to snap under the pressure. Thankfully my leather jacket is stopping his teeth from tearing into my skin, but if he carries on for much longer he's gonna be breaking bones.

I punch him in the side of the head, but he doesn't let go. I fall back onto my ass in the dirt, grinding my teeth together as he tries to climb on top of me, probably hoping to go for my throat.

I don't have a choice. I take the balisong and I drive the honed edge of the blade into his body, over and over again. He yelps, and then whimpers as he finally releases my arm. I have blood all over me, my shirt and jeans are covered in it, red and warm and sticky, reeking of copper. A twinge of guilt snaps inside me as he staggers and falls onto his side, chest rising and falling too quickly. His eyes roll, whites showing, as he watches me get to my feet.

Poor bastard. He was just doing what he's been trained to do his entire life: Attack. Kill. Such a shitty situation. If I hadn't acted when I had, he would have done some serious damage, though. He would have barked more, and I couldn't risk it. It's a miracle no one came out the first time he sounded the alarm. I stoop down and place my hand on his laboring chest.

"Sorry, buddy." I whisper the words, and his ears swivel in the direction of my voice. He whines, and I know I should do the merciful thing and finish the job. I just can't, though. I don't have the stomach for it. I step over the dog, heading for the back door. It opens first try. The Perez peach farmers are not very security conscious, apparently. Seems strange, given what a cowardly bastard Julio is.

The kitchen is neat as a pin. No dirty plates or cups on the sideboards. The tiled floor is gleaming. A pot bubbles on the stove, and I have the urge to lift the lid and see what's cooking inside, it smells so damned good. The smell of home cooked food after a week of eating gas station food will make your stomach rumble no matter the circumstance you find yourself in.

There's only one door leaving the kitchen; I walk through it to find a skinny, ill-looking guy sitting on a wooden chair in a narrow hallway with an assault rifle laid out across his lap. When he casts his bulging brown eyes up at me, I see the shock register, and then I see disappointment follow and I jam the balisong into his neck and swipe sideways, cutting his throat open from ear to ear. He didn't even get to raise his rifle. The light fades in his eyes, and I move on down the hallway without casting a look over my shoulder. The room with the four guys inside is to my right, television still blaring loudly, now with raucous high-pitched music. I can't hear a thing over the TV. The men sitting on the couches could have heard me come into the house, and they could be waiting for me to burst in on them. It's unlikely, though. Julio's guys charge at the first sign of a fight. They aren't the patient types. The door is ajar, but not enough that I can see in properly. If I can't see in, then they can't see out, either.

Quickly I dart past the doorway, trying to time my footfall with the thump of the pounding music that's practically rattling the windows in their rotten frames. I make it past the door, but I don't release the breath I'm holding until I've turned the corner in the hallway. I'm faced with a stairway running up to the second floor, and a single door to the left. Somewhere up there on the second story, someone hammers on the floor, yelling for the music to be turned down, and I lean back against the wall, waiting to see if anyone comes racing down the stairs.

No one appears, though. The music turns down a fraction, just enough that I can hear the steady thrum of my heart still keeping a slow and steady beat, like a metronome. A metronome of death.

I have two options: I could go into the room on the left and find out if it's occupied, or I could go upstairs and locate the guy up there. I allow myself the luxury of thinking about it for a while. Julio's what would kindly be termed as morbidly obese. No way is the lazy, lumbering bastard jogging up and down any stairs. I doubt he's up there very much, which makes the decision actually very easy. I need to clear the upper floor. No sense in heading straight toward my target, only to be lynched by god knows how many angry Mexicans the moment he opens his stupidly loud mouth and starts hollering for help.

I take the stairs two at a time, reaching for my gun. I may want Julio to suffer as much as physically possible, but I don't have time to be toying with anyone else. The feel of the gun's handle in my hand is all too familiar. I've held a thousand different handguns in my lifetime. Glocks. Brownings. Colts. Remingtons. Sigs. The make and model doesn't matter. I know the kinks and quirks of any weapon the second I curl my fingers around it, and this gun is no different.

I land in the upstairs hallway, scanning the area quickly. No one to be seen in the hallway. There are two doors to my left, and two to my right. I hurry forward, trying the handle on the first door I reach. It opens, and I startle the lone guy inside, who happens to be pulling up a pair of jeans.

"Motherfuc—" He fumbles, trying to jerk up his pants and reach for his gun laying on the bed in front of him at the same time. I don't give him the opportunity to do either. Rushing into the room, I squeeze the trigger, planting a bullet neatly between his eyes before he can finish the word that's made it halfway past his lips. He slumps to the ground, his head bouncing hard off the end of the bed as he makes his way to the floor. Blood starts pouring everywhere; I can't tell if it's from the bullet wound or the huge gash that's just cut his forehead wide open.

It's academic at this point. The job's done.

The next door is locked. I take a step back and kick the wood, just below the lock. I'm ready to shoot, when I lay eyes on the lifeless figure sprawled-out on the bed. A girl, young and blonde, twenty-one, maybe twenty-two? She's unconscious, naked, her legs spread wide open, and there's a needle sticking out of her arm, the plunger pressed down to the hilt. I can't stop to check her pulse. If she's dead, it's already too late. If she's dying, I won't truly be able to help her until every single threat inside this farmhouse is neutralized. I duck out of the room and try the next handle. It opens, the door creaking loudly— no one inside. The final room on the right, then. I turn the doorknob and step quickly into the room, gun raised, finger on the trigger. The curtains are drawn and for a second I think there's no one here, but then I hear it, the sound of soft, gentle snoring, and I finally make out the large, bulky shape lying in the bed.

It's Julio.

I was wrong. He *is* upstairs, after all, and he's passed the fuck out in bed. Apparently it doesn't matter that it's the middle of the day. I watch him for a moment, waiting to see if he really is asleep and he's not just faking, and then I stick my head out into the hallway, listening, trying to figure out if the four guys downstairs might be on their way up here any time soon.

The music is still raging, though, thumping hard. They're probably so coked out of their minds, they didn't even hear me shoot the dude trying to get dressed. I retreat into Julio's room, closing the door behind me.

Hmm. How to approach this situation. I slip my bag from my shoulders, quickly hunting inside it until I find what I need, and then I climb carefully up onto the bed, collecting up the piece of clothing he's left on top of the covers in my hand. Julio's stomach hasn't shrunk any in the months since I've seen him. If anything it's gotten bigger. The fucker probably hasn't seen his own dick in years. I throw my leg over his bulging waist, scowling as I straddle him, not enjoying the close proximity of my own dick to his swollen midriff. I feed out a length of duct tape and snap it off with my front teeth, and then I tap Julio on the shoulder.

Nothing.

I prod him a little harder, driving the tip of my finger into his fat.

Still nothing.

For fuck's sake.

I slap him. Hard. Julio's eyelids spring open, his mouth already forming a shout, but I stuff the material I found on his bed into his mouth, smirking a little when I realize they're his own underwear. I slap the duct tape over his mouth, forcing it closed, and then I sit back on his belly. The balisong comes back out. Julio's eyes follow the glint and glimmer of the metal as it flashes in the dark.

"Well, hello there, Mr. Perez," I say cordially. "I was wondering if I might be able to buy some peaches?"

Julio lifts his hands, but I cut him off before he can try anything. More accurately, I grab hold of his right hand and cut off his pinkie finger before he can do anything. Cutting off someone's finger is no easy task. It's not like slicing a hot knife through butter. It's more like trying to cut through a raw chicken breast with a soupspoon. Julio bucks, screaming through his own soiled underwear as I get down to business. If I was covered in blood before, I am seriously drenched in the stuff now. Julio screams through his gag, and I finish the job with one final sawing motion. I hold the severed finger up for Julio to see, and his face turns a sickly shade of white.

"I'm not really here to buy peaches," I say, tossing his finger over my shoulder. It hits the floor somewhere behind me, and I hear it roll on the floorboards. "I need some help with something, and I believe you're just the man who can help me, Mr. Perez. So I'll ask nice and we'll see how far we get, shall we?"

Julio's still screaming through his gag, his eyes bugging out of his head; he's trying over and over again to jerk his hand free from mine, but I have a tight hold of his wrist and I ain't fucking letting go. His other hand is no use to him either, since it's pinned underneath my knee. I'm not beyond kneeling on his forearm until it breaks, should he come close to wrestling that one free.

"Quit screaming so we can talk, Julio."

He doesn't quit screaming.

"God damn it." I suppose this one's on me. I should have told him what I want *before* cutting off his pinkie. Sighing, I fold the *balisong* up and put it in my pocket. Pulling back my fist to build up some momentum, I bring it down on Julio's heavily jowled face with a sick sense of satisfaction. His nose pops under the impact, and another shower of blood sprays up at me as he huffs heavily out of his nose.

His eyes are watering like crazy, already swelling up, but he's gotten the picture and stopped screaming.

"There we go. That's more like it." I rip the duct tape from his mouth, and Julio draws in a ragged, pained breath that sounds like a broken vacuum cleaner, on its last legs.

"*You...fucking....psycho!*" He's too mad to manage more than one word at a time. "You cut off my finger! You cut off my fucking finger!"

"I hope you're not going to spend too long stating the obvious, man. I get bored very easily, and every wasted minute is another wasted finger. Once we've run out of digits, I'll have to move onto other appendages, and trust me...that would really fucking *suck*. The last thing I want to do is pop your fly and go rooting to find your tiny, shrivelled up dick, Julio. *Gross.*"

Julio tries to sit up, to lean closer to me, but he only manages to heft his weight a mere inch or two from the bed. "You're so fucking dead," he hisses. "You'd better pray I can get that finger stitched back on, or I'm—"

"Or you're what?" I tip my head to one side, arching an eyebrow. "You're gonna have me killed? You'll take your anger out on the

Widow Makers? Go after Rebel? Do you honestly think you're in a position to be making threats like that, Perez? Rebel's given me the go-ahead to put you the fuck down. You're only going to walk out of this room alive by my mercy, and I'm not feeling very merciful right now. That could change, depending on how you answer my questions, though."

"Save your breath, *cabron*. I know why you're here. I know what you want, and I can't fucking help you."

"Well, that really is a shame." I locate my balisong again, flicking it open, perhaps with a little more show than is truly necessary. Julio eyes the blade with fear in his eyes.

"I can't help you, because I don't know where they took her. I don't know where she's been. I don't know anything."

"Where did the photo come from then, asshole? How did Rebel speak to her on your phone in that hotel room? He said she was alive." I grab hold of his ring finger with my free hand, making a show of holding the blade to the base of it, and Julio starts shaking his head.

"Look, a guy came out to the compound one night. This big fucking hot shot. Stacks of money in briefcases. He wanted to spend the night with three girls. I said sure. Fine. Who would he prefer? He said he has this huge thing for redheads. He picked my own girl, Alaska. I would normally have told him to go fuck himself, but he paid a hundred grand for one night. The next morning, he comes to me. He offered me a trade. He wanted to keep Alaska. Showed me these profiles of a bunch of girls he had back in Chile or Columbia. I can't remember where."

I grind the edge of the blade into Julio's skin. "This is a really long story, man. My attention is starting to wander."

"Shit, Preston. Back up. I'm trying to tell you, *ese!*"

"Get on with it," I growl.

"So she's there. Your sister is there. I recognized her from the pictures Rebel showed to me a few years back. I took copies. I've been looking for her, too."

"Why? Why the fuck would you be keeping an eye out for my

sister?"

Julio squirms, a big, ugly grub on the end of a hook. "Why do you think, *cabron*? If Rebel wants something that badly, I am going to try and get it first."

"So you said you'd trade Alaska for Laura?"

"Yes."

I punch him as hard as I can in the throat. Julio makes a gurgling choking noise as I lean down, shoving my face into his. I am all he can see, hear or worry about. "That was a seriously shitty thing to do," I tell him. "You should have called me. You should have called Rebel. Where the fuck is my sister now, Julio?"

"I told you, I don't...know!" he chokes out. "He took Alaska when he left. He said he'd send three men back with your sister in a few weeks. He left another three hundred thousand as security. His men answered the phone when I was in that hotel room with Rebel, they let her speak to him, but that was the last time I heard from him. He never showed up with her, and he never came back for his money. He must have wanted to keep both of them."

"Or you freaked him out when you put her on the phone with Rebel. You're a stupid son of a bitch, Julio. Fuck, I should just kill you right now for being such a cunt."

Julio opens his mouth, is about to say something else, but I clench my fist over his head, implying what will happen if he even dares to breathe one word. Whatever he was planning on saying dies on his lips.

"Who was he?" I demand. "This guy who showed up out of no-where, wanting to fuck your girls?"

"I don't know. I swear, I don't fucking—"

I punch him in his throat again. He coughs, rattling, wheezing, and I lean back, sighing as I wait for him to sort his shit out. When he's done, I continue. "You don't let anyone through your gates unless you know exactly who they are, what they had for breakfast and how many shits they've taken since they woke up. So you had to have known who he was, Julio."

"I didn't." He winces, screwing his eyes shut, anticipating my next blow. I decide to give him a second to finish his sentence, though. "He came with one of my regulars. Manny. He's my brother, *ese*. I allowed him to bring people in with him all the time."

"Bad business. Very bad for business," I say. "Where's Manny now? Back in the States?"

"No. No, he's dead, okay? He was shot in Downtown LA."

"*Convenient.*"

"Not convenient for me," Julio gasps. "If I could send you off after him, I would. Then you wouldn't be here, messing up my shit."

"I suppose that's true." I stop leaning quite so heavily onto his neck. "Describe this guy to me, then. What did he look like?"

"South American, olive skin. Brown eyes, brown hair. Fuck, Cade, I don't know. Wait, he was really thin. His shirt and his pants looked like they were a size too big for him or something."

"Did he speak Spanish when he was with you?"

"Of course! Why the fuck would he have been speaking in English?"

I want to pistol whip the motherfucker for being rude, but I don't think I can hit his head again without him losing consciousness. "Any recognizable scars? Tattoos? Any other defining features?"

"No. No, nothing! He looked..."

"He looked what?"

"He looked like an accountant or something. He wore nice clothes. Glasses. *He wore glasses!*"

Glasses? Strange, but then again what's to stop a kidnapper and probable rapist from having bad vision? I shift my weight over Julio, scowling. "You have three seconds to tell me something useful about this guy, Julio, or I'm burying this knife in your carotid artery and I'm watching you bleed the fuck out. Do you understand what I am saying to you right now?"

"I don't know...damn it, Cade. You're gonna suffer for this, I promise."

Ignoring his panicked chatter, I hold up three fingers, and then I tuck the first into my palm. "*One.*"

"I can't tell you something I don't know!"

The second finger goes down. *"Two."*

"Isn't this enough? You've already taken my damned finger..."

"Three." I'm bringing the knife down, fully intent on following through with my promise, when Julio shouts, stopping me in my tracks.

"WOLVES!"

The tip of the balisong stops, less than a milimeter from penetrating his skin. "Wolves?"

"Yes! Yeah, that's right. *Wolves.* Manny kept talking to him about wolves. They were whispering together about a house for wolves. It didn't make any sense to me, and this guy was spending a lot of money—I didn't want to ask too many questions."

"A house for wolves?" My incredulity colors my voice. "What the fuck is that supposed to mean?"

"I don't know. I seriously don't know. But they talked about it for hours. That's all there is, Cade. I promise you. I swear it."

Pity floods me. Julio, a thorn in the side of the Widow Makers MC for years now, looks like he's about to burst into tears. There's nothing more pathetic than watching a fat man cry. I nod my head, letting out a deep breath. "Okay. All right. I believe you. I suppose this means our conversation is at an end, then." I sit back on my heels, releasing the pressure of the knife's blade against Julio's throat.

A visible tidal wave of relief washed over the man underneath me. "You really are going to regret this," he snaps, anger returning to his eyes. "You'd better find my fucking finger, before I—"

I plunge the knife forward, sinking the metal into his neck, watching all four inches as they disappear into his flesh. Shock registers on Julio's face, his eyes growing wider and wider as he realizes what I've done. And what that means.

"But...I....told..." he splutters. Blood pumps out from between his fingers in thick, powerful spurts, almost strong enough to hit the high, grimy ceiling overhead. Julio scrambles with his four-fingered hand, trying to scoop the vital fluid back into his body, but the truth is there, written all over his face; he knows he's already lost.

"You said it yourself," I tell him, watching with a blank look on my face. "That's all there is, Julio. That's really all there is." It takes just a few moments for a man to die like this. I sit on top of his chest, enjoying every single one of them. Maybe that's wrong of me. Perhaps I've become unhinged. A normal person wouldn't stab someone in the neck and observe with cold, disconnected interest as their life force flowed out of them and they died. On the other hand, Julio should never have told me he knew where my sister was and he planned on obtaining her for his own purposes. That was a pretty big fucking mistake. What was he going to do with her, if this glasses-wearing accountant had made good on his deal and sent Laura back to him? Taunt and bully Rebel, for sure. But he would have taken his pound of flesh before he struck any kind of bargain with Jamie. He would have taken more than he should have from her, and for that he deserved to die.

He that is without sin among you, let him cast the first stone...

It's not often that quotes from JC himself play out in my mind. I'm not a religious guy, and I don't often find myself in situations that lean themselves toward righteous thinking, however covered in the blood of the lives I have just taken, I find myself feeling pretty fucking pensive. I've judged Julio and found him short. I could have just gone, taken the small fragments of information he gave to me and left him, injured and squealing like a stuck pig in his bed. I didn't, though. I doled out the punishment I saw fit for his crimes.

One of these days, someone will judge me, and *I* will fall short of *their* expectations. I'll gladly accept whatever penance they decide to serve upon my head when the time comes.

Until then, I'm going to keep on doing what I have to do in order to get my sister back.

TWO

MR. AMERICA

The woman with the needle hanging out of her arm is dead. I want to bury her and the dog in the back of Julio's yard, and I also want to finish off those four coke heads in the downstairs living room, but I have time to do neither. I have to get on the road; I have to hit Santa Clarita before dark, and the sun is already bobbing lower in the sky than I like. I duck low and weave my way through the long grass back toward the scrambler, planning the next step of my journey: ride for six hours, find somewhere to wash properly, store the scrambler somewhere safe, and get my ass on a plane.

I may have feigned ignorance when Julio started babbling about a house for wolves, but I do know what it means. Or at least, I think I do. Not a house for wolves. *The House of Wolves.* Villalobos. The Villalobos family aren't like other cartels. People don't shake in their boots when they hear the name whispered down dark alleyways across the United States. There aren't many people who would even have heard of them in the first place. Like most cartels, The House of Wolves deals in skin, coke and heroin, but they only deal with their own contacts—in motherfucking *Ecuador.*

They are the top of the food chain, a great white shark in the sea of narcotics and sex trading, and they don't bother themselves with small fry. The only reason I even know of the family is because of the constant trawling for information that's carried out at the Widow Makers' clubhouse. Jamie's not your average motorcycle club president; he's heavily invested in bringing down as many sick fucks as he can. If you deal in skin and you're stupid enough to try and sell girls online, or in any sort of bidding community, then you're basically fucked. It's only a matter of time before we find you. Our hackers are good. The Villalobos family have been whispered about for years, but no one has ever given us solid information on them. And without solid information, the risk of a full-frontal assault has just been too great.

Until now.

So. A flight out of Mexico. A small dip into the stack of money I'm carrying with me, but well worth it if it leads me to Laura.

I take off my leather jacket and then the black tee I'm wearing underneath, using the sweat and blood soaked shirt to wipe down my jacket, and then I rifle in the small bag I have stowed under the scrambler's seat, hunting for something clean to wear. A gray ACDC shirt? Perfect. I throw it on, bundling up my leather and jamming it into the small compartment under the seat, along with the bag, and then I wheel the Yamaha back to the road. Just as I'm about to start the engine, shots ring out behind me, from the direction of the Perez farmhouse. I can just about make out two guys running from the house, their muffled, indecipherable shouts carrying across the fields. One of them raises his hand and another gunshot rings out, snapping through the air.

Looks like it's time for me to get the fuck out of here.

••••

Getting a plane ticket is easy. There are plenty of security checks in Mexico, especially if you're a white American trying to fly to another country and not back into the States, however this isn't my first time at the rodeo. I pay five hundred bucks to a toothless old garage owner on the outskirts of Santa Clarita, telling him if I'm not back in a week he can keep the scrambler. I make sure to tell him, in no uncertain terms, what will happen if I did come back in less than a week and the motorcycle isn't there, too.

VICE

I ditch every single last scrap of clothing I've brought with me, and I buy a suit and tie, briefcase, polished tan leather shoes and a pair of aviators. The money I'm carrying with me goes into the briefcase.

I am no longer Cade Preston, vice president of the Widow Makers Motorcycle Club. I am Samuel Garrett, executive sales representative at Holland Radisson Tailors & Purveyors of Fine Cloth. Thank god for fake passports, and thank god for fake back-stories. The travel documents and sales pitch I prepared back in New Mexico at the Widow Makers compound were meant to be used if I needed to chase Julio down in Columbia or Brazil. I hadn't banked on Ecuador, but the paperwork holds up when customs officials inspect it. The suit I've bought is expensive enough that they don't ask too many questions— *what is your business in Ecuador, Mr. Garrett? How long do you intend to stay for? Do you plan on traveling back through Mexico on your way home to the United States?*

I already have my responses scripted out: I'm searching for a new manufacturing site; I'm going to be in Ecuador for a week. Maybe more. And no, I don't intend on flying back into Mexico.

They don't care about my responses. All they care about is the envelope of money I casually "forget" on their desk.

"You may go, Mr. Garrett. Have a nice day." Smiles all round. Handshakes. A warm pat on the back.

I know nothing about Ecuador. Like, zero. Absolutely fucking nothing. I read the in-flight pamphlet in the back of the seat in front of me on the flight, but it's in Spanish, and while I can speak the language fluently, reading it, on the other hand, is another matter entirely.

By the time we land in Eloy Alfaro International Airport, I know that the population hits somewhere under the sixteen million belt, and that there are four distinctly different regions to the country. The thing about in-flight pamphlets, though, is that they don't tell you where you might find the local coke and heroin moguls, or where you might be able to buy a shit load of guns. More's the pity.

I buy a couple of t-shirts, two pairs of jeans, a new backpack, a new leather jacket and a pair of white Adidas sneakers from the stores

29

before leaving duty free, and make my way to the first rental place I can find that has motorcycles. I could easily rent a car instead of a bike, but the past week sat on the back of the scrambler has given me time to think. Time to plot, and scheme and plan. Plus the vibrations of my cock against the gas tank feels really fucking good. You just don't get that kind of stimulation in sitting behind the wheel of a Honda Civic.

The rental company only has touring motorcycles, which isn't going to work. If the House of the Wolves are smart, they'll be holed up in the hills somewhere, probably off road, and I'm gonna need something that can handle a few dips and bumps in the terrain. The guys in the rental place barely understand me when I try and explain what I need, but eventually we get there. They give me the name of a second-hand place that won't lease me a motorcycle, but will sell me something reliable on the cheap.

Four hours later, I have a five-year-old version of the motorcycle I just left behind in Mexico, and I've gone from sixty grand down to fifty. I ride to a shifty looking café just outside the city, all too eager to leave the busy, over-crowded roads and streets teeming with people behind. There, with a giant cup of coffee glued to my hand and a stale queso wrap growing staler on a plate in front of me, I make a call from my cell. A call I am seriously not looking forward to.

"You did *what*?" On the other end of the line, Jamie sounds pissed. "You flat-out killed him?"

I stuff the queso wrap into my mouth, hoping the sound of me eating will drown the rest of my conversation with him. That's not going to work, though. I need something from him, and I can't really ask him if he can't understand a word I'm saying. I swallow the huge bite of food in my mouth and sigh. "He had it fucking coming, man. Tell me you weren't sick of his shit, Jamie. Tell me you wouldn't have done the same thing if you were in my situation."

Silence reigns supreme. I chew on another bite of my food, while my best friend, technically my boss, chews on what I've just said. Eventually, he grunts down the phone. "You should have called it in," he says. "We could have done some recon work, seen how many of his guys hung around once he left the country. Now we don't know how many of them are gonna come looking for payback."

"You know as well as I do, no one's gonna be mourning that disgusting piece of shit. If anything, those power hungry bastards will be sending us thank you cards."

"Maybe," Jamie concedes. "But still..."

I discard the wrap, wiping my hands on my jeans. "Yeah, I know. I'm sorry. But sometimes it's better to ask for forgiveness than permission, right?"

Jamie laughs. I can imagine the way he's pacing, still trying to process the information that Perez, one of our sometimes allies and nearly-all-the-time-enemies is dead, though. I probably should have given him a heads up first. I'm not looking forward to parting with this next piece of information, either. "While we're on the subject of things I need to ask forgiveness for, I should probably let you know that I'm not in Mexico anymore."

"What? Where the fuck are you, Cade?"

"Ecuador."

"The fuck are you doing in Ecuador?"

"Julio said Laura was with the Villalobos cartel. I came to find them."

"Ah. Right. So...would you even be calling right now if you didn't need me to ask one of the guys to find out where the Villalobos family is based?" He can read me like a goddamn book. He's laughing, but he's pissed at me, too. Or worried about me. Probably both.

"I would have called," I tell him. "*Eventually*."

"Damn it, you asshole. You should have let me come with you. Do you know how shitty I feel right now?" he snaps. "You're my brother. I should have your back right now."

"You and I both know you couldn't have come," I tell him. "Not with things the way they are right now." Neither of us wants to talk about the reason he *has* stayed behind. His girlfriend is sick. *Really* sick. Disappearing off on a mission with me just wasn't an option. And I would never have let him come, even if that weren't the case. He's happy now, and he's already given up so much. It's time for him to get on with his life. "Besides, you *do* have my back. You're gonna let me know where these motherfuckers live so I can go pay them a visit," I tell him.

"Yeah. *On your own.*"

"It'll be fine, Jamie. When is it *not* fine?"

"One of these days, it really won't be. And then what? Do *not* make me travel all the way to fucking Ecuador to find what's left of your body, Cade. I will be so fucking mad at you."

"You can kick my ass when you come join me in hell. How 'bout that?"

Jamie grumbles down the phone. "Sounds like a plan. I'll text you whatever we find in a couple of hours. In the meantime, if you change your mind, feel free to get back on the next fucking flight home, and I swear I won't castrate you for being a reckless dick."

"You're one to talk," I tell him. "When was the last time you didn't handle a situation like this recklessly?"

Jamie doesn't say anything. He barks out a shout of laughter, and then he hangs up the phone.

••••

It's close to eight in the evening when I receive the location of the Villalobos cartel. Orellana, to the east. Way, way, *way* the fuck to the east. It's a ten-hour ride if I use the freeways, or a thirteen-hour drive if I stick to the back roads. Adding three hours onto my journey is annoying as hell, but it also means I'm less likely to get pulled over by cops, or caught up in traffic and accidents.

JAMIE: Took forever to track them down. These guys have no paper trail. No online presence whatsoever. We had to pinpoint them using keywords from Ecuadorian police reports. As far as we can tell, Orellana is where they're based. We've scoured the area, and scrubbed the satellite images. These buildings seem to be the most likely location. It's the best we can do right now. We'll keep looking, though.

Underneath his text message, he's sent a fuzzy screenshot of a group of buildings, surrounded by trees. A whole lot of trees. So I was right. If this information is correct and this is where the Villalobos cartel is based, then they're way out in the middle of fucking nowhere. There doesn't even seem to be any roads in and out of the compound. Not even a goddamn dirt track.

I shoot Jamie a quick thank you, and then I'm climbing on the back of the motorcycle, making sure I have everything I need with me for the miles and miles that stretch out ahead of me. All I really need is a small can of gas and a working cell phone, but the toothbrush, first-aid kit and chocolate bars will help make life more pleasant if I get stranded somewhere.

The ride passes by in a blur of rickety wagons and clouds of dust. I could power through and do the stretch all in one go, but setting off so late has made that impossible. Still, I barely stop to sleep—there are no motels on the route I've selected, and without my camping gear, sleeping on the ground off the side of the road beside my motorcycle is less than comfortable. My time in the military serves me well, though. I'm used to functioning without rest. I'm barely even tired as I finally begin to see signs for Orellana.

When I arrive, I'm surprised to find a quaint little fishing village at the foot of a tall mountain range. There are no Holiday Inns here. No Motel 6s. I don't see a single storefront as I ride the motorcycle down what appears to be the main street of the tiny town. The locals hurry out onto the streets—presumably startled by the sound of the bike's engine—and they gawp at me with their mouths hanging open as I burn past them.

Everything is decaying, falling down, tumbling back into the water and the dirt. The buildings are more like shacks, some of which stand on high stilts set back from the road. Some of them stand on the river, with tiny rusting tin boats tethered to rotting wooden posts out front, bobbing on dank green water. Children in worn-out clothes run alongside me as I weave my way through the streets of Orellana; they're poor and obviously have little, but their clothes are clean, and they have shoes on their feet. Smiles on their faces.

I don't stop in the town. The building complex I'm looking for isn't down here, after all; from the looks of the image Jamie sent through for me, the complex is further up the mountain, deep in the thick rainforest that surrounds the town for miles and miles.

The scrambler handles the dirt tracks that weave up into the hillside without a problem. My bones feel like they're being jarred out of their sockets, and the noise the engine makes is amplified through the rainforest, though. I sure as shit won't be sneaking up on the Villalobos cartel at this rate.

My heart quickens in my chest as I think about what I might find up here. It's been years since I've seen my sister. *Years*. If she is with the Villalobos crew, what the fuck is she going to be like now? Doped up? Broken and in pain? Will she hate me for taking so long to find her? I hate myself for that. I won't hold it against her if *she* does. I run myself around in circles until I'm dizzy—it's dangerous thinking this way. Laura might not be here, after all. It's entirely possible that my House of Wolves guess back at the Perez farmhouse was wrong. Jamie and I have already traveled all over Chile, Columbia and Mexico looking for her, our seemingly endless journeys always as a result of some small piece of information that inevitably leads us on a wild goose chase. Why should this time be any different?

Because it feels *different this time*, a voice whispers in the back of my head, treacherous, evil, cruel thing that it is, setting me up for failure. She was alive, though. When Jamie was in that hotel room, bargaining with Julio, my sister was alive. After so long, it was a miracle. If whoever took her has kept her alive for such an extended period of time, why would they suddenly kill her now? It wouldn't make sense.

I ride the scrambler further into the rainforest, barely willing to acknowledge that either way I'm riding toward danger. Laura's not going to be camped out at this place on her own. If she is here, then she's going to be heavily guarded, and the men watching her are highly unlikely to hand her over without so much as a by-your-leave and a sorry-about-that-we-probably-shouldn't-have-taken-her-against -her-will.

It takes me forever to find the building Jamie sent me on the satellite image. My cell phone loses service, and trying to triangulate my whereabouts using landmarks is next to impossible with the high canopy and the trees pressing in from all sides. Eventually, after much swearing and sweating, I manage to find what I'm looking for. Three separate low-lying buildings rise up out of all the greenery—dark, concrete boxes with no glass in the yawning window frames, weeds and ferns sprouting from the rooves and the cracked pathway leading up to the open doorway of the first, largest building. They're little more than ruins. Whatever they used to be, they were never the home of a secretive, incredibly rich cartel. Perhaps this was a meeting point for some of the Villalobos cartel members, but never anything more. It's likely squatters live here now. The three buildings form the sides of a square, one side left open, given access to a courtyard between the structures. Rusting, twisted metal lays everywhere, and rotten mattresses, abandoned sofas, and old, smashed TV sets sit among the long grasses, like some kind of bizarre long-forgotten hotel room that Mother Nature decided to reclaim as her own.

There isn't a single soul around, and my heart plummets in my chest. *Fuck.* After riding all this way, traveling through three different countries and spending a small fortune, I'm drawing yet another blank? No way. *No fucking way.*

I kill the scrambler's engine and climb off the motorcycle, wincing as my joints complain. The pain's not enough to distract me from my goal: recon the area. Find clues. Figure out who used to live here, and find out where the fuck they are now. I'm almost about to step through the open doorway of the largest building when a voice stops me in my tracks.

"I wouldn't do that if I were you."

I spin around, gun already in my hand, my finger ready to squeeze the trigger, to find a young woman leaning up against the trunk of a tree, arms folded across her chest.

My first thought: *Wow*.

She's beautiful. Her dark gray tank top hangs loose on her frame, the front tucked into her dirty, ripped jeans. She's covered in sweat, her forehead glistening with it, which somehow makes her look...well, *hot*. Hazel almond-shaped eyes, thick, light brown hair shot through with strands of gold, tied in a messy knot on top of her head. Freckles. Freckles everywhere... Across the bridge of her nose, over her high cheekbones, over her shoulders. Her skin is a deep golden color. Perfect. Utterly flawless. She must be in her mid to late twenties, and she looks very, very amused.

I only notice the huge, serrated knife in her hand when she points it at the doorway I was about to step through. "We booby-trapped that place a few years ago. A trip wire across the doorway. Old land mines buried under the dirt floor. I can't really remember where everything is now. Personally, I don't think it's a good idea for you to go snooping, Mr. American. It would be a sad day for you." Her accent is mild; she could easily pass as an American herself, but there is something there. A soft, subtle lilt that lets me know English probably isn't her first language.

"Is that right?" I consider the shell of the building in front of me, trying to buy some time. Trying to decide how this situation is going to play out. I'm holding up a gun, and this girl, whoever the fuck she is, has a huge knife clasped casually in her right hand. Gun beats knife every time, but still. No need to automatically assume she's hostile.

"How do you know I'm American?" I ask, keeping my voice light.

A smile pulls at her lips. She shrugs one shoulder, pushing away from the tree. "You're the only person out here wearing a leather jacket in one hundred degree heat." A pout. A really fucking sexy pout. "And then there's the fact that we got a call from a friend of ours a couple of days ago, letting us know that an insane guy on a motorcycle was probably headed toward Orellana. That kind of gave you away."

Hmm. Someone from Perez's place must have figured out who'd paid them a visit, and where I'd likely be headed next. Perfect. I should have killed those four bastards in the living room after all. "I see."

"You should put away your gun, Mr. America. It's hard to have a conversation when you're staring down the barrel of a pistol."

I eye her knife, raising an eyebrow. "I don't think so, sweetheart."

"You may as well," she advises me. "There are men in the trees all around you, and their guns are much bigger and much more impressive than yours."

I cast my eyes around, searching through the camouflage of the greens and browns surround us, and I can't see anything. I got very good at spotting snipers in the desert, but I can't seem to find anyone here. "You're bluffing," I tell her.

"Maybe. Maybe not. I guess the choice is yours, Mr. America. Do you lower your gun and talk to me like a civilized man, or do you risk finding out if I'm telling the truth?"

The situation really is that black and white. I do as I'm told, or I potentially get shot in the head and I never see it coming. My grip tightens on my gun. "Sorry. You are literally gonna have to prise my weapon from my cold, dead hand." I never had my rifle taken from me in Afghanistan. I'm sure as fuck not going to lose a weapon in some rainforest in Ecuador.

The woman's smile spreads across her face. "As you wish." She gives a slight nod of her head, and I hear the bolt of a rifle being drawn. I duck to the left just in time to avoid the bullet that comes tearing out of nowhere; it buzzes my arm, clipping my jacket, tearing a hole in the leather. Miraculously I'm not even grazed, but I'll admit my heart rate has jumped up a notch.

"Well, that wasn't very nice."

"But didn't I warn you, Mr. America?" the woman says, grinning. Her teeth are perfect. She looks like she got them straightened and whitened in Hollywood.

"I suppose, in fairness, you did."

"Are you going to put down your gun now?"

I consider this for a second. "How about I keep my gun but I put it away? And you put down that very manly knife of yours?"

"But I like my knife."

"I like my gun."

"I see we are too similar, Mr. America. Perhaps a conversation is out of the question after all."

I don't say anything. The two of us just observe each other for a moment, and then she tips her head back and laughs. "No need to look so serious. I'm only playing with you." She throws the knife in the air and catches it by the handle, then slides it inside her belt, tucking it away. "Why don't you tell me your name, Mr. America? That way we can be friends, and not have all of this hostility between us."

I doubt me telling her my name is suddenly going to make us best friends, but I give it to her anyway. "I'm Sam. Sam Garrett. And you are?"

"I am Natalia, and I am very pleased to meet you." She walks straight for me, holding out her hand, ignoring the fact that I haven't lowered my gun yet. For a split second her hand and the gun are level in the air, and I think she might try and grab it. But she doesn't. She just smiles. Up close, her freckles are far more intense, and even more attractive. A rogue smile slips past my lips, and I lower the gun.

"Pleased to make your acquaintance, Natalia. Feel like telling your friends to lower their weapons now, too?"

Natalia with the freckles pouts, and then sticks her fingers in her mouth and whistles—she's pretty fucking good. I wince, angling my head away from the sharp sound. Seconds later, a single guy with an old Winchester rifle appears from the foliage. He's much older than Natalia, maybe in his late forties, and he's clearly Ecuadorian. Takes me a moment to figure out what he's wearing on his head: a pair of retro headphones with foam cushions and red plastic headband. The closer he gets, the louder the music blasting out of his headphones gets—rap music. Specifically, Run DMC. His eyes are dark and impassive as they scan over me. He doesn't say anything. He stands behind Natalia, one hand on the rifle, one hand on an actual bona fide

Walkman, clipped to his belt at the hip.

"This is Ocho," Natalia says. "He is my friend with the weapon."

"Hmm. You really had me outnumbered, huh?"

"Yes," she agrees. "Two to one. Now come, Sam Garrett. I'm sure my father is eager to meet you."

"Your father?"

"Yes. He's the reason you're here, I assume? You want to buy coca? You want to fuck? That's the only reason anyone ever comes to Orellana."

THREE

FERNANDO

I expect to be hurried off toward some vehicle they have hidden somewhere, but instead Natalia walks off into the rainforest, head down watching where she steps. Ocho waits for me to follow after her, and then he takes up the rear, hand still resting lightly on his gun. The lyrics to *"It's Tricky"* are booming out of his headphones, and the surreal nature of this moment hits me hard. I'm in fucking Ecuador, in the rainforest, following the hottest girl I've ever seen and her grumpy '80s loving hip hop sharp shooter into god knows what kind of danger. And she thinks I want to buy coke, or to screw some prostitutes? Perfect. Just fucking perfect. So now I have to choose: when I meet her father, do I continue on with the rouse? Or do I just come out with it and ask him where the fuck my sister is and have done with it? I'm tired of waiting. I am over chasing my own goddamn tail down so many different rabbit holes.

It occurs to me, however, that a coke dealer front might not be such a bad thing. Asking about Laura straight out of the gate might get me killed. It's probably better to wait it out. Chances are I might just see my sister with my own two eyes if I wait long enough, and *then* I can start killing people in order to get her the fuck out of here.

We walk through the rainforest for fifteen minutes, and then another ten. Your average person might be turned around by the time we reach the small, concrete bunker, almost completely hidden in the undergrowth, but I'm not all that average. Years of navigating by the position of the sun in the sky has taught me well; I can easily bolt and find my way back to the scrambler if I need to. I eye the metal hatch, planted square in the center of the rough cast concrete that in turn is set deep into the ground, and I quirk an eyebrow at Natalia, the beginnings of laughter building in the back of my throat.

"I don't suppose you ever watched *Lost*, did you?" I ask.

She frowns, sighing heavily. "No, I never watched this. Is it important?"

"No, I guess not."

"Good." Bending down, she uses the butt of her knife to hammer on top of the steel hatch; the clanging sound rings out, loud and clear, reminding me of the popping, warped metal sound that submarines make when they're rising from seriously deep water. Ocho turns his Walkman off and slides his headphones off his head, letting them rest around his neck. He still hasn't said a word, and from the stubborn, flat look on his face I don't really think that will be changing any time soon. Twenty seconds pass, and then the hatch flies open, revealing a young girl, early twenties, with a filter mask over her face. Aside from the mask, she's completely and utterly naked. I try not to stare at her small but perfectly formed tits as she casts a mean eye over the three of us.

She says something in Spanish, but her words are muffled behind her mask and I don't quite catch what she says. Something about shoes? Something about a bandana? Natalia scowls at the girl. She flips her knife over and puts it away again, then gathers her hair back in her hands and ties it into a ponytail.

"You tell him we're coming down," she hisses, and then she kicks at the girl with the toe of her scuffed red Converse shoe. The girl makes a disgruntled growling sound, shooting a hateful look in my direction, but she disappears, lowering herself back down into the oppressive darkness below her.

"Come on. Don't worry. You don't need to get undressed," Natalia tells me. "Normally my father is very strict about his guests removing their clothes. He's in a good mood today, though." She squats down and climbs down into the tunnel beyond the hatch, and then she's vanishing into the inky shadows, too. I can hear the soles of her shoes hitting the rungs of a ladder as she descends, and then her voice calling up from the depths.

"Are you afraid of the dark, Sam?"

"Only when it's smart to be," I mutter under my breath. If I follow her down into this hole in the ground, I am going in blind. Literally. It's dark as fuck down there, and I have no idea how many armed guards are waiting for us. One look at Ocho tells me I'm not going to be able to back out of this without a fight, though. I'm bigger, stronger, faster, and younger than he is, so I have no doubt I could take him, but where would that get me? No closer to Laura, that's for sure.

Slowly, I lower myself through the hatch, keeping an eye on Ocho as I climb down, hand over hand. He hops into the hole after me with the practiced ease of someone who's done this many times before. He closes the hatch after himself, sealing it shut with the clanking of a bolt being drawn across, and the light goes out. The ladder is much longer than I anticipated, and it takes a while to reach the bottom. Ocho climbs down four or five rungs above me, silently, a ghost moving through the pitch black. Eventually I reach the bottom of the ladder and step down onto solid concrete.

Natalia's voice echoes when she speaks. "Put your hand on my shoulder, Sam. Here. Yes." I learn a lot from the way her voice bounces around inside the dark space—we're in a tunnel, long and narrow by the sounds of things, and the walls are pressing in. My hand touches the bare skin of her arm and then her shoulder. She's much shorter than me; she's probably only five seven or five eight, yet her confidence makes her seem taller somehow. I feel like I'm looming over her as she sets off in an easterly direction, skimming her fingertips along one side of a wall. God knows where the naked girl has gone. It would be really easy for me to take Natalia down right now. Ocho, too. It's as if he can read my mind, though. I feel a sharp, angry prod in my lower back, and I know all too well what I'm being poked with—the muzzle of his rifle. He's ready and willing to shot me in the spine at the first sign of any trouble out of me. Fair enough, I guess.

Moments later, blazing, stark white light is suddenly burning into my retinas as Natalia opens up a door in front of us. It takes a second for my eyes to adjust to the light again. Once my vision is restored, I'm surprised by the space that lies ahead: a huge underground warehouse, clean, everything painted white. Strip lights overhead hum with electricity, lighting up the vast, hollow space, and well over twenty young girls, all naked, stop what they're doing and turn to look at us. The low tables they're standing in front of are covered in cocaine. Bags of cocaine, already sealed and bricked up, presumably ready to ship out. Cocaine drying in trays under heat lamps. More coke in small lines, arranged on sheets of tinfoil, being mixed with a variety of other white, non-descript powders. About a billion dollars of cocaine, just floating around in the fucking air.

At regular intervals, huge guys with machetes and assault rifles in their hands lean against the walls, watching everything with sharp eyes. They are unsmiling, serious-looking motherfuckers, and I suddenly get to thinking this might not be such a great idea after all.

I've seen enough coke productions in my time to understand why the women are all naked—the boss doesn't want to lose product if one of his workers decides to stuff an eight ball into a pocket to take home for later—but the guards? It makes no sense why they would be naked, and yet they are. Dicks everywhere. Natalia, myself and Ocho: we are literally the only three people wearing clothes in the entire facility. Natalia's father must be really fucking paranoid if he doesn't even trust his own guards not to steal from him. Awkwardly, the guard standing closest to us has a raging boner, his cock standing to attention. He has a tight, uncomfortable look on his face that makes me want to burst out laughing.

"Poor Matteas," Natalia says, smirking. She openly stares at his dick, head angled to one side, as if assessing its size and girth. "He just started working on the floor. It can be very...*hard* for these guys at first. My father likes to chose young, beautiful women to cut his product. Stupid really. If he picked old, fat, saggy women, none of the men would be distracted by all the bare pussy around here."

If she's bothered by all the cocks, or the "bare pussy" as she so eloquently phrased it, then Natalia does an excellent job of hiding her discomfort. She's probably been around this kind of thing her whole life, and had plenty of time to become desensitized to it all. I've seen members of the club back in New Mexico fuck their wives on the pool table in the club house; I've seen people having threesomes behind the bar, and I've seen guys being blown left, right and center. I've never seen anything quite like this, though. The women are all beautiful, and the guards lining the room all know it, I'm sure. Most of them have a stern, focused look on their faces, as they undoubtedly try to avoid getting an erection like the poor bastard to our left.

"Is this just for entertainment?"

Natalia places her hand on my arm and gestures for me to walk with her. "No. It's more...*diversionary*. If workers are coming in here every day, totally naked, then they're not plotting how to steal, or how to take power from my father. They're too busy looking at each other's bodies to think of anything else."

A good idea, I guess. But wouldn't fear alone keep them from trying anything so stupid? I felt like asking, but the bored look on Natalia's face makes me rethink that. She turns and points to the other side of the room, a hundred feet away, where a single door, painted blue, provides the only pop of color in the entire room. "My father's office is through there," she advises me. "He hates to be disturbed, but I'm sure he won't mind a visit from a foreign businessman like yourself."

I look down at myself, taking in my t-shirt, dusty jeans, and my equally dusty, fucked-up leather jacket, and I wonder how many foreign businessmen come through Orellana.

"We have to get off the floor now. If we don't, we'll be too high to talk by the time we sit down with him." Natalia stalks off toward the blue door, and the women workers, their faces covered in dust masks, all watch her with envy in their eyes as she passes them by. I wonder how many of them want to stab her in the back at the earliest opportunity. I'm willing to bet money that all of them do.

I glance over my shoulder, and Ocho hasn't followed us; he's standing in the middle of the room, staring at a girl's ass as she measures out powder into little baggies, weighing each one, and tossing them onto a bucket. She doesn't seem to care that he's checking her out at all.

Natalia knocks quietly on the blue door, stepping back, and then clasping her hands behind her back. Her fingernails are dirty. I don't know why I notice that, or why it makes me like her even more, but it does. A second later, the door whips open and a tall, incredibly skinny man is glaring at us down the length of his very straight, very long nose. A pair of tortoise shell glasses are perched on the very end of said nose; he peers at us through them like the prescription might not have been updated in a couple of years.

"Natalia. Who is this man?" he asks in a clipped voice. His accent is far thicker than Natalia's; I'm sure they would normally speak to one another in Spanish, but he must have taken one look at me and known I wasn't from around these parts, just as Natalia did back by the booby trapped buildings.

"Says his name is Sam Garrett. We found him snooping around outside the old outpost. He hasn't said why he's here yet. I brought him straight to you, Papa."

The tall, spare guy with the glasses squints at me, frowning. His skin is much darker than Natalia's; her mother must have been white. The guy straightens his back, and blows a deep breath out down his nose. "I am Fernando Villalobos, and you, my friend, have either made a very grave mistake by wandering onto my land, or you have a very good reason for being here. Which is it?"

It appears as though I'm standing before the very man I've come looking for. Hatred coils in the pit of my stomach like a snake. Is this the man who took Laura? How can that be true? He doesn't look remotely capable of kidnapping anyone. His shirt is neatly pressed and tucked into his pants. His hair is trimmed in the most conservative, boring style imaginable. If I went to see my accountant and sat down in front of this guy, I wouldn't even blink. "Oh, yeah. I have a *really* good reason."

Fernando removes his glasses and sighs. "Which is?"

"Drugs. I want to buy a fuck load of drugs."

He blinks, and then shakes his head. "I'm afraid a...*fuck load* is not a quantity we deal in, *Sam*. Who do you work for?"

"A private individual. A businessman, who enjoys his anonymity in situations such as this."

"Oh. Well I'm afraid we don't deal narcotics with people we don't know, Mr. Garrett. Anonymity breeds mistrust. Betrayal. I'm sure you understand."

"As you wish. His name is Louis James Aubertin the third. He's an investment banker in New York. He provides a service for other professional men and women in the city. They go to him when they need a little...*stimulation*." This is a lie we've had to tell before, and Jamie's already given me the go ahead to fall back on it if I need it. Jamie's father, perhaps the biggest asshole on the face of the planet, still thinks Jamie is a banker in New York. There's a pre-existing paper trail there—bank accounts, an apartment. A fake office, set up on the eighteenth floor of the Klein building on Wall Street.

Fernando rocks back on his heels, folding his arms across his chest. I feel like a teenager picking up my date for the first time, only to be accosted by her overprotective father on the doorstep. This is a lot more serious than that, given the amount of armed, naked guards close by, but still... I don't feel as threatened as I probably should. On first inspection, Fernando seems like the introspective, brooding type. Intellectual. Stern. Very cold, of course. But not terrifying. Good thing he's stayed low here in Ecuador, instead of trying to claim territory in the States; he wouldn't last five seconds in a place like L.A. or Chicago.

"I usually only deal internally within Ecuador," he says. "I have no relationship with the Ecuadorian border, or with any state officials. I can't help you transport this...*fuck load* of my product you wish to buy out of the country. How are you intending to transfer the coca back into the States? Or do you intend on shoving it all up your nose, Mr.

Garrett?"

"Ha! No. I love coke as much as the next guy, but not that much. We have a fleet of small aircraft at our disposal. We can fly it out personally without being discovered."

"And how did you come across my coke?"

"I'm sorry?"

"How did you find my excellent cocaine and know where to come to buy more of it in bulk? You see, Sam, we do not sell to people we do not know. And the people we *do* sell to know better than to even breathe the name Villalobos when they are trafficking our product. So...I ask you again. How did you know to come *here*, to this place, to buy *my* drugs?"

Ahh. *Shit.* He does not look happy. The whole accountant vibe he had going on a second ago has morphed into something far less friendly. He has a glint in his eye, sharp and cruel, that hints at madness. "I beat it out of a very fat Mexican," I tell him. "And then I killed him."

Fernando's expression is all ice. He studies me with cool disregard for a moment, and then pinches the bridge of his nose between his index finger and his thumb. "I may have heard something about that."

"I used to go stay at his compound. He always had the best girls in his stables. *And the best blow.*"

"So you are interested in women, too?" he says.

I shrug, doing my best to look nonchalant. "I'm a guy, aren't I?"

Fernando looks at the ground, brows banked together, as if he's thinking furiously. Taking a step to the right, he holds out one hand, gesturing me into his office. "Come in. I need to make a phone call. You'll excuse me for a moment, I think." It's not a request. He's merely informing me of what's about to happen, and I honestly don't like the sound of it. A phone call to whom? I cut a sidelong look at Natalia. She seems to be locked in some kind of intense, silent communication with her father, and I can't decide if that is a good or a bad thing. Bad, I'm sure.

"I have something for you, Sam," she tells me. "My father will be back in a minute. I'm sure the two of you can discuss the matter of a purchase further then. In the meantime..." She gives me a tight-lipped smile and heads past her father, into the office.

I make a point of smiling warmly at Fernando as I enter his office. Better for me to pretend I'm completely oblivious to the danger of this situation than to break out into a sweat. Fernando nods slightly, and then he hurries off down the length of the floor, making a beeline for Ocho. His shoulders seem to have inched up some, like he's bracing for something; why Fernando Villalobos would be worried about anything here, in his home, with all his men and their weapons around, is a mystery.

Fernando's office is unassuming. No art on the walls. No frills of any kind. Bare tile floor. Regular desk. A small lamp, which is turned on, since there doesn't actually appear to be an overhead light.

"Have a seat." Natalia pulls out a seat in front of her father's desk, gesturing for me to park my ass in it. She seems to have forgotten about my gun. Either that, or she's placing a great deal of trust in me, and she doesn't expect me to shoot her father where he stands.

"Sorry it's so dim in here," she tells me. "My father has very sensitive eyes. Normal fluorescents bother him."

"That's okay." I sit down, watching her as she goes and sits in the seat Fernando must have occupied a moment ago. Sliding open a drawer, she produces a small silver mirrored plate, along with a narrow metal tube. It glints in the half light—a solid gold blow pipe.

I know what's coming next. Sure enough, she places a small wrap of paper down onto the desk in front of her and begins to unfold it. "I'm sure you'll want to sample our current product, yes?"

"Oh, that's not necessary."

She looks up at me, frowning. "No? That's normally our buyers' motto—try before you buy. People are normally ripping this stuff out of our hands. Not cheap."

"I'm sure that's true. But it's also bad business. I'm not here to enjoy myself. I'm here to make a deal. If I'm out of my head, how can I have a proper conversation with your father?"

Natalia smiles, splaying her fingers on the table in front of her. She studies her fingers, each and every one, before she speaks again. "Mr. America, you had better stick this pipe up your nose, and you had better inhale deep. If you don't, my father is going to have your hands removed, and he's going to mount them on the wall of our living room. Is that what you want?"

Well. When she puts it like that...

I hold my hand out, and she places the blowpipe in it, smiling. "A good choice," she advises me. The coke is already pre-cut and fine as icing sugar. She scoops a healthy amount out of the pile with her fingernail, and then she taps it out onto the silver plate, passing it to me. I've done coke before. It would have been impossible to avoid, living a life like mine. I'm hardly a seasoned pro when it comes to snorting narcotics, however. I already know how hard I'm going to have to work to prevent the top of my head from blowing off once the drugs hit home.

Sliding the pipe up my nose, I hold the other end to the small silver plate, and I inhale. Fireworks light up the inside of my head. *Fuuuuuck.* My head automatically kicks back—it feels like my nose is bleeding—and lights flash and flare behind my closed eyelids. A crushing wave of euphoria hits me hard. My body feels like it's been transformed, turned into silk, into the softest cashmere. My pores prickle and my head hums, my ears whistling as the cocaine gets to work. By and far the cleanest, most impressive buzz I've ever experienced.

"Is it good, Mr. America?" I open my eyes, and Natalia is leaning across her father's desk, eyes narrowed, watching me intently.

I sniff, shaking my head, trying to piece myself back together enough to form a sentence. "Yeah. Fuck yeah. *Damn.*"

She laughs. "What does it feel like?" she asks.

"I'm sure it feels the same for me as it does for you."

"I've never taken cocaine." Her voice is calm and collected. She says this as if it should be obvious—that there's no way she would ever do such a crazy, reckless thing.

I blink at her. My vision seems to have sharpened. Everything in the room has focused, the light growing to blinding proportions, the colors so much bolder and brighter. "That is the strangest thing I've ever heard. The daughter of a cocaine dealer, never having taken cocaine. Just seems so..."

"Unbelievable?"

"Yeah."

Natalia smirks. With the drugs coursing through my veins, she's even more beautiful, even more vibrant and alive. "My father forbids it," she informs me.

"I see. And you always do what your father tells you?"

The smile grows bigger. "*Always.*"

"You should probably rebel every once in a while. It's good for you."

She just shakes her head, scooping another bump of coke onto her fingernail and sprinkling it onto the silver plate. "Rebellion is called mutiny in Ecuador, Mr. America." She passes me the drugs. She doesn't let go of the plate. For a moment, we're both holding onto it, and she's giving me a pointed look that penetrates deep. "*And mutineers get shot at dawn.*"

She lets go of the plate.

"I'll bear that in mind, then."

"See that you do."

The second blast of euphoria hits me even harder this time. It's like a sledgehammer to the side of my head, sending me reeling back into my chair. I can feel my pulse everywhere, throbbing like the beat of a demented drum, and my fingers have gone completely numb. In fact, my whole body feels kind of numb, like I'm made out of cotton wool. It should be a worrying sensation, and yet it feels good. Really, really fucking good. My lips are tingling like crazy, and fuck...even my dick is getting hard. I want to risk a quick look down to my crotch, to see if my increasingly large boner is all that noticeable, but when I open my eyes, Natalia is watching me again with an intense, fascinated look on her face, and all other thought flies out of the window.

She isn't "morning-sunrise" kind of beautiful. She's "out-of-control-burn-your-fucking-house-down-forest-fire" kind of beautiful. And she's looking at me like she wants to shove me back into my seat, pull down her panties, and sit on my face so she can ride my mouth.

I'm sure her father would not approve.

I could be imagining this, of course. There's a very good chance I'm just seeing what I want to see, because my dick is now harder than granite, and my eyes feel like they're shooting laser beams out of them.

Natalia licks her lips. "Would you like some water?"

"Thank you."

She gets up and leaves the room, which strikes me as strange. If she's not watching me, then who is? I suppose the men out on the production floor would put me down pretty quick if they thought I was up to no good. But still... If one of Perez's guys left me alone at his compound, they'd find themselves headless and in need of a shallow grave. Not even Jamie would leave a guy sitting alone in an unlocked room.

Natalia doesn't come back for quite a while. I sit in my chair and I don't move, though. I can feel my breath, pulling and pushing around my body; it's as though the cells that make up my body are bigger than they should be, more sensitive, and I can feel every last one of them. I'm not in my right mind. I'm smart enough to realize that the drugs have fucked me up, and I shouldn't go making any rash decisions, so I keep my ass parked in my chair and I wait.

Eventually, Natalia comes back carrying a large glass carafe of water and two small tumblers on a tray. She sets it down on Fernando's desk, and begins to pour the liquid into the two glasses with all of the gravity and measure of a Japanese geisha preparing tea.

When she holds out a glass for me, filled almost to the brim with water, I accept it, holding my breath, not wanting to spill it. Natalia throws back her glass of water like it's a shot of tequila, down in one, and then she leans forward on her elbows, observing me as I slowly sip from my glass.

"You're not like most men who come here," she tells me.

I frown. I *need* to be like most men who come here. If Fernando's going to be tricked into thinking that Sam Garrett is a real person, right along with Louis James Aubertin the third, and that we want to start selling his narcotics north of the border, I need these guys to think I'm driven by addiction, desire for power, or a desire for money. Anything else is going to look suspicious. And a man with unclear motives is a dangerous man. "How so?" I ask.

Natalia sits back in Fernando's chair. She looks like she wants to kick her feet up on the desk, but then thinks better of it. "You're thinking all the time. *Think, think, think.*" She taps her temple with her index finger. "Every word you say is measured. Like it's passed a rigorous vetting program before it is allowed out of your mouth. It makes me think you are trying to hide things."

I press my fingertips against the sides of the cold glass in front of me, trying not to appear surprised by her very accurate assessment of me. "I promise I'm not doing it on purpose. And of course I'm hiding things. Every single guy you meet is trying to hide something, I can pretty much guarantee it."

"If you're referring to your erection, Mr. America, you really need to try harder."

I bark out laughter—I can't help it. She does *not* look like she has any business saying the word *erection* let alone actually noticing mine, and yet she doesn't seem embarrassed. Not even slightly pink in the cheeks.

I shift in my chair, angling my hips up for a moment so the bulge in my pants is even more prominent. "That is entirely your fault," I inform her. "Coke turns me on."

"Evidently."

"And so do exotic, half Ecuadorian women with sexy accents."

"How do you know I'm only half Ecuadorian?"

"Because your skin is almost white. And your eyes are green."

She harrumphs. "Skin and eye color don't seem to be a very reliable way of assessing someone's heritage, Sam."

"So you are one hundred percent Ecuadorian?"

She smiles a small, weighted smile. After a drawn out second, she says, "No, actually. You are right. My mother was born in Philadelphia. She moved to Ecuador when she was only eleven."

"And she still lives here?"

"No."

"She went back to Philadelphia?"

"No. She died, of course."

She says "*of course,*" as though it was the natural progression for her mother, like it was fated. Could be she *was* fated to die, the second she met Fernando Villalobos. "I probably shouldn't ask how she died, should I?"

Natalia gives me an accommodating smile, sighing. "Probably not."

"Then I will keep my mouth shut." I hold up my water glass, and Natalia reaches across the desk and toasts me. I'm about to say something else when the door behind me opens, and Fernando returns with a very thick, chunky-looking cell phone in his hands. No, not a cell phone. A sat phone. We used ones very similar in the military. Fernando gives me a jagged edged smile as he crosses the room toward us.

"Are you quite relaxed, Mr. Garrett? It's a very mellow high, no? We are always complimented on the soothing qualities of our coca. You feel more alive than you ever have, but also more in love, too. No hostilities here. No arguments or fights because of our product."

I am feeling pretty damn mellow; not even the drugs are enough to slow down the thunder of my heart, or dampen the buzzing in my head, though. I tap my fingertips against the side of Fernando's desk. "Did you figure everything out on your phone call, Mr Villalobos? You weren't gone for very long."

Fernando nods. "Not particularly. I called to confirm your credentials, Sam. My contact in New York is unreachable at the moment, however. I was only able to verify that your employer is very well known in certain circles. If there is anything you wish to tell me, now is the time to do it, my friend, when you cannot be caught out in a lie."

I shrug, but underneath his desk, where he can't see, I'm digging my fingernail into the grain of the wood, pressing hard, until I can feel splinters biting into my skin. The pain helps keep me focused. Helps keep my face straight. "I'm not lying. We want to buy from you, and I want to make a huge, fat profit back in the States." I look at Fernando and then at his daughter, hoping they don't see anything in my expression that might make me look suspicious. "Why is that so hard to believe?" I ask.

No one speaks for a moment. After a long, nerve-racking pause, Fernando inhales sharply. Taking his tortoiseshell glasses from his face and sliding them into the breast pocket of his neatly pressed button-down shirt, he clasps his hands together in front of him. "You're right, of course. I'm sure you understand, though. Like your employer, we are very private people, Mr. Garrett. We don't like to be disturbed, or have strangers show up announced. It makes us...what is it you say in America? *Antsy?*"

"Yeah. Antsy."

"We shall know if you're a legitimate customer in good time," Fernando continues. "Until then, you will be a guest. Eat, sleep and relax in my home."

"Oh, that's not necessary. I'm sure I can find somewhere comfortable enough in Orellana that—"

Fernando's cold, sharp look cuts me off. "But really, Mr. Garrett. *I insist.*"

FOUR
THE BLUE DOOR

Fernando tasks Ocho with escorting me from the premises, gun pressed into my back, Jurassic 5 now buzzing from his tinny speakers—I can hear the lyrics of the music perfectly as I climb back up the rungs of the ladder towards the surface, and I can still hear it perfectly when I'm standing there, waiting for his head to pop up out of the ground behind me like a gopher. A number of things occur to me during those few fleeting seconds while I'm waiting, the first of which being that I could easily kill him right now if I wanted to. One swift kick to the throat as he emerges from the ground would be enough to do it. I don't want to kill the guy, though. Apart from getting a little pokey with the muzzle of his gun, he's kept his mouth shut, and he hasn't been even remotely offensive. I'll feel bad if I kill him just so I can go darting off into the trees, fleeing the situation before I've really gleaned any useful information. If letting him live means I get to see inside the Villalobos family home, then so be it.

I don't think I know a single soul who has entered the Villalobos estate. I have no idea what to expect, and I have no idea if my sister will be there. Thankfully she wasn't chained to a desk down in that bunker, working her ass off cutting coke, naked as the day she was born. That's something to celebrate at least.

Ocho prods me with his gun, pointing this way and that into the rainforest, directing me, and we walk for what feels like an unbelievably long time, until we finally hit a dirt road that cuts through the trees. We head west. I count in my head, not wanting to pull out my cell phone to check the time in order to monitor how long we walk for, just in case Ocho thinks I'm going for my gun and shoots me in the back. I reel numbers off in my head until I reach six hundred, and then I start over again. I've ticked off seventeen minutes in my head by the time we emerge from the forest into a small clearing, where an Escalade and a brand new Jeep Patriot are parked side by side. Ocho grunts. Once he has my attention, he tosses me a set of keys and opens the driver's side door of the Escalade.

He jabs me with the gun.

"Me? You want me to drive?"

He jams the muzzle of the gun into my ribcage, and I don't ask again. I climb into the vehicle, and I go to slide the key into the ignition, only there is no ignition. A small START button brings the engine roaring into life the moment I hit it. Ocho grunts again, slamming the passenger door closed behind him, and then he's pointing, gesturing for me to go left. I do as I'm told. We pass back through the town of Orellana, and then head over the river via a narrow, unstable looking bridge. The landscape whips by in a blur, and Ocho says nothing. Only points. Eventually he directs me to take yet another dirt track off the pot-holed, bumpy road we've been traveling down, and we drive for a short period of time before the roadway suddenly becomes paved, and we're winding our way up a bare, exposed hillside, into the mountains.

I count fourteen hairpin turns before we're spat out on top of the mountain, and we're faced with the biggest, grandest, most over the top villa I have ever seen in my life. And I've seen some ridiculously big houses. Huge, the building stands three stories tall, with five-foot high windows on the upper floors. A row of ostentatious pillars prop up the façade, twelve of them all evenly spaced out in a row, bared like teeth against the cool blue sky that seems to stretch on forever into the distance behind the mansion. God knows how they got the building materials up here to create such a monstrosity. The road was barely enough to take the Escalade. There's no way heavy lifting machinery made it up here. No way in hell. Ocho stabs his finger toward the right, gesturing for me to take a small pathway that leads around the side of the house, and I take it, pulling up around the back into a fully constructed motherfucking parking lot, filled with four-by-four vehicles and, unbelievably, golf carts.

"Lot of people live here, huh?" I ask. Ocho probably doesn't hear me over his Walkman. He gets out of the car and walks around the vehicle, opening my door for me and jerking his head back toward the house. Still, not a word comes out of his mouth. I could speak to him in Spanish, but I don't think he's in a very chatty mood. And besides, Fernando doesn't know I understand Spanish yet. Better to keep that card up my sleeve. Might be useful if he takes any calls or talks to his men in his native tongue, expecting me to be oblivious to his words. I follow Ocho, allowing him to shepherd me into the mansion through the back door, through what once would have been the servant's entrance. The place looks old enough to have once been staffed, in any case. Orellana was very little more than a shanti boat town kind of affair, and yet this mansion would be quite at home in Victorian England.

Inside, the floors are pale, polished marble, shot through with threads and fractures of gold and gray. It looks wet somehow. Liquid, like the calm, flat surface of a milk bath, yet it's reassuringly solid underfoot. There are more pillars in the foyer, and strange, musty paintings on the walls of austere military figures in colorful, unfamiliar uniforms. Sabres are mounted to the walls. Bronze cast busts of angry looking men with moustaches rest on walnut sideboards, and ceramics of graceful and elegant naked women pose an on shelves—all of which seem to be headless. A woman in a full-blown black and white maid's outfit hurries into the foyer, a tray of empty glasses in her hand; she looks up, sees Ocho, sees *me*, yelps, and nearly drops the tray.

"Dios Mio!"

Ocho growls at her, and the woman crosses herself, as if the mere sight of us is enough to put the fear of god into her. She turns on her heel and disappears back the way she came, muttering frantically under her breath.

"I am *not* the first white man that woman has seen," I mutter under my own breath.

Another sharp prod from Ocho. He places a hand on my shoulder, and he hurries me down a wide, beautifully decorated hallway, until we round a corner and we're faced with a massive sweeping staircase, carpeted in a plush, rich cream. Ocho's eyes flicker upwards, and I get moving. No point in hanging around, pretending like I don't know what he wants from me. I need to behave myself until I've been able to recon the entire house, search every room, and find Laura. That's going to take time. More time than I anticipated, now I've seen the size of the damn place.

Up the stairs we go.

On the second floor, I can hear talking. The sound of many people talking. I can't make out the words, or even the language, but as Ocho guides me down a series of hallways, the talking gets louder. He reaches the end of a particularly long, straight hallway and then throws open a blue painted door to the right, revealing the source of all the chatter—a small room, packed with people, at least twenty of them. Twenty-five, perhaps? Most of them are men. Women walk around the room, scantily clad, some of them not dressed at all, some of them wearing sheer material that gives the hint of nipple here and the suggestion of ass there. A tall guy with raven-black hair sees me standing in the doorway and smiles, heading straight for me. He's Caucasian—most of the people inside the room are—and he's wearing a white tuxedo.

"You're late. What took you so long?" he asks, slapping me in an overly friendly manner on the shoulder. He shoots Ocho an annoyed look and hisses at him, frowning. "Well? Go on, Ocho. You're not needed here now. We have everything under control."

Out of the corner of my eye, I see a woman in a pink bra and panties drop to her knees, and the man standing in front of her slowly slides his bare cock into her mouth. I blink, looking away. Ocho isn't paying attention to the guy with the black hair; he's looking at me, looking at me intently, eyes narrowed. I think he's gauging my reaction to what I've just walked into, so I make a show of smiling and allowing my eyes to wander again. Are my pupils still blown from the coke? Do I look turned on right now, or angry as fuck? Because I *am* angry as fuck. I don't think I've ever been angrier than I am right now. I can't let it show, though. That would be seriously disastrous.

Ocho makes a low rumbling noise, but he doesn't argue with the guy. He backs out of the room, closing the door behind him, and the tuxedo guy is suddenly grabbing hold of me by the arm and dragging me off to one side.

"Who are you? Where have you come from?" he demands, talking out of the side of his mouth. He's smiling, eyes wrinkling at the corners, as if he's reacting to something funny I've just said, but his voice is low and urgent.

"I came from New York. My name is Sam." Giving him any further information than that would be foolhardy. I don't know who the fuck this guy is, after all.

"New York, New York," the guy chants. His fingers continue to dig into my arm. "Nope. I don't know anyone in New York. Fucking awesome."

He has no accent, well trained to make it sound as though he could have come from anywhere, but as he talks I hear a hint of a Southern twang slip through, giving him away.

"Did he mark you, yet?" the guy asks.

"Mark me?"

"Yes. Y'know. Did he brand you?"

My look of confusion must speak loudly enough, because he rolls up his sleeve and holds out his arm, showing me what he means: a small, angry, red burn mark in the shape of a wolf's head, with a large V underneath it. "He marks his property," the guy tells me. A shadow of doubt flies across his face then, appearing out of nowhere. "Unless..."

"Unless?"

"Unless you're a player, not a member of the Servicio."

"I don't have a fucking clue what you're talking about right now."

"Did you pay to come here? *To fuck*? Or are you one of us, one of Fernando's *servants*?"

I take a step back, putting a healthy amount of space between us. "I'm neither. I just came to buy drugs."

The guy in the tux visibly calms. He tucks his hands into the pockets of his pants and rocks back onto his heels, a manic light flickering in his pale blue eyes. "You have no idea where you are, do you?"

I refrain from answering. I don't like the madness hovering over his head, this strange Southern, dark-haired man; I'm beginning to think he might be a little crazy. He tips his head back and laughs.

"You've strayed far from the path of civilization. No one just comes here to buy drugs. He'll have you playing this game soon enough, or he'll turn you into a pawn in it, Sam. You'd better clue yourself into your surroundings and quickly, otherwise you might end up the used instead of the user." He steps back, a quirky, unsettling expression on his face. I think he's going to go and stand back by the door, but before he can reach it a tall, blond-haired guy with neck tattoos places a hand on his shoulder and stops him in his track. The blond guy already has a woman on his left arm. She's completely naked, apart from what looks like a necktie looped tightly around her throat, biting into her skin. Her dark brown, almost black hair is arranged into a perfect mess of curls, which fall way down her back. Her breasts are perfect, nipples peaked and standing to attention. The blond guy hugs her to his side as he reaches out and strokes his fingers down Tux Guy's cheek.

"Care to introduce yourself?" the blond guy asks.

Meeting my eye instead of the newcomer's, Tux Guy smirks, a false air of confidence rolling off him. He sighs. "Of course. I'm Plato. I see you've already met my friend Persephone?"

Plato's fingers skate over the creamy, perfect skin of the woman on the blond guy's arm; he traces them over her stomach, up, so that he's skimming the swell of her breast. The girl doesn't move. She remains glued to the spot, allowing Plato to explore her body, seemingly unfazed, as the blond guy watches on.

"Oh yes. She's fucking perfect. And so are you."

Plato looks hungry, but it seems false. Like he's acting. "Would you like for me and Persephone to put on a show for you?" he asks the blond guy. He steps closer to the man, so close that their chests are almost touching. The blond guy's eyelids droop as he looks from Persephone to the other man.

"Yeah. Yeah, I want you to fuck her good for me, man. I'm going to watch."

Plato pouts. "Is that all? I was hoping..." His hand disappears between their bodies, and suddenly the blond guy is stiffening, his shoulders growing tense. He makes a low, warning growl in his throat.

"I'm not fucking gay," he hisses.

"I never said you were," Plato offers. "But that doesn't mean I can't suck your dick. And it doesn't mean you can't fuck my ass, either."

I stand back as the three of them move toward a low couch in the center of the room, where Plato begins to slowly strip out of his suit. His attention is fixed on the woman and the man in front of him, but his gaze flashes to me every so often. He's trying to see if I get it now. And I do. This place is full of rich bastards, willing to pay to have their deepest, darkest desires fulfilled. It is also full of people, held here in this room against their will, who are forced to submit to whatever is asked of them. On pain of...I don't know. I'm not sure what the punishment would be if any of these "workers" refused to do their jobs, but I'm sure it can't be good.

In no time at all, Plato is completely naked and he's inside Persephone, fucking her hard and fast while the blond customer watches, stroking his hard cock through his black pants. I can see the desire in his eyes. I can see violence, too. This whole thing has started off pleasant enough, but I know men like this fucking blond dude, and I know what he really wants to do. He wants to hurt them. He wants to watch the pain in their eyes—pain that he causes—and he wants to get off on it.

The room is full of violence, shame and terror, all of which is thinly disguised by a grim patina of desire and lust. The woman on her knees, blowing a guy a few feet from me, is fingering her own pussy, palming her tits as she works her lips and her tongue up and down the guy's shaft, but her moans are forced. She's not enjoying herself, and she sure as shit doesn't want to be here. Plato's cock is rock solid as he uses it to pound Persephone in the ass, but I get the feeling there might have been some sort of stimulant involved on that front.

I stay exactly where I am, and I try to keep my head down. The occupants of the room all seem to be fairly involved in their activities at hand (or mouth, or ass, as the case might be), but I don't want to draw attention to myself, so I stand perfectly still and I watch.

The blond guy with Plato and Persephone finally gives up the pretence and gives in to what he really wants. He grabs hold of Plato by the hair and kisses him roughly, jamming his tongue into his mouth. Plato responds, sucking on it and groaning while Persephone rocks her hips against his, the two of them still fucking. The blond guy lets go of Plato's hair and runs his hand down Plato's back, until he's reaching in between his legs and he's cupping Plato's balls. With his other free hand, he cups and squeezes Persephone's tits, so that he's touching and caressing them both while they writhe against each other.

The next twenty minutes are pretty damned uncomfortable. I lean back against the wall, watching the door, waiting for Ocho to return to see that I'm not enjoying myself, but he doesn't show up. Instead, I'm treated to the vision of Plato sucking the blond guy's dick. I know shit is going to get real when the blond guy strips off, but things don't go as I expect. He doesn't bend Plato over and screw him in the ass. He bends over himself, burying his face between Persephone's thighs, and he has Plato fuck *him* in the ass. Dark haired Persephone comes loud, and she comes hard. It's a real orgasm, by the looks of things. Some of the other men standing around the edges of the room, quietly talking to other beautiful women in various states of undress, all stop their conversations to watch as Plato puts on the performance of a lifetime.

His skin is shining with sweat as he works himself in and out of the blond guy, who grabs handfuls of the thick carpet beneath him, head bowed, eyes closed tightly. A couple of the guys on the peripheries of the party subtly take hold of their erections through their pants, running their hands up and own themselves as the small space fills with the sound of Plato's exertions.

"Goddamn he's good," someone mutters close by.

"The best."

"Well, he's had practice. Three years' worth."

Three years? Plato has been here for *three years*? That doesn't seem as though it can be true. Surely not. How long can a party like this continue, after all? A night? Nothing more. People sleep. People have work. Responsibilities. Even if Plato is here against his will, the people who have paid to attend this...*event* have to return to their lives at some point.

One of the men watching the display before us steps forward. His pants are unbuttoned, his dick in his hand. He doesn't even hesitate as he pushes himself into Persephone's mouth. She accepts him; her eyes are clamped shut, and her hands are balled into fists, but she accepts him. The guy shudders pleasure as she licks and sucks at him. The blond being fucked by Plato watches with stunned, wide eyes as the other well-dressed man fucks Persephone's mouth. He moans, a ragged breath of ecstasy escaping his lips, and then he's coming, his dick pulsing as he spills his come everywhere into the carpet.

"Holy fuck," someone whispers.

"Quite the show."

Next to me, a tall guy with a black button-down and black leather gloves turns to the woman kneeling naked at his feet and strokes a hand over her hair. "Do you see?" he whispers. "This is how it goes. This is everything. This is what is expected of you."

The woman looks shocked. She can't be more than twenty, and her bottom lip is wobbling. Her tits are small, less than a handful, and they look bruised, as if someone has been biting them. Small wheels of purple and black mark her skin on her stomach and on her shoulders, too. On the flesh between her thighs. She shivers as the guy wearing the gloves reaches into his back pocket and produces and short, rigid whip with a flayed leather tassel on the end. He runs the end of the whip down her back, between her shoulder blades, stopping short just above the curve of her buttocks, which look as though they've already been treated once or twice with the whip prior to now.

"Behave yourself and you'll come to like this," the guy whispers. "Misbehave, and it's within my power to make your time here the most unpleasant thing imaginable. Unbearable, even."

I have a rage inside of me the likes of which I have never experienced before. I am boiling. My veins are filled with bubbling battery acid, and if feels like my lungs are about to explode. I clench my hands into fists.

"Do you understand?" the guy whispers.

The girl looks up at him, and there are tears in her eyes. Her whole body is trembling. "Please. I just want to go home. *Please.* I swear I won't tell anyone about this. I promise, I—"

A gloved hand flies out, cracking across her cheek, sending her sprawling out on the floor, and that's it. I have had enough. I'm reaching for my gun before I even realize what I'm doing. It's instinctual, and I've never been very good at ignoring my instincts. A loud crack splinters through the air, and then I'm staring at the naked blonde girl on her knees, because her face is splattered with blood and her eyes are bugging out of her head.

The room is silent.

The guy who was schooling her on how to behave a moment ago sways a little, a bizarre, confused look on his face, and then he slumps to his knees right in front of the girl, slowly touching a hand to a smoking hole in his chest. He looks down at the hole, and at the blood that's slowly beginning to trickle from the wound, and then he laughs. Just once. One surprised, disbelieving snap of laughter. His eyes roll back into his head, and then he topples forward, head first into the blonde girl, who shrieks and scrambles back, terrified.

Plato and his companions have stopped fucking and are all looking at me like I've lost my mind. In fact, *everyone* is looking at me like I've lost my mind.

"You...that was...really fucking *dumb*," Plato says. His dick is still hard, which is kind of off putting, but impressive. None of the other assholes in the room have managed to maintain an erection. Their balls look like they've well and truly shrunk up inside their bodies.

"You have no idea what you've just done." Plato grabs his boxers and his pants from the floor, hurrying towards me. Another guy steps out, trying to block his way. He's huge, well over six feet; he looks like he's just processed the fact that I killed a man at their fuck fest, and he's really not happy about it.

"I hope you like pain, new guy. We're about to break every bone in your goddamn body." He rushes forward, murder in his eyes, and I hold up the gun, closing one eye and aiming the thing directly at his head. My hand is steady. I don't need to close an eye to squeeze off a shot and put an end to this motherfucker, but it makes it look like I mean business. The guy stops in his tracks, and his face turns a frightening shade of crimson.

"You're not seriously going to shoot two of us," he snarls. "Fernando will have your head for this."

"He can have it, if he demands it," I say. "I have seven bullets left in this gun, though, and I'm a crack shot, asshole. I'll take eight of you before I leave this room, and I'll die without a single regret."

"You're insane."

"No, man. I have just had *enough*." And it's true. Years of men abusing young girls. Years of raiding warehouses in the middle of the night, to find teenagers handcuffed to gas pipes, while lines of guys take their turns with them. And years of looking for my sister, never finding her, thinking with each new obscene horror I find that this could be what she's been going through for so long. It's taken its toll. Every second has left a black mark on my soul that's slowly but surely tarnished me. There's no good left in me. There's nothing to keep me from killing as many of these sick motherfuckers as I can and welcoming death with open arms.

I'm about to pull the trigger, to kill this motherfucker right where he's standing, but then a small voice whispers in the back of my head: *Laura. What about Laura? She* could *be here. She could be here, and then what? If you die, she'll* never *escape this place.*

My finger eases off the trigger. The guy breathes out slowly, his hands twitching by his sides, eyes narrowed into slits. I can tell he wants to be the one to do it. He wants to be the one who kills me. No matter what happens here today, I won't be giving him the satisfaction, though. I'll bury a bullet between his eyes before that happens, or I'll kill him with my bare fucking hands. A man like him will never best a guy like me.

Plato grabs hold of me by the arm and drags me back, hissing under his breath. "Come on. You have to get out of here." He's managed to get his boxers on, which I'm more than pleased about. He shoves me backward, and then he's dragging me toward the door.

Persephone gets to her feet, tits wobbling everywhere; she holds a hand out, grasping at thin air, shock all over her face. "Don't! Don't open the door!"

Plato casts a troubled look over his shoulder. He shrugs. "I don't think it'll be that bad." And then he's opening the door and pulling me through, slamming it shut behind us.

I stand in the long, empty, beautifully decorated hallway, staring at the now closed door. "That thing's been open the whole fucking time? What the hell, man?"

Plato pants, out of breath, like he just ran across the finish line of an uphill marathon. I recognize the fear painted across his face. I recognize the wide-eyed look of panic in his eyes. "Once you walk through that door, you stay in that room until he tells you otherwise," he says.

"What? *Why?*"

"Because Fernando's a psycho. He has rules, and those rules can't be broken, no matter how stupid they are."

"And if you don't stay inside?"

"Then Fernando feeds you to his wolves." He says this so matter-of-factly that I think he's joking for a second. But Plato isn't laughing. His face is pale, and a thin sheen of sweat has broken out across his forehead.

"I don't suppose that's a metaphor for a severe beating?" I ask.

Plato shakes his head. "No, man. That's about as literal as it gets."

"How do you know?"

"How do you think, asshole? He waits until nightfall and then drags us out of there onto the front lawn. *He makes us watch.*"

FIVE
AN APOLOGY

I consider leaving, just bolting from the house and taking Plato with me, but the man violently shakes his head when I make the suggestion. "We wouldn't make it a hundred feet from the house. The forest's full of booby traps. Fernando's obsessed with hunting and trapping. He'd fucking love to come back to the house later to find the two of us staked through on metal spikes. And believe me, that's exactly what would happen. Plenty of people have tried to run before. And every single one of them has died."

"Then what?"

"We stay here, and we wait."

"No way. That asshole back there won't wait long before he comes out and tries to rip my head from my body. Loitering here is just asking for it."

Plato laughs a stony, cold laugh. "You don't get it, man. No one apart from Ocho can come and go without being dealt the same hand. Player or Servicio, it doesn't matter. Once you're through the blue door, you do not leave. The players love the restriction most of the time. It feeds into their fantasies. They have an alpha pool running between them—who can own and dominate the most girls...or *guys*...while they're trapped inside the room." He looks away, rubbing his hand over his jaw. "Why did you do it, man? Why couldn't you just leave well enough alone? Now you've probably gone and gotten us both killed. And for what? A newbie chick that's probably getting fucked by eight guys already now that she doesn't have her sponsor in there to protect her?"

"That guy was *not* protecting her."

"He *was*. If a guy brings a girl here and he's sponsoring her, training her, then no one else can touch her. He might fuck her. He might punish her if she doesn't do what she's told, but none of the other sick fuckers in there can lay a finger on her. It's one of Fernando's laws."

I just look at him. None of this is making any sense to me, but then again I've seen and heard plenty in my life that hasn't made a lick of sense. It's just...*Fernando*? Seriously? The guy I just met at the bunker was quiet and reserved. Nervous, almost. He didn't seem like he'd have the mettle to feed a living, breathing human being to a pack of wolves, that's for sure. What kind of guy has a room like this in his house, where his *law* is enough to keep grown ass men and women trembling behind an unlocked door?

Plato leans back against the wall, his bare skin resting against the plasterwork, and he sighs heavily. "This is highly inconvenient, y'know? I was planning on killing myself next week. I've been stashing toothpicks under a floorboard in my room. I was going to swallow them and eviscerate myself from the inside out. Now all of my scheming is totally wasted. "

"Evisceration is any better than being eaten?"

"I'm a selfish person, my friend. I don't give anything without deeply resenting it. So yeah...another animal consuming my body really isn't going to sit well with me."

I consider asking him how that ties in with the fact that he's constantly giving away a part of himself when he fucks the people in the room we just left, but I decide that pointing this out isn't going to help either one of us, so I button my lip. "Just go back inside, man," I tell him. "I won't say a word. Fernando will never know that you snuck out for five seconds."

Plato pulls a face. "Of course he will. Look." He points up at a small, white, inconspicuous camera that's mounted high on the wall in front of us; it's tiny, and exactly the same color as the paintwork, but I should have noticed it. It should have been the first thing I saw when I walked down here with Ocho, but I'm so spun out and turned around that it slipped my attention.

"Ahh."

"There are five of them inside the room as well." Plato waggles his eyebrows in an ironic fashion. "Fernando likes to keep an eye on things from his office. Wherever he is right now, he already knows about this. It's too late. So heading back inside is pointless. It'll only make him madder. Better to stay here and hope he's in a good mood when he gets back."

Natalia said as much when we were on our way to meet him earlier—that he was in a good mood. Hopefully this incident won't sour that. I'm not holding my breath, though. I've had a lot of experience with cartel bosses, and I can't say any of them have ever taken kindly to me killing their guests.

Shit. This is going to be terrible.

I pull my cell phone out of my pocket. I could call the club. I'd only need to ask once, and Jamie would be on a plane in a heartbeat, bringing the full force of the Widow Makers MC along with him. I stare at the cell phone screen, trying to construct the request in my head:

I'm sorry, man. I fucked up. Big time.

Hey, Jamie. I used your name to get into a cartel boss's house, and then I killed someone. Now it looks like I'm gonna be fed to a bunch of wolves.

Hi, Jay. Remember when you said not to make a scene down here? Well...

I put my phone back into my pocket. How many times has Jamie put himself on the line for this? How many guns have been pointed at his head already? The answer is too many. I'm going to have to figure this one out on my own.

And if I can't?

Well, then.

So be it.

VICE

••••

It doesn't take long for the head of the Villalobos cartel to show up. Plato tenses at the sound of tires crunching on gravel, and then he turns white as an over-bleached sheet when the front door of the building opens and the sound of people arguing floats up to us on the second floor.

I strain to listen, but the shouted words aren't in English and none it makes sense. I recognize the voices, though—Fernando and his daughter. She sounds upset, anger spiking in her words. Fernando's side of the argument is less heated, clipped and cold, which is somehow far more worrying than if he were yelling.

"Oh, god," Plato groans.

Footsteps on the stairs, and then Fernando appears in the hallway, back ramrod straight, shoulders drawn back, marching toward us with steel in his eyes. Behind him, Ocho follows with his headphones still glued to his ears, and his assault rifle primed in his hands. Natalia brings up the rear, her brows banked together in a severe frown, and two twin spots of color reddening her cheeks.

"Father," she snaps. Fernando stops in the middle of the hallway and turns to her. He glares at her, and she seems to lose her fire. She bows her head, and sucks in a deep, shaky breath. "Father, I ask that you—"

"You do not ask anything of me, child. You are obedient, and you behave as a lady would behave. Now go back downstairs and find Arissa. She needs help unloading the supplies, I am sure."

She glances quickly down the hallway in our direction. Shuffling her feet, she looks like she wants to stay, to say something more, but she wears her fear openly. She doesn't want to disobey her father. More than that, she is afraid to.

She stares at the floor a second longer, and then she turns, hurrying away with her hands curled tightly into fists. Fernando watches her go, and then he slowly turns toward us. Plato huffs. He sounds resigned now, and I can't help but feel as if his lost hope might have chased mine away with it.

"You have been in my house for less than two hours, Mr. Garrett, and it seems as though you've already caused quite a scene. Can you explain yourself?"

Clearing my throat, I crack the knuckle of my index finger, smiling. "I apologize. I wasn't aware of your house rules until I'd already broken a few of them. Had I known you frowned upon homicide and people freely roaming around your home, I would have refrained from both."

Fernando doesn't look all that pleased by my attitude. His expression is similar to my father's when I told him I planned on joining the military. I've only known this guy for a few hours, so it's kind of impressive that I've let him down so spectacularly already.

"Ocho is a mute, Mr. Garrett. He has no tongue to speak with. If he had, he would have explained everything a little more efficiently. In these situations, I normally like to go over my rules personally, but I didn't have time earlier. Can you please tell me how this came about? Why did you kill that man?"

Fuck. I can't tell him I was incensed by the way that bastard was treating the girl at his feet. I'm supposed to be into fucking women and treating them like they are my possessions. If I tell him I took offence to how that asshole was talking to the girl, it will look very strange indeed. "He wouldn't share," I say. "I wanted the girl he was with, and he was being a cunt about it."

I'm praying to god the cameras inside that room don't have sound. I didn't exchange a single word with that William guy before I shot him dead. If I was meant to be arguing with him over that girl, then the fact that I simply took out my gun and pulled the trigger will seem highly irregular, too.

Fernando tuts. "We are very respectful here, Mr. Garrett. If one of the players inside that room has claimed a girl, she is his until he is finished with her, or he invites someone else to join him. Is that clear?"

"Seems very civilized now, when you put it like that." I can't seem to keep the disgust out of my voice.

Fernando scratches his face in a nervous, twitchy manner. "As you were unaware of the rules, I will accept a sincere apology from you in this instance, and you may wait downstairs for me." He looks at me expectantly.

"What about him?" I point a thumb at Plato. He looks like he's about to keel over and pass out.

"Him?" Fernando steps toward me and places a hand on my shoulder. His fingernails are perfectly manicured and trimmed, with a tiny crescent of white rimming each nail. It looks like he actually spends time shaping and cleaning them. His hands aren't manly in the slightest. "Plato knows better. I'm afraid, where he is concerned, a simply apology is not going to be sufficient."

"He was helping me. He shouldn't be punished."

Fernando tips his head to one side. "Are you telling me how to run my household, Mr. Garrett? Because, rest assured, that would be very ill advised."

"I'm merely pleading his case. What kind of a man would I be if I let someone help me at the risk of their own safety, and then I did nothing to preserve theirs?"

Fernando considers this. "Very noble. I shall think on the matter. In the meantime, I'd like to have a word with Plato in private."

"It's okay, man. Just go," Plato hisses. "This is the best possible outcome, believe me." It doesn't look like the best possible outcome from where I'm standing, but hell. I don't think I'm going to accomplish anything standing here, forcing the point. Plato looks at me with wide, urgent eyes, and I make a vow to myself. This poor bastard is not being fed to any animal, be it a pig, a wolf or a fucking monkey. I'll work it out. I'll make sure he's safe.

"All right, then. I'll be downstairs."

"I think you are forgetting something," Fernando says quietly. "Your apology?"

"Oh. Of course." I can't remember the last time I apologized to anyone, let alone for something like this. Do I feel bad that I killed that sick fucker? Nope. Do I feel like I should be scraping and bowing because he's dead? Abso-fucking-lutely not. But the situation will spiral out of control if I don't. I angle my head to the floor, averting my eyes. "I'm sorry, Fernando. Please accept my humble apologies. I should have respected your hospitality, and I let my own anger get the better of me. I promise, it won't happen again."

With cold, dead eyes Fernando stares straight through me for a moment. "Your apology is accepted, Mr. Garrett. I'll be will you shortly. For now, Ocho will show you where to wait for me."

And just like that, I am dismissed.

SIX
BEND OVER

"**One hundred kilos. That is the smallest amount that we deal** in, Mr. Garrett. We find this sorts the chaff from the wheat. Only serious buyers come to us, and buying our cocaine in these quantities demonstrates your intent."

We're sitting in a poorly lit, barely furnished office much like the one back at the bunker, and I'm beginning to feel like I'm in way over my head. There's a large, round, black button mounted on the wall behind his head; will I be ditched out of my chair, through a trapdoor, into a tank of shark infested water below, à la James Bond, if he hits the thing?

"In case you were wondering, that is a cost to you of two million American dollars. Do you have that amount with you?" He knows I don't have two million dollars just sitting in my back pocket. He's being an asshole, but I can't call him out on it. I have to play ball. I smile confidently.

"Carrying that amount of money around with me in a foreign country wouldn't be very smart now, would it? I have fifty thousand. That's what I can give you as a show of good faith."

I don't want to buy *any* coke, but if I don't keep up this pretence, I'm gonna be in serious shit. If handing over every single last dollar I have with me means I buy his trust, even for a couple of days, then it will be worth it, though. Despite my apology, Fernando is obviously still not happy with me. He sits back in his chair, his face falling into shadow, and for the first time he looks sinister and evil enough to be the head of this cartel. "Fifty thousand. Okay. And you will have the rest of the money for me in three days' time. And your boss will bring it here, yes? You are his right hand man, but I would prefer to forge our business deal with the man in charge."

"That won't be a problem." It *will* be a problem. It's gonna be a *huge* problem. Jamie knows I'm probably going to be using his New York cover, but he has no idea that I'm promising away two million fucking dollars, or that he is now expected to show up. Nothing to be done about it now, though; the lie will have to hold water for the time being.

"Okay, Mr. Garrett." Fernando holds out his hand for me to shake. "We have ourselves a deal. But know this. I am still waiting to hear from my friends in America. If they tell me anything about you or your employer that might give me cause for concern, there will be consequences. I will leave that to your imagination."

He gets up, splaying his fingers out on his desk as he leans forward on it. "Now. My rules. If you go through the blue door, you may not leave that room until I give my express permission. We both know you have discovered this rule already, so there will be no excuses now. Second rule. You may not kill any of my guests without my express permission. Lucky for you, the man you killed, William, owed me a great deal of money and wasn't planning on paying it to me any time soon. If you had killed one of my wealthier clients who pay on time, I would not have been so lenient."

"I understand. No more killing people. Promise."

Fernando shakes his head slowly. "There is only one more rule, Mr. Garrett, and it's a simple one to follow. I do not allow anybody in this household to interact with my daughter on a romantic, flirtatious or sexual level. She is a brilliant and smart woman, but she is not worldly wise. She does not realize people here would take advantage of her given half the chance. This is why I must insist that you only speak with her if Ocho is present, or some other member of the household staff."

Damn. No speaking to Natalia without a chaperone? I mean, he's filled this bizarre mansion out in the middle of the forest with twenty to thirty sexual deviants and criminals. He needs to warn them off his daughter, especially when those motherfuckers are the kind of guys to take what they want without asking. I get that. But she's a grown-ass woman. She's twenty-six or twenty-seven. She should be able to make her own decisions for herself. This is my liberal American brain talking, though. And Natalia has *not* grown up in a liberal American environment.

"I won't talk to her without someone present," I tell him.

"Good. And try not to curse in front of her, Mr. Garrett. The last man who used profanity in front of Natalia was severely punished."

"Oh?"

"Yes. I cut out his tongue with a blunt knife. Now he can never make that mistake again."

On the other side of the open office door, Ocho shifts uncomfortably from one foot to the other. So that explains that, then.

"My men will be by your room later on this evening to collect your fifty-thousand-dollar collateral, if that is convenient with you? I would be grateful if you would please remain in your assigned room until that time, please? A number of players from the blue room are being released this afternoon, and I would hate for any of William's friends to run into you in the hallways. Just as I have not punished you for your indiscretions, Mr. Garrett, it would also be very hard for me to punish them for theirs should they decide to follow in your footsteps."

"And Plato?"

"Don't worry, Mr. Garrett. You will see Plato again soon, I am sure of it."

••••

My bedroom is luxurious and way more than I was expecting. Dark, slate-gray drapes hang from high windows, and the bedclothes, also slate-gray, match the thick, rich rug that covers the polished floorboards. I have an en suite bathroom—clean towels, and tiny little bottles of body wash and shampoo stacked in a glass bowl beside a huge shower. I've stayed in plenty of five star hotel rooms that weren't anywhere near as nice.

Five star hotel rooms don't generally come with video surveillance, though. I spend an hour going over the place with a fine-tooth comb, searching every piece of furniture and picture frame, the light fittings and the air vents until I'm satisfied that there's nothing in here. Looks like Fernando only watches over the common areas of the house, along with the party room. At least I can keep my own privacy here.

I kick off my boots and my clothes, stretching, revelling in the freedom of being naked. It's three thirty in the afternoon—quite an eventful day thus far. I take a long, blisteringly hot shower, scrubbing the dirt from my body, and once I'm done I dry myself off and crash out on the massive bed that takes up a considerable portion of the room. I don't mean to sleep. I don't even mean to close my eyes, but the next thing I know, it's dark out of the windows overlooking the rear of the property, and a weird, cold sensation is prickling across my still-bare skin.

My heart steps up the pace, sending my pulse skyrocketing upward. Something isn't right. It's dark, but I can feel it—eyes on me, eyes traveling over my body. There's someone in the fucking room with me. I sit up at the same time they strike.

"Get his legs! Get his fucking legs!"

Hands claw and grab at me; I can't tell how many men are in the room with me, but there are more than I can fight off. And they're fucking strong. I'm surrounded by American accents, which is weird. I try to wrestle myself free from the men that are holding onto my arms, thrashing my legs to prevent more of them from taking hold of me by the ankles, but it's a futile struggle. It feels like there are two guys per limb, holding me down, and I can't fight against those odds. Not naked and unprepared as I am. I still give it a fucking good try, though.

"Goddamn. Fuck! He kicked me in the balls."

"Quit fucking around, Art. Just get the fucking job done already."

"I'm trying! Ahh, Jesus, I'm gonna throw up."

I lash out, trying to connect with someone else, with something vital and delicate, but they've got me now. "What the fuck are you doing?" I snarl. "Get your fucking hands off me."

A light switches on in the bathroom, followed by a small lamp on the table beside the bed, and a soft, warm glow fills the room. Not much light, but enough that I can make out the crowd of men kneeling on my bed, holding me down. I can see plainly enough the tall, red-headed guy standing in the doorway, wearing a black suit with a white button-down underneath, surveying the scene with distaste. He steps inside my bedroom, pulling the door closed behind him.

"Well, this is messy," he says. "I thought I said ask him if you could search his belongings?"

The guy holding my right wrist, pressing his other hand down hard onto my chest, makes an amused sound. "No. You told us to go fuck up his shit," he says.

The red-headed guy in the suit thinks for a second and then nods. "Yeah, you know what? I think you might be right. I did say that, didn't I?"

I writhe, rage bubbling through me as I try to get free. "*What the fuck is going on?*"

The guy in the suit enters the room properly now, casting a bored glance around the space, his eyes traveling over my scattered belongings. He reaches out and picks up my cell phone. "My employer is a trusting man. To a point. He hires men like me to be extra suspicious on his behalf. You could say...I am Fernando Villalobos's paranoia. And I was *very* paranoid when I heard that a guy from New York had showed up today on a motorcycle without so much as a phone call ahead of time. I suggested we do a little investigating before we welcomed you into the fold with open arms."

"I've hardly been welcomed with open arms." I jerk my right leg free and swiftly kick all in one motion, sending the guy who was holding onto me flying onto his ass. The guy holding onto my other leg scrambles, trying to grab hold of me, but I bend and kick out again, smashing the sole of my bare foot right into his face. He hollers, letting go of me altogether, and then I'm straining, doing my best to free my arms so I can start swinging properly.

I'm almost free when I hear something that makes me freezes, though: the safety of a gun being removed. Looking up, I see that the guy in the suit is now standing over me, and he's pointing the business end of a Glock into my face.

"You really are a handful, huh?"

"You don't know the half of it."

"You certainly don't seem like a straight laced businessman, Mr. Garrett."

"I never said I was. Why the fuck would my employer be hiring a straight laced businessman to come out here on a trip like this?"

"True." He grunts. "If you have nothing to hide, why are you railing against being searched, then?"

"I wouldn't have given a shit if you'd knocked politely on the door and asked, motherfucker. When you sneak up on a guy in the dark, pin him to a bed while he's naked and start messing with his stuff, of course he's gonna react fucking badly."

Suit Guy smiles. "I guess you're right. How about this, then? We would like to look through your belongings, Mr. Garrett. Do you consent?"

"Let me go, and then ask me."

He ponders my demand, then seems to agree to it. He jerks his head in a terse, irritated motion, and then his lackeys let go, releasing me from the bed. I hop up, grabbing the towel that had been wrapped around my waist when I passed out on the bed. No one bothers to look away as I cover myself. I have zero modesty left; I've been naked in front of so many people in college, in the military and at the club that I couldn't give a shit if some guy gets an eyeful of my cock and balls. What pisses me off is that none of the assholes hide the fact that they're checking out what I've got, assessing me. I suppose they've all been in that room upstairs. They must have seen what goes on there. They must have watched so many naked men and women fuck in there that it's all just meat to them by now.

I fold my arms across my chest, clenching my jaw. "Have at it, jackhole. I don't have anything to hide."

Suit Guy smirks savagely, twitching a finger. His men get to work. I only had my small backpack with me when I arrived, filled with the clothes I bought at the airport and the money I knew I would need at some point. The guys go to town, tearing the bag apart, looking for hidden pockets or zips that might be concealing nefarious secrets. The bag is in pieces by the time they're satisfied that there's nothing to be found there. They quickly move on to my jeans, my leather jacket, and the Adidas sneakers I was wearing when I arrived. Soon the pants are destroyed, as is my leather, and the brand new shoes. One of them holds out my wallet to the guy in the suit, who shoots me a sly glance as he flips it open.

"Any surprises in here, buddy? Anything you'd like to get off your chest before I empty this thing?"

"Nope. Go for your fucking life." I'm not stupid. It's not like I have a Widow Makers MC membership card in there or anything. The wallet is still kitted out with my ID from the airport. The credit cards have Sam Garret's name on them. The driver's licence also his. I'm not dumb enough to have plastered the inside of my wallet with pictures of Laura, thank god. Suit Guy looks visibly disappointed when he doesn't find anything that proves me to be a liar.

"You realize we're going to have to search you personally, Mr. Garrett?" he says. That seems to put a smile back on his face.

"You think I've got a wire shoved up my ass?"

He shrugs. "Could be the case. We can't be too careful." He nods to one of his boys, signalling that he should come forward and check me, and I growl low and deep in the back of my throat.

"You can search my bag and my clothes and my cell phone, motherfucker, but not a single one of you is going near my ass."

"I'm afraid you really don't have a choice."

"I guess we'll see about that." I will *never* submit to a cavity search. *Never*. I'm on my feet now, and I am fucking ready. I can take all of his guys without a problem now that I'm not half asleep, flat out on my back. I flick a warning glance out of the corner of my eye to the guy who is slowly approaching with his hands out, and I bare my teeth. "Do you know how to break every single finger in a man's hand in under three seconds, with nothing more than a towel?" I ask him.

He stops dead, blinking at me. "No, I don't," he mutters.

"That's a pity. Because *I* do."

The guy looks back at the redhead, lifting both eyebrows. "Harrison?"

Harrison doesn't say anything. He doesn't move. He's still holding his gun, but it's loose in his hand, pointed at the floor, and he doesn't really seem to be paying attention to the situation. His lackey swallows and resumes his approach. I kind of feel sorry for the poor bastard. He tries to jump me as soon as he's in arm's reach, but I grab hold of him by the wrist, spin him around so that his arm is trapped behind his back, and then I do as I promised. I lean my kneecap into the small of his back, pushing, and I pull his arm back toward me at the same time, straining it so that it's almost popping from his shoulder joint. It's very easy from there to snap the bones in his fingers. Index, middle, ring and pinkie. I must be getting soft in my old age, because I don't break his thumb. I could. It wouldn't take more than a second, but without his thumb he's useless for six weeks. He'll lose total use of his dominant hand, and who the fuck knows what happens to guys who suddenly can't even hold a pen or wipe their own asses around here?

I let him go, and he tumbles to the floor at Harrison's feet, screaming, holding onto his hand for dear life.

"God," Harrison snaps. "Fucking pathetic. One of you guys just fucking deal with this, okay? None of us can leave until we're sure he's clean."

I survey the other men. None of them are volunteering to be next in line to have their fingers broken. Harrison sighs, lifting up his gun. He aims it at my head, his finger on the trigger.

"Be a good boy and bend over now. This will all be over in a moment."

VICE

I take three long steps forward, so that his Glock is pressing up against my forehead, right between my eyes. "No. Fucking. Way. You're going to have to kill me first."

"Don't tempt me, friend."

"If Fernando wanted me dead, he would have shot me himself the moment he laid eyes on me. Or maybe later, here at the house when I broke his rules. But he didn't. I guess that means he wants this deal to go through, *friend*. So do what you have to do. But I won't be cowed by you. And I sure as hell am not letting anyone stick anything in my ass. It's your call."

Harrison's eyes lower until they're no wider than slits. He isn't happy, not one bit, but I know he isn't going to shoot me. Not yet anyway. He lowers the gun and spits onto the floor at my feet. "It isn't often that someone refuses me something, Mr. Garrett. I'm not a fan of rejection, and I'm not a fan of being told no. I assure you I will get what I want. Either now, or later, when Fernando's tired of the little charade you're playing." He holds up my cell phone in his hand for me to see. "Tell me the passcode."

"Why?"

"So I can read your messages and confirm you're acting on behalf of this New York banker, moron."

"There's personal information on there."

"I'm counting on it. Don't worry. I couldn't give a shit about your pussy pics and your stashed porn files. It's your conversations with your boss I'm interested in. Give me the fucking code."

"No."

"I mean it. This isn't a fucking joke, okay? You haven't just checked in for a spa weekend at the Ritz Carlton. Your *life* is on the line right now."

I make a show of thinking for second, and then I hold up my hands, surrendering. "Okay. It's five eight five nine. But seriously, man. Don't look at my private photos. They're pretty graphic. I'd hate to think of them in the wrong hands."

Harrison smirks, and I know all too well that he's going to make a big deal out of the files he finds in my gallery. He's in for a fucking surprise. When he rifles through my phone, he'll find about seventy pictures of a naked eighty-three year old woman at various stages of undress as she obviously performs a strip tease. It's quite disturbing. In the text messages, he'll find the most sordid, graphic sexts between myself and Mavis—texts so nasty and dirty they'd even make Carnie, the Widow Makers' recently promoted prospect, blush. In my emails, he'll find eighteen folders of spam, and a number of coded, confusing messages from a contact called "Trident," that will leave him scratching his head for days.

What he won't find is anything incriminating about Laura, or any correspondence between Jamie and me. It'll drive him crazy. The code I just gave him is the key. If the code "five eight, five nine" is entered into my cell, my real phone screen isn't unlocked, but a proxy screen complete with apps, contacts, notes and photos. He'll never be able to tell it's not real. And he'll never gain access to the stored information I have on countless different South American cartels, the places I've buried bodies, or the entire towns I've razed to the ground on my journey to find my sister.

Harrison taps the code into the phone and swells up when it unlocks, his chest puffing up with pride, like he hacked into the damn thing himself. "I'm sure Fernando will be discreet," he says, but he and I both know Fernando will only be looking at it once he's been through it with a fine tooth comb. "Get dressed," he tells me. "Everyone's gathering outside. Fernando wants you down there, too."

"What for?"

Harrison rolls his eyes, pocketing my cell phone. "Just do it, man. He doesn't like to be kept waiting."

It's only after he leaves, the rest of his men following behind him, that I realize how badly this could have gone. I've been facing Harrison and his guys the whole time. I didn't turn around, and none of them tried to sneak up behind me to get a jump on me. If they had, they would have immediately known I was lying to them.

They would have seen the huge Widow Makers MC tattoo that

sprawls across my shoulder blades, and I, my friends, would have been fucked.

SEVEN

THE HOUSE OF WOLVES

I **find some clothes that haven't been completely destroyed, and** I head outside. On the lawn in front of the huge mansion, a small crowd of people are gathered together, looking uncomfortable and frightened. It hits me then—at least five or six of them have red hair. How strange. They're dressed in white robes, men and women both, clutching the material tightly closed up around their chins. Their feet are bare in the short, neatly cut grass. These are Fernando's Servicio, as Plato called them.

Off to the right, another crowd of people hover—a mix of men, all dressed in expensive clothes from suits to leather jackets, jeans to Georgio Armani slacks. They have this lean, hungry look about them that sets them apart from the other group. These are obviously Fernando's guests, his players, the men who have paid to use and abuse the other human beings a few feet away from them.

On the far stretches of the lawn, Fernando is talking to a line of guys who are all carrying rifles. He appears to be giving them orders. A moment passes, and then the men run off across the lawn, disappearing into the vegetation line, where the land turns from well-maintained country garden to overgrown, wild rainforest.

I'm scanning the scene before me, hunting for Plato, sure I'm going to find him in chains, tied up and butt naked in the dirt, when I see him standing in amongst the Servicio. Our gazes meet, and I see that his bottom lip is badly split open, and there's a violent purple bruise under his right eye. In spite of the injuries, he smiles broadly and gives me a thumbs up, which sets my mind at ease. He wouldn't be so happy if he thought Fernando was about to feed him to a pack of wolves, surely?

Alone, standing on her own to one side, Natalia is shivering in the cool night air, arms wrapped around herself as she stares off into the dark. I'm about to make my way over to her when I see a shadow shift close to the house, and Ocho emerges, still carrying that damn rifle of his. I'm reminded of Fernando's warning not to speak to his daughter unless someone else is present. And I'm reminded of what happened to Ocho when he broke that rule.

I like my tongue. I like being able to speak. Most importantly, I like making girls come with it, and I can't do that very well if it's been cut out of my fucking head with a blunt knife. I forget about making my way over to Natalia and stay put instead.

"A wise move, my friend." Harrison spits into the grass, grinning at me wildly like a mad man. "Live to fuck another day. It's a good motto to have around here."

"I'm sure you could give two shits if I live to fuck another day," I mutter.

"Don't be so sulky. I was just doing my job. I'm sure you can understand what that's like." When I don't say anything, he continues. "You're ex-military. You know what it's like to take orders. You weren't just fucking around in the desert, doing whatever the fuck you wanted there, either."

"How do you know I'm ex-military?"

Harrison rocks back on his heels, peering into the darkness. "Come on. It's obvious. Might as well be written all over you, asshole. You have that way of walking. Talking. Breathing. If you're not ex-military, I'm the fucking Queen of Sheba."

I grunt. "But not you. You just wish you were. You were probably out there as part of a private security company, right? The hired help who couldn't make it into the Marines? Running around the hot zones, wearing night vision goggles and khakis from fucking J Crew."

He laughs a sour laugh. "The pay was good. And J Crew khakis are really good quality."

"I'm sure they are." I'd normally take a few more shots at him; he's the type of dude who'll snap and explode if you rile him up enough, but then four guys emerge from the house, carrying a white shrouded object that can only be a body wrapped up in a sheet, and I've suddenly lost all interest in the man standing next to me.

"Is that...?"

"The guy you shot in the chest? *Yeah.*" Harrison leaves, walking off toward Fernando, and I make a decision: I follow after him, wondering what the hell is about to happen. Plato hisses my name, trying to get my attention, but I ignore him, trying to appear confident and curious as we approach Fernando. The older man wipes his forehead with a fresh, pure white handkerchief, then tucks it neatly into the breast pocket of his blazer. He nods when he sees Harrison, and then holds out his hand for me to shake. His grip is probably a little tighter than it needs to be.

"I see you've met Harrison," he says stiffly. I hear what he really means to say in the frigid tone of his voice: *I see Harrison busted down your door and had someone violate your asshole.* Harrison shifts uncomfortably, looking off into the forest. He doesn't tell his boss that I refused to spread my butt cheeks for him. I don't feel like offering up the information either, and Fernando continues on non-the-wiser. "Your antics earlier have left us in an unfortunate position, Mr. Garrett. I have a body to dispose of, and only one way of doing that quickly and efficiently. In truth, I love feeding my dogs. But I try not to give them human flesh too often. It makes them bold. Inquisitive. They get a taste for it, and...well. They have taken people coming in and out of the house before. Unfortunate. Very unfortunate."

I'm betting Fernando doesn't get postal service up here, then. No mailman in his right mind would loiter on the front doorstep if he suspected he might be set upon by a pack of savage animals.

"I thought you might like to watch up here with me when the wolves arrive. Luckily they are already in the area," Fernando says, throwing an arm around my shoulder. "Normally we must call them with an alarm, but not today. Some of my men are out in the forest, herding them in this direction as we speak."

"I wouldn't have thought wolves are native to an environment like this," I say.

Fernando shakes his head from side to side. "There are many areas of Ecuador that are inhabited by wolves. Admittedly, the Inter-Andean valleys are more suited to them than here, perhaps. But understand, the wolves in my forests are not wild. *I* brought them here. I have trained them to survive in this place, and they have thrived. Now, there are over a hundred wild wolves living in these mountains. I like to think of myself as their guardian. Their shepherd, if you will. I'd like you to witness their beauty for yourself. You will see why I love them so much. Come." Fernando heads off in the direction of the tree line. He doesn't have a weapon with him. None of his riflemen follow after him, though they watch with sharp eyes. Harrison elbows me in the side.

"Careful he doesn't slit your throat out there, man. His *dogs* love lapping up blood from the dirt."

"Fuck you."

"Whatever." He shrugs. "Just don't say I didn't warn you."

I don't have my gun now, either. I searched for it among my scattered possessions after Harrison and his men left, but it was nowhere to be found; he obviously took it with him when he left my room, and asking for it back seemed inappropriate. So I follow after Fernando with my hands in my pockets, my fingers closing around the handle of my small balisong knife. His men clearly left it for me because of its size. It's tiny, but they have no idea what I can do with the smallest sliver of sharpened steel. It'll definitely be enough to protect myself from a hungry wolf. I'm hoping that's the case, anyway.

When I reach Fernando, he puts his arm around my shoulders again, and points into the trees. "All of Ecuador used to be forest and jungle for hundreds of years. Before the conquistadors arrived, the indigenous people of this country were farmers and hunters. Excellent hunters. The wolves were a spiritual animal to us. They are still spiritual to me. If I find out that someone has harmed a wolf here, I am not a happy man. I had a favorite wolf many years ago, Kechu. He was silver, with brilliant blue eyes. Very rare. He was brave. He was so courageous that he would come up here to the house and sit on the lawn, and he and I would watch each other for hours. It felt like we were communicating in some way.

"And then, one day, I came back home after visiting family for a few days, and I saw Kechu chained to a post out here by the trees. He was struggling to get free, whining and afraid, and I was filled with rage. I stormed into the house, demanding to know why my favorite wolf was being treated that way, and my father explained what had happened. Kechu had attacked my eight-year-old sister, and ripped out her throat. He had killed her.

"I was distraught. I loved Kechu, but I had loved my sister more. It felt as though he had betrayed me. I realized after a little while that I was wrong, though. Kechu had not betrayed me. He was following his natural instincts to kill, to eat, and my little sister had been easy prey for him. I took my father's gun, and I shot Kechu here." Fernando taps my face with his index finger, above my right eye. "He was my favorite wolf, Mr. Garrett, but he had done something I could not forgive. Even though it was his nature, and even though his actions were not a personal attack to me, they still could not go unpunished. I did what I had to do, even though it broke my heart."

In the distance, a single, low howl splits the night air apart. Back by the house, the group of men and women gathered in white robes mutter and mumble to one another, panicking like sheep as they shift against one another, trying to move to the rear of the party, further away from the forest. The howl goes up again, and this time it's joined by another, and then another.

"Their song is quite haunting," Fernando says. "I've always loved it, though it seems to disturb some of my other guests."

Yeah, no shit. I'm not surprised they find it disturbing, if you've been feeding their friends to your little pets. The words are on the tip of my tongue, but I manage to keep my thoughts to myself.

Fernando squeezes my shoulder, sighing. "What do you think of my story, Mr. Garrett? Do you think I did the right thing in killing Kechu?"

"I think once an animal turns against its master, there really isn't anything else you can do."

He seems pleased by this response. "Exactly. I am pleased you understand. You remind me of him, you know. In a strange way, I think of him every time I look at you, and it's like I'm visiting with an old friend. I think I will call you Kechu, if it doesn't bother you too much." It's not a request. He's going to do it, regardless of if it does bother me or not. I'm not stupid enough to ask him not to, though. And I know what he's doing: he's giving me a warning. He will accept me, we can become friends, but no matter how much he likes me, if I fuck up and do something to offend him, or hurt those he cares about, he will shoot me in the head without thinking twice.

"I don't mind," I tell him. "I don't mind at all." I should be giving him a warning of my own. If I find out my sister has been here, if Fernando has even laid eyes on her for one fucking second, I will do worse to him than shoot him in the head. I'll be murdering him with my bare hands, and I will be taking my goddamn time with it.

The wolves arrive then. They appear like ghosts, forming out of the shadows, taking shape slowly, gradually. It feels like my eyes are playing tricks on me as they slink forward out of the darkness, as if they aren't really there, only the suggestion of them as the prowl up toward the house. Their paws make no sound on the short grass. They make strange chittering, yipping noises to one another as they weave around each other's bodies, eyeing the situation before them.

Are there ten of them? Fifteen? The way they move around one another, dipping in and out of the shadows, makes it impossible to count. Their coats are stunning—brindle, gray, black, tan and stone, all blending together as they shift and press cautiously forward.

The guy I shot, William, has been taken out of the sheet he was carried out in and has been laid out on the grass, arms spread out wide on either side of him, his eyes closed, his skin pale and ashy; the way they've arranged him makes him look like some sort of offering. A sacrifice. A worried rumble goes up from Fernando's players. The men in black have all looked stoic and cool up until now. Some of them have even looked turned on by the whole situation, their eyes bright and shining, filled with anticipation, their hands rubbing at their cocks through their suit pants. Now they don't look so excited. They look concerned as the wolves pad silently toward them, as if they are made out of the thick silence and the oppressive darkness of the night.

"I'm gonna fucking shoot that one if he comes any closer," one of the guys hisses. "I don't like the look of it."

The wolf pack splits, warily hedging around William's body. They smell the air as they investigate. They are trying to work out what level of danger this prone man lying in the grass poses to them. I see the moment they catch the scent of death on him. A ripple of excitement runs through the pack, and the largest of the animals, a huge male with a black streak through his gray ruff, darts forward, snapping his teeth at the body. He grows braver when William doesn't defend himself.

Then, in a whirlwind of fur, flashing teeth and ripping claws, the wolves descend upon the body. It's mayhem. I cringe as they make short work of William's shirt, tearing it from his torso, and then it's flesh they're tearing from him and not fabric.

Blood spackles their muzzles. They eat in a frenzy, fighting over various different organs they yank from the body. It's fascinating to watch the hierarchy of the pack in effect: the largest gray wolf is clearly the alpha. A smaller, black wolf must be his second, because he gets to remain at the body, eating, while others dart in and out like fish, grabbing a mouthful here and there where they can. If either the gray or the black wolf bares his teeth, snapping, the others hunker down, golden eyes on the floor, backing away.

"It's a miracle, no?" Fernando asks, folding his arms across his chest.

"Something like that," I reply.

The huge gray wolf tips his head back and howls so loudly, the sound echoes off the surrounding mountainside. His pack stops eating and interweaves their own cries and howls in with his, creating a beautiful yet terrifying chorus of ecstasy that makes the hairs on the back of my neck stand on end.

They eat until there's nothing left but bones.

EIGHT

A WORD TO THE WISE

I lock my bedroom door when I return to my room. A locked door isn't going to do much good if Harrison or any of Fernando's other men decide they want to come pay me another visit, but at least the sound of them kicking the damned door down will wake me up this time. I shower again, feeling dirty after watching the wolves gorge themselves, and then I climb into bed, staring at the ceiling. I already know I'm not going to be able to sleep for hours. I don't intend on resting, anyway. I just need to wait here long enough to allow everyone else to go to sleep, and then I'm going on a hunt of my own. I need to find out if my sister's here, and to do that I need to do some snooping.

I should have asked Plato where his room was. It's likely that Fernando keeps all of his workers together, in the same area of the house. That's how most of these sick fuckers keep the people they buy and sell like stocks and shares, anyway. I should have asked Plato a lot of things. That guy back in the party room said he'd been here for three years. If anyone knows anything about Laura, it'll be him. The opportunity to quiz him didn't arise earlier, when I was watching him fuck that huge blond guy in the ass, though. Nor when I was shooting someone in the chest, and he was dragging me out of that terrible fucking place. I also have no idea if he's loyal to Fernando, even if his loyalty is only out of fear. There's every chance he'll go running to the old man and sound the alarm if I start blabbing about a missing blonde woman who bears an uncanny resemblance to me. I need to figure out whether his bravery today when he helped me was a flash in the pan, or if he actually does want to get the fuck out of here.

I lie in bed for three hours. When I get up and creep out into the hallway, I already know I've been seen. Not by any of Fernando's guards, or by any of his guests. No, the house is deathly silent. Not a soul stirs anywhere in the building as far as I can tell, but that can't be said for the small white lenses Fernando has mounted all over the walls. Technology never sleeps, after all. I'm positive I've already been captured on camera as I make my way down the hallway; it'll only be a matter of Fernando's security detail informing him that I was up and about in the night, and that will be it. He'll know I was sticking my nose in places it doesn't belong, and I had better have a good excuse when he confronts me or there will be hell to pay.

Good thing I have some time to think on that. As it stands I don't have an excuse at all, let alone a good one.

Down hallways and down staircases I go, clutching my balisong in my hand, ready to plunge it deep into the chest of any man who might stand in my way. There are so many bedrooms, so many narrow corridors and so many fucking dark corners that I begin to doubt my plan. How the hell am I going to search this place without waking anyone up? It's like hunting for a needle in a haystack.

I head downstairs, following my gut. If I were Fernando... Wow. That's a horrifying thought. If I were Fernando, I hopefully wouldn't be hosting such fucked up sex parties, and I hopefully wouldn't be kidnapping men and women and forcing them to do unspeakable things to each other for other people's entertainment. If I were, though, if I were the most deplorable kind of person imaginable, I suspect I'd be keeping my captives under the house, as opposed to in any of the luxurious, comfortable rooms on the top floor. The basement, if there is one in this giant, soulless building, won't have any windows, which means less chance of escape. And basements are nearly always easy to soundproof, so no faint, desperate cries for help would be heard anywhere else in the house. Seems prudent to me.

I'm on the ground floor, when I hear a muffled scraping sound behind me. At first I think it's my imagination, heightened by the stress of the situation, but then I hear the sound of quiet, even breathing and I know I'm being watched. Harrison? Maybe Ocho? God knows how many people Fernando has in his employ; it could be any one of those fuckers. I duck to the right, slipping into a shadowed doorway. I have no idea where the door leads, and I don't find out. I press my back against the wall, opening and closing the door loudly enough that whoever is hanging back in the hallway will think I have walked through, and then I wait.

One, two, three, four, five...

A slender shadow stretches up along the other side of the doorframe, and then suddenly a figure is standing there, dressed all in black, with a huge, menacing knife in their hand. Scratch that—it's not a knife. It's a motherfucking machete, and it's about to come down on my head. I react, blocking the blow, sending the blade clattering from my attacker's hand.

"*Shit,*" he swears under his breath. I grab hold of him by the throat, slamming him into the wall, lifting him a clear foot off the ground as I pin him to the wall.

"Shit's right, motherfucker. You're in it up to your neck now." I pull back my arm, ready to hammer the point of my own flick knife into his throat, when I see freckles, a fuck load of them, and I squint a little closer into the darkness.

"*Natalia?*"

"*Let me...go!*" She kicks and scratches, using her fingernails, digging them into my skin. I barely feel a thing, but in the same vein I know she's leaving a mark on me.

"Quit it," I snap. "Damn it, Natalia. Be fucking quiet!" That's a stupid thing to demand of her, I'm sure—she's going to be yelling for her father the moment I set her down—but I demand it anyway. Then again...I'm not squeezing her throat hard enough to prevent her from screaming, and she hasn't done it yet. What does that mean? Why isn't she making *more* noise than she is right now? I clamp a hand over her mouth, pressing my body against hers so my chest is pinning her to the wall and not my hand wrapped around her throat.

I can feel her tits crushed up against my chest, and it's almost enough to make my dick hard, especially since she's still clawing and scratching at me like a hellcat. "Let me go, *cabron*! I need...I need to fucking talk to you."

"About what?"

"My father."

"So talk. You can do that just fine right here. Is he planning on killing me?"

"Yes. But then he's planning on killing everyone here at some point or another, so...don't take it personally."

"That might be difficult. I like being alive."

"Then you should leave here. Right now. And don't come back. Forget about the drugs. Forget about Plato. Get on your bike and go. Don't look back."

That's probably very sound advice, but I've been on this road for so long now. I have no idea how to turn away from it. I haven't got the faintest clue where I would go if I walked away from this lead. "I can't do that, Natalia. I have to see this thing through."

She huffs, pulling at the hand I have wrapped around her neck, trying to force me to release my hold. I have more strength in my little finger than she does in both arms, though, so she doesn't get very far. She gives up, allowing her arms to fall slack. "You're not as smart as you think you are," she tells me. "You think I don't know why you're really here?"

I scan her face, looking for some sign that she's grasping at straws, simply trying to get me to back off, but all I find is wildfire burning in her eyes. She's defiant and angry. If looks could kill, I'd already be six feet under. "What do you mean, why I'm really here?" I demand.

"I knew as soon as I laid eyes on you, *Cade*. She told me you'd come for her one day, and I didn't believe her. I didn't believe for one second anybody would ever be so stupid."

It feels like an invisible hand is clenching hold of my heart. I narrow my eyes, trying to steady my breathing, but I feel like I'm about to fucking lose it. "Who? Who told you I'd come for them?"

Natalia grits her teeth together, scowling at me. "Who do you think? Your sister. *Laura* told me that you'd come. Now get your fucking hands off me so we can talk."

••••

"She's dead."

Natalia doesn't pull any punches. She just comes straight out with it. We're sitting at a counter in the kitchen—Natalia insists there are no cameras in here—and she's brewing tea. Her machete sits on the counter beside the kettle. Neither of us wants or needs the tea, but this way we have an excuse for being in here if we're found. "She was here for years. I'm not supposed to get friendly with any of the girls who show up here and get transported up into that room, but she was here for so long that it seemed inevitable. During the times when there were no guests at the house, no parties being held, my father sometimes lets the men and women from the blue room read in the library. Laura and I would meet there and talk. I wanted to know about the States, because…well, because I don't know anything about my mother. I don't know anything about where she came from. And Laura told me about you. From the very first time we spoke, she insisted you were going to come and get her."

"And now she's *dead*?" I can't believe it. Can't seem to make sense of it. It can't be the case. "My friend spoke with her on the phone a little over three months ago. She *can't* be dead."

"She can." Natalia reaches across the counter and takes hold of my hand. "She *is*."

"Then how? How did Jamie speak to her?"

"My father records all of his guests when they first arrive here, as proof of life. Sometimes, if he finds out the girl or the guy is from a wealthy family, he will make a ransom request and send them back home. When Laura arrived, he found out your father was some big lawyer or something. He was going to ask for a ransom, but then...I don't know. He decided to keep her. He didn't want to let her go after all, so he kept her. It happens all the time. He doesn't like to let go of his prizes."

I feel like I'm about to throw up. So...the voice Jamie heard on the phone was Laura's? And she was asking for his help? But the plea was recorded years ago? Can it be true? It makes sense that Fernando would make recordings of his kidnap victims as proof of life. And Julio never said he'd actually seen Laura, just that he'd been shown her picture as part of a portfolio of women he could pick from in exchange for his own woman, Alaska.

"When? When did she die?" I ask. My voice is hard. I barely recognize it.

"Three years ago." Natalia looks like she's about to burst into tears.

"How?"

"Cade—"

I get to my feet. "Fucking tell me. Right now."

"Overdose. Some of the other girls here drink and do drugs, to cope with..." She trails off, clearly uncomfortable with voicing the realities of her father's actions. "Laura didn't, though. She always wanted to have a clear head. She was always looking for ways to escape. And then her friend Sylvia got caught running from the house one night, and my father..."

"He punished her?"

Natalia nods. "He fed her to the wolves."

"And my sister couldn't take it anymore?"

Natalia looks down at the two mugs of piping hot tea in front of us. Her eyes are shining brightly, filled with tears. "I loved Laura. She looked out for me. She helped me once, when one of my father's men thought they would try to take me. She stabbed him in the neck with a letter opener. I don't know what would have happened if she hadn't found us."

I sit in silence, staring at the grain in the marble counter, doing my best to tune out the loud, high-pitched screaming that's filling my head. I can't hear anything around it, though. I can't seem to think in a straight line. Everything is jumbled and confused. I feel like I'm barely holding onto my sanity.

"Cade? That is your name, isn't it?"

My head snaps up, and I find Natalia standing in front of me; I didn't even notice her slip around the counter.

"Yes," I whisper.

"I hate my father. I am nothing like him. If I could have left, I would have a long time ago. But I am a lot like Laura and those other girls upstairs, Cade. I'm watched over twenty-four hours a day. There's no way out for me. Nowhere to run to."

"You're not."

She gives me a puzzled look. "I'm not what?"

"You're *not* like my sister and those other girls upstairs. Your father's never made you spread your legs for a man while other people watch on. You've never been beaten and abused, and forced to do things repeatedly against your will."

Her expression turns dark. I see the flicker of pain in her eye, the twitch of the muscle in her jaw, and I know before she even opens her mouth that I've spoken out of turn. Her words come out as a whisper. "Hasn't he?"

I jerk back. "He wouldn't let any of those fuckers near you. He's so fucking protective of you."

"Oh, he is. And you're right. He doesn't let any of *them* near me."

"Fuck. You're not serious. You're telling me—"

She spins around, wiping her eyes with the backs of her hands. "Enough. This isn't about me. It *was* about Laura. Now, it's about you leaving here before my father realizes who you are and has you killed."

I am rocked, numb to the core. I don't know what to say to her. It's obvious that she doesn't want me to say anything at all, but... god. His own daughter? How can that sit right even in his warped, fucked-up mind?

Natalia's shoulders are shaking, hitching up and down; she's crying.

I want to get up and go to her, comfort her in some way, but who the fuck am I to be doing such a thing? I have no right. I don't have the first fucking clue how to make her feel better. I don't have the first fucking clue how to help her, either.

Natalia's soft crying fills the cavernous kitchen, and for the first time in a long time I feel truly dead inside. My hope, the one thing that's been fuelling me for so long, is now gone. Extinguished in a heartbeat. The suspicious part of me would be doubting what Natalia's saying is true, that she's lying to protect her father in some way, but that can't be the case. If it were, she would never have told me Laura was here in the first place. She would have kept her mouth shut and let Fernando kill me whenever the fuck he felt like it. But no, she tried to warn me, and she knows things about Laura. She described her to me. She told me things about her only someone close to her would know.

And now she's sobbing, trying not to, struggling to keep her shit together, and I can't think of a single thing to say to her to make it better, because it's fucked. It's all fucked, and I am a hollow, empty, treacherous thing that can't be trusted. I didn't save Laura. I didn't fucking save her, and now I can't be expected to do anything about Natalia. If I even *try* to help her, it'll probably end in disaster, with both of us dead.

She turns around and her cheeks are streaked and wet, but she looks angry again. "Don't you feel sorry for me, asshole. I don't want your pity. I don't need it."

Of course she doesn't need it. Pity isn't going to help her; it's only going to make her feel like shit. "I don't pity you. I'm angry *for* you. I'm going to kill that son of a bitch for what he's done to my sister. I'll twist the knife that little bit deeper now, knowing what he's done to you, too."

"You can't. Don't you think people have tried before? He's insane. Harrison and his men protect him all day, every day."

"I can take care of Harrison just fine."

Natalia slumps against the wall, looking miserable. "No. Seriously.

Laura is gone, and the people here are already too damaged to put back together. Why lose your life over so many lost causes?"

"Lost causes are my specialty." I stand, watching her. She's the most stunning, graceful, breathtaking thing I've ever seen, even in her misery. In another life, one where we are both different people, I might have pursued her. I can imagine how she would fit perfectly into my arms. I can picture all too well what she looks like covered in sweat, naked, panting my name as she rides my cock. These are dangerous daydreams that simply aren't practical here in this terrible, dangerous place, though. I slide my hands into my pockets, digging my short fingernails into my palms.

"Good night, Natalia."

She stops me just before I leave the kitchen. "You're not going to leave?" she whispers.

"No. I told you. I'm going to murder your father. I'm going to wait for the most perfect opportunity, when the time is exactly right, and I'm going to take his pride and his dignity from him, before I take his life." I pause, and then ask her one simple question. "Would you like to watch?"

She doesn't even hesitate.

"Yes. Yes, I would."

NINE
AND THEN, THE RAIN

Two days pass, and I don't see Natalia again. I don't see Plato, and I don't see Fernando. The only person I interact with is Ocho, who brings me my meals, and who, being mute, is zero fucking fun to talk to. I stay in my room watching bad Ecuadorian television in a language I don't understand, and I do push ups. That is my entire existence: Ecuadorian Days of Our Lives, and a thousand push ups a day.

On the third day of what appears to be my solitary confinement, Fernando shows up with Harrison on his heels. Fernando looks pissed beyond measure; Harrison, on the other hand, looks gleeful, like a kid on Christmas morning.

"We agreed that your Mr. Aubertin would be here today, Kechu. Please, can you explain to me where he is?" Fernando's furious, his voice clipped, his hands shaking by his sides as he addresses me. I frown, looking over his shoulder at Harrison.

"I couldn't tell him to come," I say. "Harrison took my phone. And I've been locked away in this fucking room for days. I tried to explain to Ocho, but I don't think he understands English."

Fernando turns, pinning Harrison in his severe gaze. "You took his phone?" he says slowly.

"Yeah, well, I mean we had to. He could have had anything on there."

"And what did you find?"

"Nothing."

"Nothing?"

"Well." He shuffles his feet, looking awkward as fuck. "There were some weird pictures on there. Some fucked up text messages. But nothing untoward."

"And you did not return it back to him?"

"I didn't think it was important."

"How are you to know what is important and what isn't important? Give him back his phone."

Harrison, unsurprisingly, has the damned thing on him. It's probably been giving him a boner, knowing that he's taken my toy away and it's been sitting in his pocket this whole time. He thrusts it out to me, the dark look on his face just daring me to say something to him. I take it, smiling pleasantly.

"Thank you, Harrison."

Fernando waits for the exchange to be over, and then he pivots on the balls of his feet and slaps Harrison across the face, hard. Harrison's head whips around with the force; his eyes are the size of dinner plates. He's shocked. He's overflowing with anger too, but he's not that stupid. He knows he can't do anything to retaliate. "Leave," Fernando commands. "Kechu and I must talk alone."

Harrison looks stung that he's being sent away. No doubt he wants to stick around to listen to Fernando threaten me in some way, but it looks like today is not his lucky day. He leaves, and Fernando places a hand on my shoulder.

"I already know about your conversation with my daughter the other night, Kechu. She came to me very first thing the next morning and told me herself."

What the fuck? She told him about our conversation? I glance sideways at Fernando as he guides me out of my room and down the hallway. He doesn't seem as mad as he should be, but then again the man always seems cool and calm. He's had two days to allow the information to settle, too. Still, I'm ready to fight, ready to jam my knuckles into his throat and throw him over the bannister, down two flights of stairs if I have to. He sighs, slowly shaking his head. "She explained that you ran into each other in the kitchen, and you held a conversation at her insistence. I was perhaps too quick to tell you that you should not talk to her alone, Kechu. This house is big, but it's only *so* big. You're bound to run into one another, and it would be discourteous of you to ignore Natalia. I have reconsidered my rule. You may talk to her as and when you see fit. However, if I discover that you have tried to abuse her good nature, or *mine*, in any way, there will be repercussions. Is that clear?"

"Absolutely." So she was covering our asses, not informing her father of my identity? The wall of relief that hits me is massive. He's gonna know exactly who I am before too long. I'm going to tell him myself, as I'm digging the pointy end of a fucking screwdriver into his eye socket, but I'm not ready for that yet. I like to think while I work out, and for the past two days, as I've been counting off my push-ups, I have been thinking very deeply indeed. How long did Laura suffer here? How long did she hold out before she finally decided she couldn't handle it any longer and she took her own life? A very, *very* long time. So I'm not going to rush this. I'm going to wait, bide my time, and I'll know when the perfect opportunity presents itself. In the meantime, I'm going to continue playing this game, figuring out my enemy, and I'm going to be patient.

Fernando leads me downstairs, through the foyer and out the front door, where the mud splattered Patriot is waiting for us, engine idling. "I apologize for Harrison's behavior. He can be a little petty some-times. Overzealous. It's a trait I've noticed in many of you American men. Anyway, now that your property has been returned to you, please feel free to contact your employer and let him know that he is expected. And in the meantime, I'd like to take you hunting with me and my men. I'm sure you have spent time with a rifle in your hand before, no? I find hunting to be a stress-relieving exercise. I'm positive you would benefit from some time outdoors, after being cooped up for so long."

He makes it sound like he had nothing to do with the fact that I was barricaded in my room for forty-eight hours, when he is the only person who could have ordered such a thing. I'm not about to point this out, though.

Hunting. In the forest. With the man responsible for my sister's death. This is going to be difficult. Every time his back is to me, I'm going to be filled with the temptation to put a bullet in the back of his head. I won't give in to that temptation, though. Fernando Villalobos will see his death coming, unstoppable and undeniable, and he will know it's being dealt to him by my hand.

"I love to hunt," I tell him, smiling easily. I'm probably a sociopath. I can put up a front like this without a second thought. I can lie and mislead people until the cows come home. I don't flinch. I don't hesitate. The words just fall from my lips, and no one is ever any the wiser. Fernando nods, holding his hand out, gesturing for me to climb into the passenger seat of the Patriot.

"Perfect. The others are already waiting for us. Let's go and find them, shall we?"

••••

Natalia is the first person I notice when we arrive at our rally point. Another six vehicles are already parked, half concealed by the trees and undergrowth, and eight men with rifles are standing around, leaning against the cars, chatting amiably in Spanish as they wait for us to arrive. Natalia's eyes meet mine as I get out of the car, and my dick stirs in my pants. I can't fucking help it. She's too goddamn beautiful for words, and I'm a hot-blooded male with an overactive imagination. When I look at her, I see too much. I see her naked, pinned to a mattress beneath me. I see her eyes rolling back into her head as she comes. I see my own tongue, burying itself into her pussy as I eat her out from behind.

Her cheeks color, as if she can read my thoughts, and I have to make sure I'm not sporting some serious wood. I'm not, thank fuck. I don't know how I'd explain that away to Fernando. The prospect of hunting gets me hot and horny? Yeah, I don't think that would pan out too well.

Natalia slings the strap of her rifle over her shoulder, looking away. One of Fernando's guys says something to her and she nods, walking away with him to collect empty bags from the back of one of the vehicles.

Fernando gives instructions to his men in Spanish, and then he relays them to me in English, obviously assuming I haven't understood him the first time around. His orders are simple: we're here to hunt for small game. Anyone that shoots a wolf will regret it for the rest of their incredibly short lives. We're to pair off into twos and rendezvous at regular intervals.

"And it's the rainy season," he continues. "It's going to pour down for an hour or so. I hope you're not afraid of a little water, Kechu?"

"I'm sure I'll manage."

"Good. You and I will hunt together. Later, after we have stopped for food, you will go back out with Ocho, and I will go with my daughter."

Fernando's men disperse; five separate groups head in five different directions, and for the next hour and a half Fernando and I stealthily move through the forest, not speaking, not breathing a word to one another. He uses a total of five rudimentary hand signals, which I pick up very quickly: slow, stop, listen, look, and fire.

I snap off four shots, making all four kills. Fernando seems impressed each time I take an animal down, patting me on the arm, nodding encouragingly, as a father might to his son. The entire time we're stalking through the trees, I'm thinking about what it will feel like to end *his* life. My mouth is filled with the taste of copper. It's only when I catch myself literally biting my tongue that I realize where the blood in my mouth is coming from.

Finally, Fernando raises his rifle to his shoulder, and squeezes the trigger, the first time since we started the hunt. The way he handles his weapon, and the way he aims, takes sight, and shoots all in one smooth, fluid moment, defines him as an expert marksman, and yet he only clips the deer in the shoulder.

Strange.

I'm on the verge of asking him what went wrong, when Fernando hands me his rifle and starts rooting through his pack for something.

"I find these kills with guns so impersonal, don't you? I'm the kind of man who likes to get his hands dirty." From the bag, he produces something that surprises me—a fucking ball hammer. It's old, or at least it looks like it is. He spins it around in his hand, and then jerks his head in the direction of the fallen deer. "Come. Best not to keep her waiting."

Twenty feet away, through the dense vegetation, the deer he's shot is lying on its side, writhing and groaning, its eyes rolling with wild panic in its head, and frothing at the mouth.

"There she is," Fernando says. He stands for a second in front of the injured animal, hands on his hips, still gripping hold of the hammer, admiring the poor creature at his feet. "I always feel so guilty afterwards," he says. "But not in this moment. When I'm holding the hammer, ready to bring it down, I feel nothing but anticipation. You understand this, I think, Kechu."

"I think you're probably right."

Fernando hums softly under his breath while the animal thrashes and moans. He moves very slowly as he bends down on both knees and strokes a hand down the side of the deer's face. "There, there, beautiful girl," he murmurs. "There, there." And then, with the speed of someone half his age, he hefts the hammer over his head and brings the weighty metal end down on the side of the deer's head. Not once. Not twice. Not three times. I lose count of how many times he raises and brings down the hammer. The deer is dead after the first couple of blows. Fernando doesn't seem to care, though. He doesn't stop until the animal's head is caved in, shards of broken bone all over his arms, all over the ground, pulped brains and blood clumped together on the backs of his hands. His shoulders are rapidly hitching up and down, his breath labored when he finally stops.

"Quite a rush," he says, panting. Using the sleeve of his shirt, he wipes at his forehead, streaking even more blood over his face. "Next time, you should use this," he tells me, holding out the hammer. I take it, my expression flat and even. If he expects me to react or shy away from his violence, then he has another thing coming. He's showing his true colors for the first time, though, and they truly are forming a sinister, foreboding palette, all blacks and reds and violent oranges. He's a soulless man. I can see that now, as I look into his eyes.

He's on his knees, covered in pieces of the deer, out of breath, and I am holding his hammer; it occurs to me that this could possibly be the perfect moment I've been waiting for. How easy would it be to bring this thing down on *his* head? We're alone out here, with no witnesses, and no one to stop me. And yet, now doesn't feel like the right time.

The small walkie-talkie Fernando's carrying clipped to his belt blasts static at us out of nowhere, splitting apart the silence, and the moment is gone, disappeared in a puff of smoke. Loud voices stream out of the walkie's speakers, and then Fernando is getting to his feet and responding, speaking into the receiver.

One of his teams has shot and killed a cougar. They're excited about the kill, and from the looks of things, so is Fernando. "Do not move it," he orders. "I want to be the one to skin it."

He doesn't strike me as the sort of man to ever break a sweat, and yet he takes off running, ducking around trees and jumping fallen logs in his hurry to reach the kill. I run after him, easily keeping up; my fists pump the air, and with every step I take I see the hammer in my hand, and I think about smashing him over the head with it. Before I know it, he's found his men and the dead cougar, though, and I return his hammer.

Natalia's leaning against a tree, arms folded across her chest, rifle propped up beside her; when she sees me, she shifts—probably a subconscious action, but it makes her look guilty of something. Fernando doesn't see, too busy with the impressive looking cougar, but Ocho does. He frowns, shooting a suspicious glance between me and Natalia, then he backs off into the forest, his head bent low, eyes on the ground, as if he's looking for something. I suspect he's thinking about Natalia's strange reaction to me, though. That shit's probably going to be back to bite me in the ass sooner rather than later.

Fernando poses with the dead cougar for twenty minutes, while men take shots of him with their cell phones. Anyone would think he'd caught the thing himself. Once he's satisfied that the moment has been documented well enough, he orders his men back out in their teams.

"Where did Ocho go?" he demands, looking around for the man.

I keep my mouth shut tight. Natalia doesn't say a word either, though she saw him walk off as well. None of his other men witnessed where he went, so no one gives Fernando the answer he's looking for. Does *not* go down well.

"You. You," he says, pointing at two of his men. "Come with me. Natalia, would you prefer to continue hunting, or do you wish to join us in looking for Ocho?"

"I think I'd prefer to carry on with the hunt, if that's okay with you, Father?" She needs to hide her anxiety a little better. Her voice sounds too high, too airy. It makes her seem afraid. Fernando doesn't seem to notice, however.

"So be it." Fernando casts his eye over his remaining men, until his gaze finally rests on me. "Kechu, you will look after my daughter, won't you? You're a good shot. Don't let anything eat her."

I'm shocked. A few days ago he was telling me to stay away from her, warning me not to speak to her alone or swear in front of her, otherwise he was going to cut off my tongue. Now he's telling me to take her out into the highlands of Ecuador by myself. "Of course, I'll take excellent care of her. I promise."

Fernando nods, and then he dashes off through the trees. Natalia doesn't wait for the remainder of her father's men to disappear back into the rainforest. She collects her rifle up and slings it over her shoulder, hurrying off without another word. We're a hundred feet away from the other men when she spins around and stabs me in the chest with her finger.

"What are you thinking? Why are you going off with him alone, when he's carrying a gun? Didn't I tell you he wants you dead?" The alarm in her voice is palpable. Her pupils are dilated, huge and black, blocking out the majority of her irises. She looks and sounds terrified, which catches me off guard.

"Whoa, why the hell are you so worried? I can take care of myself."

"I told you," she snaps. "Laura was my friend. What do you think she would say if she knew I was letting you gamble so dangerously with your own life? She would want me to make you leave this place."

"Funnily enough, Laura was always trying to get me to do what *she* wanted me to do instead of what *I* wanted to do. And she never succeeded. Why should this be any different?"

Natalia huffs out a frustrated breath. "This game you're playing has run its course, Mr. America. It's time for you to go back home."

"I'm not going anywhere."

She's clearly losing patience with me. Pacing back and forth along an invisible three-meter long line in front of me, she buries her hands in her hair and growls like the little wolf that she is. "I already told you I'm not like my father, Cade. I don't like watching people die. I especially don't like watching people die when they don't need to. You could easily tie me to a tree and run. Your motorcycle is still where you left it. When my father finds me, I could tell him you didn't hurt me in any way, and he will probably give you a head start before he sends people after you."

"I told you. I'm not going anywhere." Her worry is quite endearing. Her hair is tied into a messy bun on top of her head, and the strands that have escaped her hair tie are plastered to her neck. It's hot and humid, and the damp air has left a high sheen on her skin that makes her look like she's covered in massage oil or something. For all that, she's not dirty, and she doesn't smell bad, though. She's only a few feet from me, and I'm practically dizzy from the clean, fresh floral smell that's coming off her. No wonder she hasn't caught anything yet—every animal in a five-mile radius can smell her soap on her, and they've undoubtedly fled in the opposite direction.

I can't get over how fucking perfect she is. She's like no other woman I've laid eyes on before. I'm sure as hell not going to come across another woman like her in the future, that's for sure. Her freckles are insane. She's wearing another one of those strappy tank tops, and I can't stop staring at the countless galaxies and constellation of dots that mark her skin.

"You're being stubborn. And stupid," she snaps. "You American men always think you know best. No one can ever tell you otherwise."

"I'm pretty sure that's just men in general," I retort, smiling. "At least that's what Laura would have said." It's so weird talking about her in the past tense. In other ways, it isn't though. For so long I've been worrying about Laura, desperately searching for her, leaving no stone unturned in my wake, but there has always been this ugly, terrible seed of doubt buried deep within my subconscious. I've suspected that she was dead for a long time. Now, using the past tense sticks on my tongue, but it doesn't hurt as much as it might if her death had come to me as a complete surprise. I'm still crippled by the knowledge that I failed her, but my heart has been prepared for this moment for what feels like an eternity.

Natalia laughs softly. "You're right there. I suppose I ought to know better than to try and tell you what to do. Laura told me you were...what was the word she used? Ah, yes. Pig-headed."

"*Pig-headed*?" That's definitely a name Laura would have used for me. I can almost hear her calling me the exact same thing right now. I shake my head, sadness washing over me. "What else did she tell you about me?"

Natalia's cheeks turn a delicate shade of red. She glances away, fiddling with the strap of her rifle. "Well. She said you were always a bully when you were little. You'd never let her play with you and your friend from next door. You were fiercely protective of her, though. You would never let anyone else pick on her. She told me you were strong and protective. She said you had a dog called Arry that you loved more than anything when you were in school, and that you cried when it got loose and ran away." She pauses, watching me slyly out of the corner of her eye. "She said you never knew, but your father hit the dog with his car and it died. No one ever told you, because they knew how upset you would be."

"God damn it. I fucking *knew* that dog hadn't run away."

She laughs, her voice all silvery and gentle. "And...Laura said that I would like you. She said you were handsome, and that women were always throwing themselves at you, and you never noticed." Her cheeks have turned an even darker shade of crimson now, and she can't seem to focus on anything apart from the rifle strap in her hands. "I can see now why she would say that," she whispers.

"You think I'm handsome?" I'm teasing her, using a playful tone, but it embarrasses her, I think. She throws her head back, tilting her chin at me defiantly.

"And so what? You'd be a liar if you told me you didn't think I was beautiful. I know you do. I've seen the way you look at me."

"How do I look at you, Natalia?"

She huffs and puffs, getting herself all flustered, and it's the most adorable thing I've ever seen. "Like you already think you own me. Like I'm already yours, and you're planning how you want to enjoy me."

"I'd be lying if I said I hadn't pictured us fucking, Natalia, but I'd never think I *owned* you. One person can't own another. You can only own someone's heart, and that has to be given freely in the first place."

She shuts up. I don't think she was prepared for me to admit I've been fantasizing about her. She must have thought I'd deny it point-blank, but fuck. What's the point in that? I'm a cards face-up kind of guy. I don't like guessing or teasing, and I don't like wasting time. In the past, being so forthright has gotten me into trouble, *lots* of trouble, but it's better to be honest than to hide behind lies all damn day long. I won't do it. I'd rather be shot down in flames than never know where I stand.

"If my father heard you say you daydream about me like that, he would kill you on the spot," she says.

"Good thing he's not around, then."

"He could be."

"We'd better lose him, then. Care to lead the way?"

She gives me a rueful smirk, an *"okay, wise guy"* kind of smirk, but she sets of walking in a northerly direction, shifting her rifle from one shoulder to the other. Walking four feet behind her, I get a stellar view of her ass as her hips swing from side to side, and I have to remind myself that I can't actually pursue this woman. I fucking *can't*. I'll lose my dick before I get to exact my revenge for Laura, and then what will I have to live for? No more meaningless sex, and no more jerking off. I might as well be dead, too.

"You can't go any faster?" Natalia calls over her shoulder. "My grandmother used to move through the forest faster than you."

"I live in New Mexico. Do you have any idea how rare it is to see a tree there, let alone this many of them, all pressing together trunk to trunk like this?"

"Stop complaining. I know you're not *from* New Mexico. You're from Alabama. They have plenty of trees there. Laura told me. Bayous, too."

I'm beginning to resent the fact that this woman knows so much about me, when I don't really know anything about her. Nothing at all, really. Asking questions of her seems unkind, though. Any answers she might be able to give me will inevitably lead back to her father, and I don't want to upset her unnecessarily. A part of me doesn't want to hear it, either. She never said the words, but they were there, hanging between us like a motherfucking noose all the same: her father won't let another man near her normally. No man...*except* him. I feel sick to my stomach.

A low rumble of thunder overhead scatters birds from the trees, and I feel it—a shiver of electricity through the air, powerful enough to make the hairs on my arms stand to attention. Natalia looks up, studying the small patch of sky that's visible through a tiny chink in the canopy overhead.

"It's time," she says. "The rain is coming. We'd better find somewhere to wait it out, otherwise we'll be soaked."

"I don't think there are that many watertight buildings out here," I observe.

"Oh, you'd be surprised." Grinning, she sets off running, just as her father did earlier. It's much harder to keep up with her than it was to pace him, though. She's nimble and small, light on her feet, and I'm a hundred and eighty-five pounds of muscle, packed onto a broad, 6'3" frame. Suffice it to say, I am not graceful or silent as I crash through the undergrowth behind her.

I'm starting to feel the burn in my lungs when the heavens open and the rain begins to fall. Describing this as rain feels misleading. This is more than rain. This is a torrential downpour, so sudden and violent that it's like being hosed down by riot police. And I should know, I've been doused by the five-oh more than once in my lifetime.

It's deafening, layers of sound crashing and warring over one another, millions of water droplets hitting fat, broad leaves, mixed in with the grumbling, resonating vibration of thunder overhead.

Natalia doesn't even hunch over to protect herself from the downpour. She runs with her back straight, her hair soaking wet, water flicking off the ends as it swings from side to side like a pendulum. I can't see where we're going anymore. I just follow after her and hope to god I'm not about to tumble face first over a cliff face.

She stops abruptly, pointing upward. "Can you climb?" she gasps.

I look up, and there are small lengths of wood hammered into the trunk of the closest tree—the trunk is huge, and the lengths of wood seem to be spaced evenly enough to be used as hand and foot holds. The most rudimentary ladder ever. I shake my head, trying not to laugh.

"If *you* can, *I* sure as hell can."

"Good." She bolts up the tree like she's been climbing the thing her whole life. That could well be the case; as I grab hold of one of the makeshift handholds, I see that it's worn and scuffed. It's probably been nailed to the tree for a really long time. We climb ten feet, and then up another five, and I realize I seem to spend a lot of time climbing ladders with this woman: first down into the bunker, and now up into this tree. Another five feet, and suddenly we're pretty fucking high up in the tree; I scan up ahead, trying to see how much

115

further she's going to take me, but all I can see is her perfectly shaped ass and I suddenly don't care anymore. I want her to keep climbing forever, if it means I get to appreciate the view for a little longer.

No such luck, though. Another few feet, and Natalia reaches out, taking hold of a wooden handrail. She hops onto a narrow single plank walkway that's affixed to the side of the tree, and then she's turning and smiling at me. "My grandfather built this place for me when he was alive. He never told my father. It was our little secret. We used to come here together when he was still healthy enough to climb." She hurries across the walkway and onto a large wooden platform, walled in on three sides, with one side left open. Most importantly, a roof covers the tiny tree house, shielding it from the worsening downpour.

The plank creaks loudly as I cross. Seems the walkway was designed to hold someone much smaller and lighter than myself, but it manages okay under my weight. It's clear something non-human has been living in here; a pile of branches and leaves have been stashed in the corner, and there are pieces of mashed up, dried fruit scattered everywhere. Natalia sits herself down, hugging her knees to her chest. There's probably enough room up here for three or four grown adults, but it's definitely not a huge space. She looks around, smiling, as I sit down beside her.

"Well? What do you think? Watertight enough for you, Mr. America?"

I plant a hand against the closest wall, admiring how well built the structure is. Seriously, the place is solid. "I think it'll do just fine," I say. I shake my head, spraying her with water from my hair.

She shrieks, screening her face with her hands. "Stop! I'm wet enough already!"

"You can't get any wetter. It's too late. No point in trying to prevent something that's already happened."

She sobers a little, lowering her hands. "I could say the same to you, no?" She peers over the edge of the wooden platform, considering the drop. "It seems as though your purpose for being here is now over. Laura is gone. She is dead, and nothing can be done to change that. You can't prevent *that*."

"True."

"Then go. I know I keep saying it, but you will only end up hurt or dead if you stay here. Laura wouldn't want you sacrificing yourself now, for nothing."

"It wouldn't be for nothing. Yes, my initial reason for being here, to take her home, is impossible to fulfil. But I have a new purpose now. I'm determined to complete it before I even *consider* leaving Ecuador."

Natalia rests her chin on her arms, which are folded around her legs. She looks down at the toes of her shoes, frowning. "Revenge is not a purpose, Cade. It is a poison. An addiction. A vice that cripples most men."

I laugh under my breath, stabbing my fingernail into the water-logged leather of my boots. "I'm afraid you're wasting your breath. I've never been very good at curtailing my vices."

"Maybe you should try harder."

"Why would I do that? I *like* my vices."

The idea of this seems to entertain her. "You *like* wanting to kill people? Do you think it will make you feel better once my father is dead? Do you think you will suddenly hurt less, miss Laura less, because you have ended his life?"

I'm silent for a second. There are plenty of things I could say in response to her question. I consider saying something about justice, that it's not how it makes *me* feel afterwards that matters. That I'm just doing what I think is *right,* to balance the scales of right and wrong in the universe. I consider telling her that I'm planning on killing her father to prevent him from hurting any other innocent people in the future. I could say I'm plotting out Fernando's downfall in order to help the people that are currently held captive in his house. But at the end of the day, none of these are the true reason for me remaining behind in Orellana.

"I *do* think it will make me feel better," I say quietly. "He's stolen something precious from me. My sister. Years of my life while I've been searching for her. My happiness. These things are all invaluable, I understand that. Nothing I could take from him with make up for what I've lost. But I know exactly how it will feel when I make Fernando beg for his life. I already know how sweet the vengeance is going to taste. It'll blaze through me, righteous and all consuming, and for a moment I'll feel vindicated. It won't last long. As soon as I've seen the light flicker out in his eyes, and as soon as his body has gone cold, I know the hurt and the pain and the loss will return. But I *need* that moment of victory. I need to know that he's paid the highest price imaginable for his sins. That's all there is to it."

Natalia closes her eyes, breathing out slowly. She sounds like she's about to burst into tears.

"What is it? You don't want him dead after all?"

"No. It's not that. It's just...my entire life, I've been surrounded by violent men. I've watched anger and hatred eating them alive on a daily basis. I think I'm beginning to lose hope."

"Hope of what?"

She pauses. The sound of the rain hammers down on the tree house roof, stealing the silence for a second. "Hope that there are any kindhearted, gentle men left in the world," she says. She speaks so quietly that I have to strain to hear her over the roar of the rain.

I don't really know what to say to that. I'd love to tell her that I am capable of such a thing, of having a kind heart, but I don't think that's true anymore. I haven't felt like that in a long time. Truthfully, I probably lost any soft edges I may have ever possessed long before Laura even went missing, back when I was in the military, scraping people off the desert floor. It's easy to blame the turmoil of my soul on Laura's disappearance, but it's only partly responsible. I've been fucked up and angry for a very long time.

I do something I really shouldn't. I reach and I stroke my hand over her wet hair. Her eyes are still closed, but she tenses even before I've touched her, as if she's expecting me to do it. If there was any way for me to be a gentle man again, she would inspire it in me. "I'm sure there's someone out there that fits the bill," I tell her quietly. "The world's a big place. And there are millions of guys who haven't been jacked up by war, or drugs, or murder. All you have to do is find your way out of this forest, and you can have your pick of any of them."

She smiles, and it's a painfully sad smile. "But what if I don't want my pick of them? What if I've already set my sights on someone else? Someone dangerous, who enjoys his vices a little too much?"

Oh, fuck.

I've felt the tension between us. I've been hyper sensitive to it, but I've been trying to ignore it, because Fernando's a fucking psychopath. Natalia isn't helping matters by insinuating things like this. Still, I'm concerned, but I'm also really fucking happy at the same time. "We all want things that aren't good for us, Natalia. Sometimes the wanting is the fun part. It's just the *having* part can be too damned dangerous sometimes."

Finally, she opens her eyes. Beautiful dark cat's eyes. "Are you saying I'm not worth the risk, Mr. America?"

She doesn't get it. She thinks I'm worried about my safety, that I won't chase after her because her father might come for me. I twist a piece of her hair around my finger, intrigued by how long, how soft, how silky it is. "I'm not afraid of Fernando, Natalia. Not for my own sake. But you...I worry about what he would do to you if he discovered something he didn't like."

She sits up a little straighter, angling her head to one side. "He's ruled my life since I was old enough to walk. Shouldn't I be allowed to make my own decisions by now? Take my own risks." She smiles. "Have vices of my own?"

I can't fucking help myself. I lean closer to her, doing my best to ignore my dick, which is demanding I take charge of this situation right now and fuck her senseless. "You want *me* to become your vice?" I whisper.

She watches me for a second, eyes wide open, and for the first time she really looks at me. None of this furtive sidelong glance bullshit. No looking away as soon as I turn and see her. She *really* looks at me, and she seems fascinated. She reaches up with her hand, just as slowly and carefully as I did when I stroked her hair, and she cups my face in her palm. Her hands are cold, but the contact feels like it's burning into me. "No point in trying to prevent something that has already happened, right, Mr. America?"

I know with every bone in my body that I should back the fuck away right now—this can only end in pain and misery, after all—but the bone in my pants has other ideas. I can't hold back anymore. Not with her looking at me like I'm some kind of goddamn miracle. And not with my blood charging around my body, filled with adrenalin, making me feel high and drunk all at the same time. I need her. I need to act now, before common sense prevails.

Rushing forward, I take hold of her neck in one hand and pull her to me, bringing my lips down on hers. Her mouth is fucking amazing, her lips so fucking unbelievably soft. I've kissed plenty of girls before, but none of those kisses have lit up the inside of my head like it's filled with motherfucking C4 explosives. She feels so fucking small and vulnerable beneath my hands. I kiss her harder, guiding her lips open, and then I'm sliding my tongue into her mouth, past her teeth. She tastes so goddamn sweet, like cherries, and strawberry, and mint all mixed together. She sighs as I massage her tongue with my own, licking, laving and tasting her, exploring her mouth, and the sound of her moaning softly nearly catapults me into outer fucking space.

She's shaking, her body trembling violently, and I can't tell if it's because she's soaking wet and the damp has penetrated down deep into her bones, or if it's because the kiss is overtaking her and she can't fucking breathe.

I should pull away and give her a second, but I don't. I wrap my arms around her and I pull her to me, crushing her body against mine. She laces her arms around my neck, and then there's no going back. I lift her into my lap, my hands on her waist, guiding her, and then she's straddling me.

How the fuck did this happen? How did we end up here, when I've been on my best fucking behavior? It makes zero sense. Her mouth on mine makes sense, though. The feel of her tits crushed up against my chest. The way she arches, grinding her hips against mine, as I stack my hands on the small of her back. All of these things make perfect sense to me.

Natalia pulls back, breaking off the kiss. Her lips are parted, pouting and swollen from the fever of our kiss, and her eyes are burning with need. "Fuck me, Cade. *Please.* Don't overanalyze. Don't think about what will happen when the rain stops. Just give me what I need."

I can't say no to this woman. I don't *want* to say no to her. In the back of my mind, I'm aware that I'm about to cartwheel head fucking first down a vertical slope, and I'm liable to break every bone in my body on the way down. There's nothing to be done, though. No ripcord. No escape hatch. No eject button. There's only Natalia, and the way she's staring into my eyes, as though she can't possibly look away.

"I'll give you what you need. On one condition."

Her fingernails dig into the back of my neck, pressing in just hard enough to send a frisson of pain ricocheting around my body. "Anything," she whispers.

"You don't let him touch you again. You hear me? You *never* let him touch you again? You fucking call for me, and I'll be there. *I'll be there no matter what.*"

Natalia blinks. Her eyes fill with tears, but she doesn't let them fall. "Okay. I promise."

I growl, grabbing hold of the bottom of her tank top. It peels from her body with ease and makes a wet slapping noise as I throw it over my shoulder. Natalia gasps as I bury my face into her cleavage, licking and biting at the swell of her tits. They're glorious, seriously fucking glorious, and I haven't even taken her bra off yet. She writhes against me as I slide my hand down, rubbing my fingers between her legs; her head kicks back, and she gasps, a look of surprise on her face.

"Oh god, Cade..."

The bra has got to fucking go. I rip the straps down over her shoulders, and then I'm pulling the cups of the plain black material down too, revealing the beautiful tanned skin of her breasts. Her freckles really are everywhere. I manage to rein myself in for a second, wanting to drink her in. She's perfect. In the past I've been with women of all shapes and sizes, each beautiful and unique in their own way, but no one ever has or ever will compare to Natalia Villalobos without her shirt on. Her hair is still soaking, sticking to her skin, which is damp and hot. I gather her hair in my hands, taking hold of it in one hand, and then I pull gently, so she has to tip her head back. She has to curve her back in order to oblige me, which means her chest rises, her tits level with my mouth.

"Holy fuck," I hiss. Her nipples are perfect, a delicate pink color that makes her seem fragile, though I already know that isn't the case. Carefully, I use the tip of my tongue to flick and tease the bud of her right nipple, and I have to bite my fucking lip when she begins to shiver and shake on top of me. My cock is straining against my soaking wet jeans, demanding to be let free, but I'm not done yet. I want to play with her for a while first.

I release her long enough to fully remove her bra, and then my hands are all over her, palming and squeezing her tits, gripping her tightly at the waist, squeezing her ass through her jeans. She can feel how hard I am as I thrust up against her pussy. She *must* be able to. Every time I do it, her breath catches in her throat and she makes a sound of frustration mingled with intense pleasure.

"I'm going to take care of you," I promise, growling into the skin just below her collarbone. "I'm going to make you come so hard all over my cock, Natalia. Are you ready? Are you ready for me to fuck you 'til you scream?"

She pants, grinding herself against me, and I know without a doubt that she is *more* than ready. I could strip her out of her pants right now and fuck her hard enough to bring this tree house down, and she wouldn't complain. I can literally smell how turned on she is, and it's enough to drive me insane. They say men and women are susceptible to each other's pheromones, and right now this is science at its goddamn best. I can't get enough of her. My hands can't stop roaming crazily all over her body. She cries out as I unfasten her jeans and slide my hand past the wet fabric, only to find even more wet fabric underneath. This isn't the same kind of wet, though. Not rainwater wet. More like, *I-want-you-inside-me-right-fucking-now-look-how-fucking-ready-I-am* kind of wet. It's such a turn on.

In one swift movement, I pop up onto my knees, take hold of her, wrapping one arm around her body, and then I'm laying her out carefully on her back. I need to get her pants off, and I can't do that if she's straddling me.

"Tell me to take your pants off," I growl.

"Take them—"

She doesn't get to finish the sentence. I cut her off as I rip and tear at her clothes. I yank her shoes off one at a time, and then her jeans are gone, thrown into the corner of the tree house. Her plain black cotton panties are soaked through with her need. I drop down, pushing her legs apart, and then I'm sucking on the material, greedily licking at it, my head spinning with the taste and the smell of her. She's incredible. She bucks and hisses as I rub my thumb over her clit, and I have to touch myself. I fucking *have* to. I pop open the button on my pants, pulling my jeans down over my hips so my hard-on can spring free.

I begin working my hand up and down the length of my cock, and it's *so* close to being too much. I want to push myself inside her. I want to be balls deep in her pussy, while I finger her clit. I want to feel her tighten as she comes. I want to feel the wetness of her all over me. She looks like she's so close to coming already—her eyes are closed, her lower lip fastened between her teeth, her chest rising and falling frantically.

"Open your eyes," I command. "Open your eyes and look at me."

She opens them, her pupils are so dilated they almost look like they're blown. She fixes her gaze on my face, and I slowly shake my head, allowing a wicked smile to tease at the corners of my mouth. "Not there," I tell her. "Look *here*." I stop rubbing her pussy for a second to take hold of her by the chin, guiding her head until she's looking down, at what I'm doing to myself, at my hand stroking up and down my hard cock. Her eyes grow wide, and then even wider as I tug my sodden t-shirt over my head, disposing of it so that I'm practically naked, aside from my jeans, which are still shoved half way down my thighs. Natalia sees the curls of black ink creeping over my shoulders, and traces the lines of my tattoo with her fingertips. She can't see the full back piece right now, but I can see that she's intrigued. I'm hardly going to hit pause to explain about the Widow Makers right now, though.

"Are you ready?" I ask her.

"Yes. I want you. *Please.*"

I'm all too aware that this might be a nerve-wracking experience for her. I'm looking for signs that she's not ready for this, that she's scared or anxious in any way, but all I can see on her face is her desire. She reaches down in between her legs and tentatively touches herself, her eyes locked on mine. The tip of her tongue darts out of her mouth, wetting her lips, and I have to physically stop myself from throwing myself on her. My will power is getting a real workout right now. If I weren't quite so in charge of my faculties, I might already be inside her, but I have a tight rein over myself. I'm all about the perfect moment. I won't push my cock inside her until she's panting, begging, frantic for me.

"Roll over onto your stomach," I command.

Natalia hesitates for a second, and then flips over onto her stomach as I've asked her to. She looks back over her shoulder, and I can see the want in her eyes. I get the feeling this is an entirely new experience for her—to want someone with such a fierce intensity—and I think it scares her a little.

If I thought her ass was amazing in jeans, without them it's fucking phenomenal. Her little black panties are cut high, exposing her flawless ass cheeks. My dick throbs like crazy in my hand as I study it. "On all fours," I tell her. "Okay." She leans back onto her knees, and I take hold of her panties by the elastic, pulling them down over her butt. She tries to help, wriggling her hips, but I gentle slap her ass cheek, tutting under my breath.

"That's my job. Don't move until I tell you to."

She doesn't speak. Her breathing is labored, out of control, and her muscles are jumping and trembling, but she holds steady, waiting for me to give her a command.

Free will.

I understand the mentality of the men who fuck Fernando's Servicio in the blue room. They love power, just like I do, but their needs as dominants have darkened. To them, being in control isn't enough. They have to take something their submissives don't want to give. They *steal* their pleasure from them. When I'm fucking a woman, being dominant is so much hotter for me because she lays herself bare, trusts and accepts, and the give and take of power is a flow, back and forth. Natalia may be obeying my every need and wish, but that doesn't mean she's powerless. She has *so* much power over me right now. I'm listening to her very intently. I'm studying her body language, so I will know the second she's no longer enjoying this experience. And the second she's not enjoying it is the same second I cease to enjoy it, too.

"I'm going to fuck you now. I'm going to fuck you so hard. It's going to be intense. I'm going to need you to stay with me, beautiful. Concentrate. You're only allowed to come when I say so. Do you think you can do that?"

Natalia shivers. Water drips slowly from the roof ahead, splashing down onto her back. I stoop down and run my tongue from the top of her ass, all the way up her spine, in between her shoulder blades to the base of her neck, and the shivering gets harder. "I can't hear you," I whisper into her ear.

"Yes. I can do it," she gasps.

"Good."

I run my fingers over her pussy, rubbing her between her legs, and then slowly I guide myself into her. Just a little. She's so fucking wet. The heat and the slickness of her pussy damn near makes my eyes roll back into my head. "God...*damn*...it..." I growl.

Her body is perfection. She's feminine, soft as silk, even though she's toned at the same time. I can't stop running my hands all over her. Carefully, I ease myself out of her, and then I drive my hips forward on the same movement, gritting my teeth together as I slam myself home.

Natalia cries out, and the sound of her pleasure echoes around the forest, loud enough to be heard above the roar of the rain.

"Shhh, beautiful. Be quiet." I lean forward, taking hold of her by the throat. I push myself into her again, just as hard, and Natalia leans into my hand, using the pressure to cut off her gasp this time. Once I know that lightly choking her isn't going to freak her the fuck out, I curl my hand around her throat and I squeeze.

There's no holding back after that. I fuck her. Holding her by the hip with my other hand, I thrust myself into her over and over again, maintaining the pressure on her throat to keep her from crying out. She can still whimper, though. She can still moan. Every time I rock my hips forward, sliding my dick as far as I can inside her, my balls slapping her pussy, she lets out the tiniest sound—a sound of pure ecstasy that makes me feel like I'm going to explode inside her. She breathes out of her nose, frantically huffing as I power into her.

"Hold on." I grind the words out from between my clenched teeth. "Not yet, Natalia. Wait. *Wait...*" I'm not even sure how long I can make myself wait. It won't be long, that's for sure. My balls feel tight and full, and my cock is tingling like crazy. Every time I push myself forward, a thousand tiny fireworks are going off beneath my skin, all over my body, hot and prickly. I allow my head to roll back as the tension builds.

My eyes snap wide open when I hear something below us, though. Something over the sound of the rain, and of Natalia's breathing, that shouldn't be there. I keep on fucking her, but I scan the forest floor below us, watching, searching.

And then, there he is. Natalia jolts when she sees what I've seen: her father, stalking closer to our tree house, his rifle raised and nocked in the crook of his shoulder. He's alone, his men now gone, and I have the distinct impression he's not hunting for small game anymore. He's hunting for *me*. Natalia freezes, her body going tense underneath me. She's scared, I can tell. She glances back at me over her shoulder, and there's a look of blind panic on her face that makes me want to scoop her up in my arms and protect her.

Jesus. This is a dangerous moment. If Fernando finds us, naked, me still inside his daughter, up a fucking tree, then he's going to kill us both. He doesn't know about Natalia's hiding place, though, she said it was a secret she shared with her grandfather and no one else. All we have to do is pray he doesn't see the ladder. We have to hope he doesn't look up.

Natalia reaches back and grabs hold of my thigh, digging her fingernails into my skin. She's terrified. Slowly, I curve my body over hers, and I move my hand from her neck to cover her mouth. She digs her fingernails in deeper. Her father stops below us, less than twenty feet away, and the tension of the situation is killing me. Somehow I'm still hard. I'm rock fucking solid inside Natalia, and my dick is tingling with an intensity that requires attention. I slowly begin to angle my hips down, sliding myself out of her pussy, and then driving myself back inside her. Natalia breathes heavily through her nose again, a tiny moan escaping her.

"Shhhhh," I whisper into her ear. "I mean it. Don't make a sound."

It's improbable that Fernando would be able to hear such a tiny, imperceptible noise over the crackling, dripping, and splattering of the raindrops falling from the leaves in the trees, but still...she needs to fucking hold her breath.

I slowly work myself in and out of her, and she presses back against me, grinding against me so I'm as deep inside her as I can go. I kiss and bite at the back of her neck, and she shakes underneath me; I can feel her pulse hammering just below the surface of her skin. I know she's frightened, but I also know she wants this as badly as I do. Her body wouldn't be reacting the way it is if she wanted me to stop, that's for sure. Against all better judgement, I continue to fuck her as her father prowls around below us.

Natalia bites down on my finger as I slam myself into her harder. I can feel the pressure building in her. She wants to cry out. She wants to scream at the top of her lungs. I know this because I do, too. And yet we're both silent as church mice as I fuck her senseless.

Rainwater runs down my back and over my shoulders, now. Natalia's skin is slick and wet, too. Steam rises off her body as she digs her fingernails into my skin, holding on for dear life. On the ground below, Fernando stops, his head cocked to one side as though he's heard something. Natalia's back locks out, rigid, and she pushes back against me, hard. I don't let go. I thrust deeper, harder, watching her reaction and her father's movements at the same time.

She urgently taps my thigh, and then she's arching her back, her head bent back at the same time, and she's coming. I lift her so that she's up on her knees, her back pressed against my chest, the back of her head resting on my collarbone, and I get to see her fall apart. She's silent, but the ecstasy on her face is something else. She closes her eyes, and her lips part, her chest rising and falling quickly as she writhes against me. I reach my hand down between her legs and I rub her clit as she comes; the warm, slick, wetness of her pleasure is all over my fingertips, and I can't stop myself any longer.

I come, slamming my cock inside her like a freight train. I'm not sure if I'm making any noise now; the world feels like it's disintegrating and falling apart around me. My ears are ringing like crazy. Natalia whimpers in my ear, whispering things softly to me.

"Don't let me go. Please, don't let me go."

I feel like I've just been smacked in the side of the head. I can't think straight. Fernando is still paused, listening, and it feels like it doesn't matter how still I am now, because the sound of my frenzied heartbeat is going to give us away. My cock is still hard inside Natalia; every time she twitches or shifts, a bolt of pleasure rocks through me, sending a shiver through my body.

Fernando stands there a moment longer, and then he seems to shake himself. He moves off, still staring down the sight of his rifle, and the rain grows harder.

Only once he has disappeared into the forest, vanished from sight altogether, do either of us move. Natalia sags, lying flat on the floor of the tree house. Her sigh is one of relief. "Thank god," she whispers.

"That your father didn't see us?"

She shakes her head, smiling. "No. Thank god you finally took me, Mr. America."

TEN

THE MOUNTAIN

Back at the Villalobos estate, Fernando has locked himself away in his study. I haven't seen him since Natalia and I walked back through the gates, tired and soaked to the bone, but strangely happy. We don't kiss as we say goodbye to one another. We don't even look each other in the eye, in case someone sees something passing between us that shouldn't exist. She just goes her way, and I go mine. With my cell phone now returned to me, I make a call I've been dreading.

"Get your ass home. *Now.*" Jamie's never told me to do anything before. *Ever.* Seems like today is a day of firsts, though. He is majorly pissed, and it's all my fault. I should never have told him Laura is dead. I shouldn't have told him I plan on killing Fernando, and I probably should have kept the fact that I just fucked his daughter up a tree to myself, too.

"You're mad. Fucking certifiable. You've lost your fucking *mind*," he hisses down the phone. "Come home. Get on the next flight out of Ecuador. I mean it, Cade."

"And leave Fernando breathing? I don't think so, man."

"I loved Laura, too, okay? Fernando won't go unpunished. We'll figure it out here, though, together, like we always do. And once we have a sane plan of action, we can make sure he pays for what he did to her. This, what you're doing, is more than ill advised, though, brother. It's fucking stupid, and it's going to get you killed."

"We've all got to die someday."

"See what I mean? Fucking stupid, Cade. Fucking *stupid*. We dragged each other out of hell in the desert. We've been through nightmare after nightmare ever since we got back. You think I'm going to let you die on your own, in another fucking country, in another fucking continent, without coming to get you? You know we're going out in a blaze of glory together, you asshole."

"Do *not* come down here," I snap into the phone. "This situation's already precarious enough as it is. If you show up, the shit is royally going to hit the fan. I just know it."

"*Cade*." His voice is hard and terse. He's so angry with me, I can hear that plainly enough, but what the hell am I supposed to do? Let him come down here and get himself killed? There's an extremely high probability that I'm going to end up getting shot in the back of the head out here; I'm not going to condemn my best friend to the same fate as me.

"*Jamie*. Do not come down here. Promise me."

"I'm not eleven years old, asshole. I'm not making promises. If I'm hit with even the slightest suspicion that things are going sideways down there, I'm getting on a plane and I'm dragging your ass out of there whether you like it or not. Do you hear me? Don't forget, I'm the president of this club, Cade. You're meant to do what the fuck I tell you."

"That's low. You're pulling rank on me now?"

"If I fucking *have* to. You think I'll let some hurt feelings get in the way of your life? You're wrong, man. You're so, *so* wrong."

I sigh heavily. He's not going to back off here, I know it. It's shitty that he's trying to order me home like some fucking subordinate, when we've always been equals. Jamie calls the shots, sure, but he's never treated me like I need to bow down to him. There's a very good chance I'm being pig-headed here, and he's just trying to look out for me, I'm aware of that, but it still stings.

"I'll be careful," I tell him.

"Damn right you will. And you've got to stop fucking the girl, man.

Trust me. That is going to blow up in your face in no time at all."

Jamie can hardly talk about fucking the wrong girls. He's in love with a woman he shouldn't have gone anywhere near with a ten-foot pole. He knows how hypocritical he sounds, because he says, "Learn from my mistakes, brother. I know you're mad, and I know you're hurting, I am too, but please...just don't do anything stupid."

I grind my teeth, closing my eyes. "Okay. I'm gonna play this smart, I swear."

Jamie's quiet for a moment, and then he huffs out a deep breath. I can imagine the look of worry on his face right now, as he paces back and forth in the Widow Makers' clubhouse. "All right, dude. I'm trusting you," he says. "Don't fuck this up. Don't put the club at risk. And whatever you do, don't get yourself fucking killed."

••••

The next morning, Harrison drags me out of bed at 6 a.m., and Fernando questions me relentlessly about where I disappeared to with his daughter for four hours. His anger is palpable—the kind you feel like a slap in the face. The man is all over the place. One minute he's asking me to stay away, the next he's telling me to take his daughter out into the forest. Now it seems as though we're firmly back in "*stay-the-fuck-away-from-her-asshole*" territory.

"I am sure you've had a chance to speak to your employer by now, Kechu," Fernando snaps. "When can we expect his royal highness to arrive?" Fernando grins, baring his teeth, and it's not a happy grin. It's a death mask, and I want to smash my fist right fucking through it.

"He's dealing with a private matter at home," I say. "He should be here in no more than a week or so." A week should be enough time for me to get my shit together and make this man dead. A part of me doesn't know why I'm stretching this out so ridiculously. I could slip into his room at night, one way or another, and put him down the same way I did to Julio. I could wrap the cord from the light pull around his throat right now and strangle the bastard to death; the struggle probably wouldn't even alert the guys standing guard outside his office. There are a million ways I could get what I want and get the fuck out of here, but I'm dragging my heels. I know I am.

It boils down to the fact that I'm a pleasure delayer. The wait, knowing what's about to go down, knowing that he won't see it coming, is almost too sweet and satisfying to turn away from. And now, there's also Natalia. I fucked her. I shouldn't have, but I did, and what stands between us isn't as simple as a casual hookup. I look at her and I feel bottomless. I feel like I'm falling. I feel responsible, and protective, and violently angry all at once. It's fucking scary.

I've avoided feeling this way about a woman since before I was deployed. I don't want or need to be feeling this way now, but I have no choice in the matter. She's under my skin, now. I try not to think about what will happen to her when I leave here, because the truth is I just can't see it. I can't see me leaving her, period, and I have no idea how the fuck I'm going to make that work.

So fucking dumb.

"A week is too long, Kechu. I'm beginning to think your boss does not respect my time."

"He does. He's also a loyal man, though, and he won't leave his family when they need him. Like you, I imagine. If Natalia was sick, or in some sort of trouble, you wouldn't leave her side, would you?" I know this is a tricky hand to play as soon as the words are out of my mouth. Fernando's expression is thunderous.

"You would be wise to leave Natalia out of this, Kechu. Don't think to use my love for my daughter to excuse your Louis James's behavior."

I hold my hands up—*I surrender.* "Forgive me. I didn't mean to use Natalia. Mr. Aubertin will be here as soon as he can, you have my word." I don't give him Jamie's word, though. He hasn't given it, and I don't want to sully his reputation as an honest man. I'm more than happy to give him *my* word, though. I'll make promises all day long, and I won't give a shit about breaking them. Later, when I'm killing the son of a bitch, how will any of it matter anyway?

"All right. You may leave now. Perhaps you ought to get out of the house today, Kechu. We are expecting guests who might not be happy to see you. Word of what happened to William has spread among even more of my clients. These are volatile men with volatile habits. I cannot ensure your safety while they are here."

"Understood. I'm happy to make myself scarce."

I am, too. Jamie might have pissed me off, but in fairness he has a point. I should probably have some sort of contingency plan in place, for when the time comes and I need to make a quick exit.

Natalia is nowhere to be found as I leave the mansion. Not that I can go looking for her. With the bi-polar mood Fernando is in today, if anyone suspects I'm purposefully seeking her out, especially Ocho, then I'm in big trouble. I leave the grounds of the Villalobos estate on foot. There are gardeners everywhere, trimming and clipping at bushes, edging the lawn, working tirelessly to make the place look beautiful. I see Ocho meandering along the workers along the perimeter of the grounds, walking parallel to me as I head toward the long, wide wood chipped pathway that cuts into the forest.

Obviously he didn't fall into one of Fernando's game traps and get killed yesterday when he wandered off alone, more's the pity. I can't shake the feeling that he's bad fucking news. He's always there. Always lurking, always watching. He sees everything, and he probably hears everything, too. I don't believe for a second that he doesn't speak English. Or at least understand it. I keep a steady, even pace. I'd love to break into a run and lose the fucker, but running around places like this generally makes you look guilty. I don't need a slug to the back just because I want to shake Ocho.

So, walking. I walk into the forest, and I continue to walk. I don't deviate from the track the cars use to travel to the estate. Without anyone here to guide me, I'm all too aware that I could put a foot wrong and get blown up by one of Fernando's booby traps. And wouldn't that just be fucking perfect?

I know where I left the scrambler. I need to make sure it's got gas and that it's still running okay. I head south when the track splits. The journey from the bunker to the Villalobos estate didn't seem all that long when I was in the car with Ocho the first day I arrived in Orellana, but now, on foot, it feels like miles and miles. The sun is high in the sky by the time I reach the bunker. Natalia told me the old ruined outbuildings here, decayed and standing in ruin, were rigged with traps, too, so I don't go inside. I skirt around the small settlement, heading to the west, to where I stowed the scrambler.

Only, when I get to the small clearing where I left the Yamaha, the clearing is empty.

"What the fuck?" I *know* this is where I left it. I have no doubt in my mind. I'm not in the habit of forgetting where I leave vehicles, even if it is in the forest and all you can see for miles is trees. I search the area, scanning the ground for signs of the bike, but I don't find anything. The ground is soft; after all that rain yesterday, even the deepest, most defined tracks from a set of tires would be gone. Mud sucks at my boots as I cross the clearing, swearing under my breath.

Natalia said the bike was still here. She thought it was yesterday, at least. That means it must have been taken recently, and she's not being kept in the loop. Am I surprised by this? No, not really. It was a miracle they let me keep my gun on me for so long. I think if I hadn't used it to shoot William, I'd probably still have it. But a mode of transportation? A means of escaping without them knowing? Fernando wouldn't stand for that, especially if he thinks there's a two-million-dollar deal on the line.

"*Fuck.*" I crouch down, resting my elbows on my knees, trying to think. This isn't the end of the world. Yes, having the scrambler would have been perfect. It's designed to excel on rough, uneven terrain and that's what I'm dealing with around here. But there are Humvees and Patriots back at the estate, too, which are also designed for navigating crazy landscapes. I can take one of those when the time comes. And hell, maybe it'll be safer if there are two people inside.

God, I don't even know why I'm even considering something like that. Natalia may not want to come with me. If her father is dead, what's to say she won't want to stay here, at the estate? It's worth a small fucking fortune. The compound and the Widow Makers' clubhouse is a far cry from the luxury she's used to.

"You look like the world has ended."

I jump up, my balisong already in my hand, fully prepared to stab whoever is standing behind me. It takes a full second for me to process the fact that it's a woman's voice I've heard, and that it's Natalia hovering on the edge of the clearing, with a backpack slung over her shoulders. Her hair hangs down in a long braid. She's wearing a long-sleeved shirt with the sleeves rolled up, and some serious hiking boots, like she's planning on taking off up a mountain.

"So you found me, huh?" I smile at her, flicking the knife over in my hand to retract the blade.

"Not hard to do," she replies. "You left a track that could probably be seen from outer space."

She's right, I'm sure. I'm used to moving through desert and bayou, and I'm good at concealing my movements usually, but in this kind of overgrown, wild forest, even my best efforts are for nothing. I raise an eyebrow at her. "I'll try not to be too offended. Are you out here following me, or are you about to fly the coop?" I point to her bag.

She pulls a wry expression, looking off into the trees. She doesn't want to look me in the eye. "I thought," she starts. "I thought I should probably take you to her. To Laura." I'm shocked. Too surprised to speak. When I refrain from saying anything, she continues. "Higher up into the mountains, we have a burial site. It's not much, but that's where my father told me she had been taken. If you would like to go, to pay your respects to her, I could show you where it is."

•••

The climb up the mountain is gruelling. We don't really speak all that much. The heat is oppressive, especially since it's the rainy season and it's so damn humid, and so we both remain in our thoughts, planting one foot in front of the other, heads bowed as we slog our way upward. We share an easy silence. It feels strange to think I met her less than a week ago. Despite my surroundings, the threat of death hanging over my head, and the knowledge that Laura is gone, I spend a good deal of my day thinking about her. It seems as though I've spent more time with her than I actually have. I recognize her tics now—the way she obsessively tucks her hair back when she's thinking; the way she taps her index finger against the table whenever she's sitting down; the way her forehead crinkles when she's confused. And most of all, how her pupils dilate every time she looks at me, like she wants to jump my bones right out of my body. I'm more than happy for her to be looking at me that way, but it carries a certain risk. One day soon, Fernando's going to notice, and there won't be any denying the fact that we're both attracted to one another.

We climb. Thank god I have good cardio. Natalia's used to the trek up to the burial site, but even she is out of breath when we reach our destination. The trees are thinner up here, so much closer to the timberline, and the mountain gives way to a broad, rocky clearing. I see the small, wooden crosses almost immediately. There aren't that many of them, maybe ten, and they're set out sporadically in between the large rocks and boulders. Red, green and orange streamers snap on the gusts of wind that buffet the mountainside. It reminds me of Nepal, of the reams and reams of prayer flags that travel all the way from Base Camp up to the top of Everest, though these aren't prayer flags. They're just pretty decorations to mark the graves.

Turning around, my breath is clear whipped away. The burial site itself is fairly barren and stark, but the view from this vantage point is truly spectacular.

"Beautiful, no?" Natalia asks.

"Yeah. Yeah, it really is."

"Come. I'll show you the place." She takes me by the hand, then. It's a small, simple gesture, but the connection between us feels all the more strong for it. Every time we touch, no matter how brief the contact, it seems as though we're cementing ourselves together in yet another way. She leads me toward the furthest cross, at the lowest point of the burial ground; as we pass by the other crosses, it doesn't escape my notice that none of them are marked. Not even with an initial, or something to indicate who lies there. I ask Natalia why this is, and she looks uncomfortable.

"The name Villalobos is not a popular one around here. Thanks to my father, people are scared of us. My grandfather and my mother are buried here. My aunt, who was killed when she was just a child. If any of the villagers suspected these graves belong to someone from the Villalobos cartel, they would dig them up and desecrate them."

"Jesus."

"I don't really blame them. My grandfather was a sweet man. He farmed in order to make money, but he also sold cocaine, too. He wasn't a violent man. He never killed anyone in the name of competition or business. Whatever profit he made from the drugs, he used to send my father away to be educated. He wanted him to be a doctor, or a lawyer. Something legal. When my father came back from school, he chose to use his business degree to expand my grand-father's cocaine production. He became very...cutthroat. Unforgiving. If someone crossed him, they were never heard from again. So now, we are feared."

Natalia comes to a stop in front of a cross with a red streamer. She dips down, resting on her heels as she runs the streamer through her fingers. "Laura's favorite color was red," she says.

It feels like I've been sucker punched in the gut. I can hardly breathe. "I know. She wore this red dress to her prom. My father nearly had a fit. Said she looked like a prostitute, but she refused to get changed." I lose myself in the memories for a moment. God, they fought so hard that night. Dad didn't want her leaving the house "looking like a street walker" and she refused to "give in to his capitalist, archaic, patriarchal bullshit." They were always butting heads, but it was because they were so alike. Later, at some point while she was away at college, they mellowed towards each other. She was his favorite, and I was okay with that, because she was my favorite, too. She was everybody's favorite. Full of piss and vinegar, always ready to call you out on your shit. She called a spade a spade, which was a breath of fresh air in our household.

"She always felt so alive to me, even when she was sad," Natalia says. She looks like she's about to burst into tears. "I want you to know...if I could have helped her escape, I would have. Things were bad back then, though. My father goes through phases. He was so watchful of me then. He was paranoid that I was going to try and leave myself. I was under constant surveillance."

I stroke my hand over her hair, sucking in a deep breath through my nose. "I know," I tell her. "I know you would have. This isn't your fault." *It's mine.* I should have been watching out for her. I should have been paying attention, not throwing back champagne the night she disappeared. And I should have looked harder for her. I should have stayed down here. I should have figured out where she was sooner.

There are so many reasons to blame myself for this. It's madness that Natalia would feel even an ounce of guilt herself. I crouch down beside her, taking the red streamer from her hands. I wind it around my own fingers, hating myself more and more by the second.

"I'll give you a moment," Natalia tells me. She gets to her feet and heads off, stopping in front of one of the other crosses, placing her hand lightly on the ground in front of it.

"I bet you're loving how complicated this thing's become," I say softly under my breath. "You always did love drama. Remember when we were teenagers, and Dad caught me sneaking out one night to see that girl...god, what was her name? Sarah Goldman. Fuck, Sarah Goldman." I shake my head, trying not to laugh. "He caught me shimmying down a drainpipe at the back of the house, and he was screaming and shouting, yelling at me, calling me a little punk, and you showed up and just sat there, eating a sandwich, watching us argue, volleying back and forth like it was a goddamn tennis match."

I almost expect to hear her voice, laughing, telling me I deserved the hiding I got that night, but there's nothing. No laughter. No elbow in my side. Just the wind teasing the red piece of fabric in my hands, and the mountains stretching on forever in every direction.

Did she ever come up here? Did she ever get to see this while she was alive? I find myself hoping so. She would have really, really loved it.

ELEVEN

MASS

A sour, terrible smell hits the back of my nose as we head back down the mountain. It's ripe and pungent, and makes my gag reflex work overtime. Natalia takes me by the hand again and tells me we need to hurry back, and I can see that she's edgy. The smell grows thicker, burning my nostrils as we hike down. At the back of my mind, I already know what the smell is, I recognize it on some level, but I don't want to acknowledge it.

After a while, the smell disappears. Natalia seems to relax, and I forget about it until we pass through a stand of trees and suddenly we're faced with a yawning hole in the ground, which is filled almost to the brim with bones. Bones fucking everywhere. And not animal bones. Not the remains of game that has been hunted and killed. No. These are human skeletons.

"*Damn*," Natalia curses under her breath. She's anxious as she looks sideways at me. "I'm sorry. I thought...I thought this was further west. The smell..."

The smell must have confused her. It was coming directly from the west, instead of from down below us, but the breeze is strange today, sending blustery gusts in loops up and down the mountain on thermals, and it's obviously turned her around a little.

I'm beginning to wonder why there's even any smell at all—the corpses in the huge, mass grave, are all skeletons—but then I catch sight of something that blows that theory right out of the water. The corpses are *not* all skeletons. On top of the mountain of bones lie three fresh bodies. All three are women, and they're naked. They're in various states of decomposition. The first body has to have been out here for at least a couple of weeks. The skin is nearly all gone, as well as the eyes, and most of the flesh on the skull. The other two bodies can't have been exposed for as long. They're bloated and purple, as if they've been submerged in water rather than left out on the side of a mountain. Then I realize, the rain yesterday was intense and didn't stop for hours. And with the bodies resting on top of the pile the way they are, they're likely to have absorbed an awful lot of fluid.

"What *is* this?" I can barely speak. I want to double over and throw up. I have seen some fucked-up things in my time, but this? This is something else. Something rotten and evil. Tears streak down Natalia's cheeks.

"This is where my father disposes of the people who stand against him. The people who try to sell cocaine in his country. And the women who say no too many times. The women who won't submit."

As I'm staring at the grave, my eyes skipping over countless bodies, I try and estimate how many people are here. The skeletons are scattered and in pieces for the most part. I give up trying to see them as whole people and instead move onto counting skulls.

Thirteen, fourteen, fifteen...

Twenty-six, twenty-seven, twenty-eight...

Fifty-two, fifty-three, fifty-four...

Oh god. So many. I can only count how many are resting on the top of the pile. Who knows how deep the hole is, how many bodies are stacked underneath. And who knows how many holes Fernando Villalobos filled before he has this one dug and filled. Something tells me this can't be the only one.

This must be how it felt for the soldiers who rolled into Auschwitz, expecting to be liberating prisoners of war, only to find the dead piled high on either side of the road.

Something occurs to me, then. Something awful and so horrifying that I can't even comprehend that it might be true. *The women who won't submit.*

Laura was as stubborn as they come. Laura wasn't a woman to submit, no matter how black the situation. I look at Natalia, and she can already see it on my face.

"No. No, she's not here, Cade. He didn't put her here. I'd know if he did. He promised me…"

Too late.

It is far too late for me to be reasoned with. The idea's in my head now, and it won't go away. That fucker could have thrown my sister's still-warm body into an open fucking mass grave? Oh no.

Just. Fucking. No.

I take off down the mountain, and I'm not walking anymore. I'm fucking running. I'm charging. I'm on the warpath, rage pumping through my veins, and I won't be able to get a hold of myself until Fernando Villalobos is lying in a pool of his own blood. I'm going to pull every single last one of his teeth out with a pair of pliers. I'm gonna dump acid on that motherfucker. I'm gonna hurt him so bad, he's gonna beg for me to just give in and let him fucking die.

There will be no mercy for him. There will be no forgiveness. There will be only pain and suffering, and finally, when I've had enough and my body is tired and I physically can't torture him any more, I'm going to shoot him in the fucking head and put him down like the fucking dog he is.

"Cade! Cade, please wait!" Natalia is behind me somewhere, running after me, but now I'm faster than she is. I'm not careful. I barrel through the forest, barely missing tree trunks, barely ducking under low hanging boughs in time.

"CADE!"

Natalia's cry echoes around off the high mountainsides around us. A chorus of shrieks split the air apart as dozens of birds take to the sky. I don't look back. I am single minded in my purpose, and that purpose is to cause Fernando indescribable agony. My journey down the mountain is a hell of a lot faster than it was going up. My legs are singing with pain, though, my knees and ankles throbbing from my headlong sprint downhill.

The sun is going down. Little more than a burned orange crescent remains hovering on the horizon. It will sink soon, disappearing altogether, and then I'll be running in darkness. Natalia probably had a flashlight in that backpack of hers. She probably had water and all kinds of other supplies, but I don't need any of them right now. I just need to get back to the estate. I just need to—

A low, eerie howl deadens the sound of the forest. One minute everything is alive, bugs chittering, birds zipping between the trees, crickets chirruping, and then it's as if the forest sucks in a deep breath and holds onto it, refusing to let it go. Another howl, long and plaintive. It's damned close. I stop dead, waiting, listening. Sound travels so well in the mountains. *So* well. It could be that the wolves are actually miles away, and their song is simply being carried on the wind, but...

Again, it comes. And this time, a cacophony of sound follows after— yipping and chattering that wouldn't be audible if the animals weren't *very* close by. Goddamn it. Fernando said it himself. These animals are brazen. They've taken people from outside the fucking house before, which means they won't have a problem taking a single person out in the forest by themselves. I'm not worried about me. I have my balisong. Plus, I've fought off crazed drug dealers and psychotic Columbian women in the past. Plus the odd Taliban extremist here and there. I can handle a bunch of wolves. Natalia, on the other hand? Does she even have a weapon with her?

Fuck.

My brain changes gear with all the finesse and power of an F16 fighter jet. I turn and run back the way I came, my muscles screaming, my lungs burning, my heart on fire.

"NATALIA!"

"Over here!"

She's easy to find. She must have been doing a fairly good job of keeping up with me, because she isn't that far behind. I find her crouched low with a serrated dagger in her hand. Her expression is grim and serious, her gaze locked on something in front of her. I don't see it for a second. My eyes need a moment to adjust to the camouflage of the forest, but soon I can pick apart all of the greens and blacks and browns, and the wolf appears, hunkered down, teeth bared, eyes glinting wickedly. He's pure black, so wild looking and beautiful, despite his obvious desire to tear Natalia's face off. She holds out her hand, gesturing for me to stop, to stay where I am.

"He won't strike if there are two of us," she whispers. "Just wait. Don't move."

I've had no experience with wolves before, and I'm betting the woman in front of me has had plenty. I do as she says, waiting to see what the wolf will do, though my hands are twitching by my sides. It feels wrong. It feels like I should be doing something to protect her.

"Steady, boy," she murmurs under her breath. "Steady now."

The wolf remains totally still; the only part of him that moves is his muzzle, which trembles as he growls. It's a menacing sound. He means fucking business, and I have no doubt he'll launch himself at Natalia if she so much as flinches.

She doesn't, though. She is even and calm as the wolf watches her with his sharp yellow eyes.

A series of excited yips echoes through the trees around us, and a cold sweat breaks out on my brow. "He's not alone, Natalia. I think it's time to go."

She nods very slowly, turning the handle of her serrated knife over in her hand. "If I back down now, he'll know he's won," she says. "I've got to see this through."

Fuck Harrison. If he hadn't taken my gun, this situation would be a whole lot different. I might not have even needed to kill the wolf; a shot in the air might have been enough to scare him off. As it stands, the animal is likely to die, and for some reason that seems like an injustice.

The wolf pounces forward, just a foot, testing the water. Natalia doesn't back down, though. She remains frozen, knife held out in front of her, ready, and her hand is stable. The woman isn't even shaking.

She's fucking remarkable. "Get ready to run," she tells me. "I was wrong. This one already thinks he's won."

"We don't need to ru—" Sudden, fast movement takes me off guard. I haven't been watching. I haven't noticed the wolf to my right, sneaking through the undergrowth toward me. I barely register the blur of color as it springs up out of the shadows, flying toward me, teeth bared and snapping, going for my throat. I don't get my arm up in time. I'm halfway there, bracing, getting ready to break the thing in half, when a flash of silver cuts through the air, and the wolf cries out, yelping. He hits me in the side with the force of a seventy-pound bowling ball, but he's not trying to tear at me with his teeth now. He's bleeding, lying on his side, and Natalia's knife is sticking out of the side of his ribs.

Then everything is chaos.

The black wolf attacks, hurtling toward Natalia, who is now unarmed. Did she...did she just take down a wolf with her knife? *Midair*? I have no time to process. I'm racing toward Natalia, but the black wolf is there first. He fastens his teeth around her forearm, clamping down, drawing blood. She screams, and the sound of her pain sends a frisson of electricity through the darkening forest. A series of howls and yelps follows—the wolves are getting excited. And now, they can undoubtedly smell blood.

I fall on the black wolf, grabbing hold of its head.

"Cade! Get it off me!"

I try to cut off its air supply, to choke it out for want of a better word, but I can tell from the rigid, taut way its body is bowed that it won't give in that easy. It just won't. There is no backing down in this animal's world. There is only success or failure, and when failure means starvation, it makes creatures like this determined. I have to kill it. I *have* to. My balisong is still in my hand, but stabbing him isn't the most efficient way of ending this right now. I grab hold of his head, taking hold of his muzzle and his lower jaw, and I twist sharply. A sickening crunching sound fills the air, and I feel the damage I've done. The wolf's neck snaps in my hands, and that's it. He's dead. It's over.

Only it isn't, because then there are another two wolves creeping forward out of the forest, and then another two, and then another three. More and more of them appear, materializing out of the darkness, and every single one of them looks ready to kill.

Natalia holds her arm to her chest, cradling it. She's covered in blood, and her face is a strange, ashy color. "They won't stop now," she whispers. "We have to get out of here."

I help her to her feet, moving slowly, trying not to startle the approaching pack. "We can't outrun them," I tell her.

She shakes her head. "This is their world. They can see in the dark. And they're way better at running through the forest than we are."

"Then what do we do?" There is always a way out of every sticky situation. *Always.* I can't see the way out of this one right now, though, and it's beginning to freak me out. I may be able to fend off a bunch of the wolves and save myself, but can I save Natalia at the same time? Can I make sure that both of us come out of this unscathed? For the first time, I wish I had been selfish enough to ask Jamie to be here. If he were at my side, this would be a fucking cakewalk. He could have handled the majority of these fuckers while I made sure Natalia was all right. Wishful thinking, though. I told him not to come. I told him to stay in New Mexico with the club, and it's too late to be changing my mind now.

Moving slowly, I bend down, retrieving Natalia's serrated blade from the dead wolf on the ground to my left, and I toss it to her. "Go for their necks. Their eyes," I tell her. "Stay calm and we'll walk away from this."

She swallows, nodding, and I can see that she's scared.

The wolves creep forward, darting ahead one at a time, testing us, trying to find the best spot to attack. There are nine of them now. Nine wolves against the two of us. The way they move is silent and menacing, and death hangs in the air.

"*Cade,*" Natalia says. The terror is plain in her voice. "This wasn't supposed to happen. I'm sorry. You were supposed to leave. You were supposed to get out."

"It's okay. It's going to be all right." I can't even convince myself of that, though. The wolves draw closer. Their teeth are clearly visible even though the light is failing, and I know how they will feel, ripping and tearing into our flesh. It will hurt. It will be agony, and it will be all my fault.

Closer, they come.

Closer.

One lunges on my left, snapping and snarling, and I slash out with my blade, growling back at it. The wolf falls back, but it's only a matter of time before it strikes again. And the next time—

A loud, thunderous siren blasts through the forest, the depth and breadth of it making the ground beneath my feet shake. I jump, ready to slash and cut with my knife, but something miraculous happens. I've never heard anything so loud before. The siren shakes the leaves on the trees. My teeth rattle inside my head, the sound is so powerful. I try to shout over it, to ask Natalia what the fuck is going on, but it's futile; my words are swept away in the ear-splitting din.

The wolves have frozen. They're no longer advancing towards us; they stand, glued to the spot, ear swivelling like crazy as they listen to the sound. Nearly all of them have a paw raised in the air. They seem conflicted. One skitters forward, and another gnashes its teeth, chasing it back.

The sound stops dead, just as unexpectedly as it started, and the wolves scatter, turning tail and bolting away from us, headed down the hill.

I can't fucking believe it.

My ears are ringing. I can barely hear anything over the loud, insistent buzzing inside my head, but I have the wherewithal to turn to Natalia and speak. "What the fuck? What just happened? What the hell was that sound?"

Natalia slumps to her knees, her chest hitching up and down as she begins to fall apart. Wiping her eyes with the back of her hand, she inhales, obviously trying to pull herself together.

"My father," she gasps. "He's calling them to him. They *know*."

"They know what?"

She looks up at me, and I see the pain in her eyes. "That it's feeding time."

TWELVE
NIGHTMARES AND VICES

Apparently a bound, helpless prey is much preferable to a pack of wolves than one who fights back. And the wolves on Orellana mountainside know when their dinner bell has been rung. As we run through the forest, back toward the house, Natalia explains her father's method of attracting the wolves so they know a ready meal is being served on the front lawns of the estate.

The alarm means live, fresh meat. And it means *hurry*.

"Someone must have...tried...to run," Natalia pants. "Someone must have...tried to escape."

Well shit. Perfect timing for us, but not so great for the poor bastard who got caught trying to leave Fernando's perpetual sex party. He said he had more players arriving today. He told me to leave the house because of it. Whatever happened after those sick fucks arrived must have been really bad for someone to risk *this*. And the risk didn't pay off.

"There's no point in hurrying back," Natalia says. "It's already too late. If my father sounds that alarm, it means he already has someone chained and ready for the wolves. There's nothing we can do."

"Like fuck there isn't."

"Cade, don't be crazy. His men will all be there. They have rifles. They know how to shoot. If you even try to stop it..." There is a hopelessness in her eyes. Something tells me she's already seen what happens when someone tries to stop her father feeding his wolves, and it didn't work out well. I can't help that, though. I have to try. I sure as fuck can't stand by and watch as one of the people Fernando kidnapped is torn limb from limb. It could have been Laura once upon a time, and the thought of that makes me sick to my stomach.

Soon, we're almost upon the house. I can hear loud shouts and jeers from the front lawn, as well as a good amount of snarling. I'm about to burst through the trees, out onto the lawn, when Natalia grabs me by the arm and pulls me back.

"No, please. Don't. Let's go around the back. Everyone will see us."

I could give two shits about everybody seeing me at this point. But she looks like she's about to have a heart attack, and I just can't put her through anymore. I let her lead me to the right, then, skirting around the side of the building. I can see people through the trees—so much movement. People running? People fighting? I can't make out much. Natalia leads the way. She guides me on an unseen path that she seems to know well, and then we're standing at a doorway, a side entrance to the house, and she's punching a code into a keypad that's affixed to the wall.

"Why are we going inside? We have to fucking stop this."

"And we will. Just trust me. *Please.*" She's so desperate for me to do what she's asking of me that I go against everything that makes any sense to me. I do it. I follow her inside the house. The heavy steel door slams closed behind us, and I feel like I've just made a terrible, terrible decision. The house is deserted. Not a soul in sight. Our footsteps echo like gunshots as we race down the marble floored hallway, and my heart sounds like a crazed metronome, marking out a frenzied tattoo in my chest.

Natalia runs through the corridors of the lower ground floor, and with every step we take the sound of the commotion outside grows louder. She's true to her word; she leads me to a wall of French doors that I haven't seen before, in a wing of the house that seems more relaxed than the austere white marble and obscenely large vases of the foyer. She rushes to the middle set of French doors and yanks them open, running out onto a deserted terrace, three or four feet higher than the lawn. There must be a hundred or so people gathered out there on the lawn. The air smells green, fresh, like recently cut grass, mixed in with something more sinister. Something metallic, like copper.

It takes me a moment to figure out what I'm looking at.

I see Harrison first. His arms are wrapped around himself, but not in a defensive way. He's cackling, his face a mask of mirth, and he looks like he's clutching at his stomach because he's laughing too hard. His body rocks forward, revealing a line of men with guns, standing off to one side, just as Natalia predicted. Just like a few days ago, when William's body was fed to the wolves, Fernando's permanent guests are huddled together on the lawn, every last one of them dressed in white robes. I scan the crowd, looking for Plato, but he's nowhere to be seen. I'm immediately worried. Why isn't he there with the other Servicio? Seems like an ill omen. There's no way Fernando would have allowed him to miss this spectacle, which can mean only one thing: *he* is the person who tried to escape. I don't know the man well enough to decide if this is the case or not, but it's a possibility. A bolt of guilt fires through me. The guy saved me. He risked his own life to try and save mine. And no good deed goes unpunished, as my father always likes to say.

"There are so many men," Natalia says, pointing out into the darkness. "I've never seen so many players here at once. My father...he would normally have told me if we were expecting so many."

She's right. There must be fifty or sixty guys, all dressed in black, talking quietly amongst themselves to one side. They're all young. They're all handsome. And they all have a faint tarnished look to them that the Versace, Tommy Hilfiger, Dolce and Gabbana just can't hide. Worse, they're all Caucasian. They all look like they're American, as far as looks can tell you such a thing, and I feel sick to my stomach. My countrymen. The people that I fought to defend. God, they make me ashamed.

It doesn't bode well that Natalia didn't know there were going to be so many. I have no idea why Fernando would be keeping his daughter in the dark, holding her at arm's length, but damn. Does it mean he knows that she's been talking to me? Telling me things?

At the very far end of the huge, sprawling lawn, I catch sight of the man. Fernando looks like he's eight feet tall. He seems to be glowing with pride as he looks down on a confusion of color and fur, just ten feet away from him. I can't see what's happening at first. Then, I make out the still form of a body in the center of the pack of wolves. Still, at first, I should say, and then jerking, twitching, dancing almost, as the wolves rip and tear and claw and bite.

They're feeding.

They're frenzied.

Their muzzles are covered in blood and gore.

And they are nearly done with their meal.

Natalia covers her mouth with one hand, supressing a horrified sob. "We're too late. Oh god, we're too late."

Even if we'd arrived twenty minutes ago, we would have been too late. "Who is it? Do you know who it is?" I ask.

She shakes her head. "I can't see." It's no real surprise that she can't; her eyes are filled with tears. She buckles at the knees, sinking to the floor. I try to catch her, but she wrestles free from my grip, crawling forward on all fours, watching the nightmare unfold before us through the gaps in the marble balustrade.

I'm at a loss. I arrived fired up to help. To stop this somehow, and now that it's too late, the adrenalin that has been coursing through my body for the past half an hour has no purpose to serve. My muscles are jumping, demanding me into action, and yet there is no course to take. Nothing that will help, now that the lifeless body out there on the lawn has been reduced to sinew and bone. I haven't felt this useless in a very, *very* long time.

"*Persephone!*" The cry rings out through the night, and it's the blood curdling cry of someone who's just had their heart ripped out. Natalia stops crying. She gets to her feet, and then we're both scanning the crowd again, looking for the person who screamed out the name.

It comes again, loud and clear.

"PERSEPHONE!"

With the large crowd of Fernando's players taking up much of the room on the lawn, we didn't notice him before now: Plato, on his hands and knees in the dirt, naked, hands bound behind his back. His face and his torso are streaked with dirt, and a river of blood is running down his back, over his buttocks and down his muscles legs.

"Oh god, is that—"

"Plato," I finish. "Yes. And the body out there is obviously Persephone."

"Oh god. Oh god..." Natalia screws her eyes shut tight. She looks like she's never seen this before. She must have, though. From the way she's spoken, she must have seen this over and over again, and yet she seemed sickened to her core. Perhaps that's the difference between men and women. I have seen so much violence and death in my life. The things I experienced while at war haunt my dreams. There seems to be a big difference between a normal person seeing something like this and when I see it now, though.

I know it's wrong. I know it's fucked-up. My soul rails against it as firmly and as strongly as it possibly can. And yet I have hurt more than this. I have witnessed such depraved, evil, dark things that I can no longer pinpoint the *worst* of the *worst*.

Across the manicured lawns, the wolves are still at work. I have no idea how long they will take over their kill, but they don't seem to be done yet. They're getting lazy, full, but they're still bickering amongst themselves, arguing over their food. Plato screams, his howl of agony plaintive and misery-filled. Harrison, who was still laughing until a moment ago, looks furious. He scowls, his attention turning to Plato. With quick, decisive steps, he heads across the lawn.

"Oh no. Oh god, no," Natalia wails. I don't need to ask why she seems so distraught. I can already see the intent in Harrison's eyes and I know he means no good. He reaches Plato quickly, drawing his gun from his belt at his waist. I'm moving then. I don't even know what I'm doing until I realize I'm vaulting over the balustrade, down onto the lawn, and there's suddenly grass beneath my feet.

"Sam! Please, come back!"

I have no idea how Natalia remembers to call me by my cover name, but she does, thank god. She sounds stricken with fear, but I am no longer in control of my own body. I couldn't stop myself even if I wanted to. I stride across the lawn, fire slamming through my veins. When I see Harrison holding out the gun, when I see that it is, in fact, *my* gun, I break into a run.

No fucking way is he shooting Plato with *my* gun.

No. Fucking. Way.

Harrison sees me coming. A wicked, morbid smile spreads across his face as he pivots, redirecting the gun, aiming it at me. He's not a marksman, though. He couldn't hit a moving target if his life depended on it. He clearly didn't get to practice his aim all that much as a private contractor out in the desert. I duck to the left and he doesn't even bother to fire. He knows it would be a wasted shot. He plants his feet, bracing, as though, he's getting ready for me, and I almost burst into laughter. He's the same height as me, the same build as me, but we are not equal opponents. Not even fucking close.

I barrel into him, one arm already extended, hitting him in the neck. With my other arm I grab hold of him firmly around his waist. He's winded, unable to breathe. At the same time he's trapped, unable to escape me to right himself.

He makes a broken huffing sound as I take him to the ground.

These guys, these fucking idiots, posers like him...they're all about the powerful right hook. That's all they have in them. Me, on the other hand? I'm trained in Krav Maga. I'm a black belt in Tae Kwon Do. I've been training in Muay Thai for as long as I can fucking remember. I'm so much more than a mean right hook. I'm a devastating chokehold. I'm a brutal roundhouse kick to the head. Basically, I'm way more than this fucker can handle, and he's about to fucking die.

"Get...off...me...mother...fucker!" Harrison gurgles, straining as he tries to get the words out. I don't get off. I jam my knuckles into his throat, making it even harder for him to breathe.

"Don't! God, please, don't!" Plato, still with his hands tied behind his back, is crawling towards us on his knees. "Don't! Fuck, man, please, just back the fuck off!"

I'm so close to killing this fucker. So close to wrapping my legs around him, pinning him to the ground, and grinding his face into the dirt. I'd do it. I would finish the job in a fucking heartbeat, but then Harrison's men are on me, eight rifles pointed in my face, and suddenly my death is upon me.

If this is the way I'm going to die, then so fucking be it. Plato risked his ass for mine. It's only right that I hand mine over to save his. There's so much going on around me that it's hard to differentiate sound. I hear two or three of the guys priming their rifles, metallic clicking all around me, but everything else is just white noise.

"Release him. *Now*," one of Harrison's men snaps. He's an American too, by the sounds of things. Another of them jabs me in the back with the butt of his rifle, hard enough to bruise. I know I need to let Harrison go, but I'm a stubborn asshole. A very large part of me would rather die than let him win this one.

"Sam, please!"

It's not Plato pleading with me now; it's Natalia. She arrives in front of me, dropping to her knees at my side, and she's crying hard. "There's already too much death," she whispers. "Persephone was enough. Don't you die, too. Don't you fucking die. You're supposed to take me away from this place."

The words are like a slap in the face. I've daydreamed about asking her to leave with me sure enough, but I never thought she'd straight up ask to come with me when I leave. *If* I leave. I feel the fire draining from my body. Letting go of Harrison, I shove the son of a bitch forward, and he topples over, falling face first into the grass.

"You have no idea...how fucked you are now, my friend," he rasps out. "Fernando's not going to be happy when he finds out you've been messing around with his daughter. When he *confirms* you've been messing around with her."

"Shut your mouth, asshole. You're lucky I don't try and stick something sharp and serrated up your ass."

Harrison's men draw closer. He's mad. So fucking mad. Mad enough that I expect him to order one of them to shoot, but before he can say the words, an enraged shout goes up on the other side of the lawn. It's Fernando. And he has his ball hammer in his hand.

The wolves appear to be done with their meal. Most of them have gone, vanished back into the forest. I see two of them slowly heading away from the house, melting into the shadows once more, leaving Persephone's remains strewn across the lawn. Fernando is the epitome of madness; he stalks across the grass, smashing his hammer into whatever pieces of her he can find—a leg, stripped to the bone; the hollowed-out shell of her torso; her skull—and the sound of shattering bone fills my ears.

So. Fucked. Up.

Natalia stifles a gasp when she sees what her father is doing. Harrison grins. "That's what he's going to do to lover boy here when I tell him what I just heard. *You're supposed to take me away from this place,*" he snaps, mimicking Natalia is a high-pitched voice. "How long has he kept you here for, little Natalia? How hard has he worked to ensure you never leave? And now this cunt shows up and he plans on taking you away from him? Oh, no. No, no, *no.* He's not going to like that one bit."

Natalia looks like she's about to fly at the bastard. I want to stop her from trying to scratch his eyes out, but I still have eight rifles aimed at my head, and one false move will get me killed. "Natalia. Stay calm. He's not going to say anything to Fernando."

Harrison wears a look of mock surprise. "I'm not? Why the fuck would I sit on a juicy piece of information like that? You've embarrassed me. Made a fool out of me. You just tried to strangle me to death. Hasn't done much to cement a brotherly camaraderie between us, Garrett."

"If you think you can get the words out of your mouth and order your men to shoot me before I kill you, then by all means, go ahead. But ask yourself...while you were sitting around on your ass, wearing those J Crew khakis of yours in Afghanistan, what do you think I was doing? Was I sipping motherfucking mai tais and relaxing by the pool? Or was I killing countless motherfuckers with my bare hands?"

"Kechu! Natalia! I was beginning to wonder where you had both gotten to! You missed all of the fun." Fernando arrives at Harrison's side, still holding on to his ball hammer. His face is splattered with blood, his hair standing on end, and his shirt is ripped at the collar. I can picture all too well Persephone struggling with him as he dragged her across the lawn. He wouldn't have cared. He wouldn't have blinked an eyelid as he hauled her out in front of everyone toward her death.

"My, my, Kechu. You have guns pointed at your head again. You have a real knack for getting yourself into trouble, it would seem. Might I ask, Harrison, what our guest has done to warrant such unfriendly behavior this time?" He sounds so civilized, so reasonable, his voice calm and even, and yet it looks like he's just crawled out of hell.

Harrison shoots me a quick glance out of the corner of his eye. He wants to tell Fernando what he just heard Natalia say, but he's also considering what *I* just said to him as well. I'll fucking *kill* him if he opens his mouth. Fernando will keep me chained on the lawn until tomorrow, when the wolves return hungry again, but it's the potential repercussions Natalia might have to endure that are bothering me most. Harrison must see the look on my face. He must see that I fucking meant what I said, and he must be pretty confident in my abilities to carry about my promise. He grinds his teeth together, scowling. "I was trying to punish this little punk, and he came out of nowhere. He prevented me from carrying out your justice."

Fernando frowns. "Why would you do that, Kechu? This man belongs to me," he says, pointing to Plato. He interfered when I brought that treacherous bitch out here. He tried to assault me in order to set her free. Surely you don't think I can tolerate that kind of behavior? If I did, the fragile ecosystem here would quickly fall into disarray. My business would not operate anymore. I would no longer be able to provide comfort and security for my daughter."

He sounds legitimately hurt, like he can't understand why I might possibly consider doing such a thing to him. "He's a human being," I snarl. "And you were about to kill his friend. He can't help caring. He can't help wanting to save her."

Fernando considers this. He looks down at his hammer, and I can already see him taking it to me in my mind. He spins the weapon around in his hand, looking perplexed. "What is it you Americans say all the time? You are walking a fine line? You are skating on thin ice? One of those things. Here in Orellana, we say, 'you are dangerously close to angering Fernando Villalobos.' It's simpler, I feel. More to the point. Please do not get in the way of my employees again, Kechu. Otherwise, I will have no choice but to take action. It's only my respect for you, and for the deal that we have made, that stays my hand here."

I'm shocked. I didn't try and butter him up; the look I gave him was contemptuous to say the least. And here he is, letting me off the hook? I'm either lucky or cursed to be in this man's good graces. Only time will tell. He gestures up at the house. "Why don't you go back inside, Kechu? There is some business I must take care of here, and I wish to speak to my daughter in private. Once I am done with her, I would like to speak with you also. I have some questions I must ask you."

Harrison looks devastated. I'm sure he thought I was about to get murdered brutally right before his eyes. Fernando turns and walks past him without even acknowledging him. Fixing Plato in his sights, he raises up his hammer. I think he's going to taunt Plato with it, just scare him a little, but that's not what happens. Plato flinches as Fernando brings the hammer down on the side of his knee. It's a devastating blow, and Plato screams, falling onto his side, unable to break his fall with his hands still tied behind his back. My stomach twists. I step forward, seconds from trying to stop this madness again, but Plato shakes his head, just the tiniest of shakes, and I know what he's trying to tell me: *Don't. You'll only make it worse. Please, just let it go.*

I turn and I bolt back into the house, trying not to listen to the anguished cries of the stranger who did his best to save me.

••••

"You see, Kechu, I've been under a lot of pressure. Pressure makes me a little crazy sometimes. Plato understands that. He knows he cannot act against me without reprisal. He's hurt right now, but he will recover soon enough. When he is healed and ready to go back to work, he will be a little more mindful of his place here in the estate. I have to be heavy handed with them on occasion. If you were in my position, I'm sure you would sympathize."

I'm sure I fucking wouldn't. Then again, I would never be in his position. Nothing could ever tempt me into the kind of life Fernando leads. He sits across from me, shuffling papers from one end of his desk to the other, and I'm hit once more by how straight-laced he appears from the outside. He looks like an administrator, or business advisor of some kind. Now that he's cleaned off the blood and gore of earlier, that is.

"I'm especially tense since we have so many guests with us at the moment. Normally when we have a large group come and visit, we hold a party in their honor. I had hoped that might be avoided this time, but my clients were disappointed that a celebration wasn't on the cards. As such, we will be holding a party in three days' time. I wanted to make sure you are aware of what is about to happen here at the house, and advise you that any discord between my guests is strictly prohibited during these times. There will be no fighting. There will be no disorderly conduct. If need be, there will be no interaction between warring factions. Do I make myself clear, Kechu? You are a guest here, just as my other clients are, however one foot wrong will see you clearly into troublemaker territory, and once there...it is remarkably difficult to go back. Do you understand what I am saying to you, Kechu?"

I grunt, staring at the heavy metal pen on his desk. In my head, I lean across, snatch up the pen, and I jam the thing right into his fucking jugular. "Yeah, I hear you. Toe the line, or I'm out."

"More than out, Kechu. You are *dead*. And, strangely, I have come to enjoy your presence here at the estate. Your fiery attitude is refreshing, when so many people come here grovelling and scraping. But there is a limit to what I find entertaining. I would hate to have to cut short this newly forged business relationship, when it could prove so lucrative to both sides. Don't you agree?"

"One hundred percent." I'm concealing my hatred right now like a boss. It's difficult, though. I just keep thinking of that mass grave. Natalia is so desperate to believe Fernando buried Laura up there on the hillside, overlooking the valley and the river below, but I know better. He buried her there, with his family? With his dead wife, and his dead father? I don't fucking think so. Fernando's disregard for life is phenomenal. He wouldn't have cared about Laura any more than he cared about Persephone, and look what happened to her. I didn't see anyone picking up the remains of that poor girl, collecting her up in order to take her up the side of the mountain to bury *her*. No. Laura met with a far more gruesome fate than Natalia is prepared to accept, and I am having no problem picturing it. It fucking haunts me as I sit on the other side of the desk from Fernando, smiling easily, agreeing to his terms.

"I'm sorry," I tell him. "I've been very rude. Our cultures and our households are very different. I promise, I'll respect your way of doing things from here on out. You don't need to worry. I won't interfere in your affairs any further. And I definitely won't cause any trouble at your party. In fact, I'm actually looking forward to it. If I'm invited, of course."

Fernando smiles, his thin lips stretching across his skeletal face. "Of course you are invited, Kechu. It would make me very happy if you would help me oversee the event, in fact. As I'm sure you are already personally aware, Harrison takes his job very seriously. Another pair of eyes and ears on the ground cannot hurt, though. Do you think you're up for the task?"

Oh, he has no fucking idea. I'm up for the task all right. I'm *seriously* up for the task. "I'd be thrilled to help out," I say. And in the back of my mind, I'm already planning how to use this event to my advantage. It's the perfect opportunity to strike against him. With so many people here, milling about in the house, strangers with unfamiliar faces, it will be easy for me to slip in and out of the crowd.

"Good," Fernando says, sitting back in his chair. "I would also like you to do me a personal favor. My daughter, Natalia, is very beautiful, as I am sure you will have noticed. Some of the men who come here get caught up in the atmosphere at these parties. It is a constant worry to me that one of them will overstep and try to harm her in some way. I would be very grateful if you would make sure that does not happen." There's a tone to his voice, something edgy and sharp that makes his words sound like a warning. *Don't* you *overstep. Don't* you *harm her.* If he really suspected that there was any chance I might do that, though, we wouldn't be sitting here having this conversation. Not in a million years. I would be wolf bait.

"It gives me great comfort to know you are on my side, Kechu," Fernando tells me, rising from his chair. "I'm not afraid to tell you that I will be disappointed when you have to leave Orellana. If you decide on staying longer, you would be more than welcome here in my home."

••••

Later, in my room, I'm expecting Harrison to drop by and pay me a visit (along with a pair of knuckle dusters). He didn't seem happy at all that Fernando didn't punish me for attacking him, and revenge seems like it would be his M.O. What I'm not expecting is Natalia, rapping against the French doors on my balcony at eight minutes after midnight, dressed in a tiny silk slip of material that makes my dick instantly hard. Her nipples are peaked, very visible through the thin fabric, and I want to run my hands over them. I don't know why the tension of the afternoon has made me crazy. It seems every time I'm about to go on a killing spree, all I want to do is fuck this girl. Seriously.

I open the French doors, letting her into the room. "I think this is supposed to be the other way around," I tell her. "Aren't I supposed to climb through *your* bedroom window?"

She smiles a small, nervous smile. There are dark shadows under her eyes, dark and bruised-looking. "I just...I couldn't sleep," she says. "I wanted to see you. To see if...you are okay?"

"I'm fine." This is only half true. I'm calmer than I was earlier, but I'm also almost certain now that Laura ended up in an open grave, with god knows how many other bodies piled in on top of hers, and that is not putting me in a good headspace.

"I can't stop thinking about Persephone," Natalia says sadly. "I should have been here, back at the house. I would have been able to talk him down."

"How many times have you tried to stop him from doing something like that before?" I ask. "And how many times has he ignored you and done it anyway?" I can tell from the way her jaw is set and her cheeks are flushed that the answer to my question, though she won't admit it, is *many*. "Today wouldn't have been any different, Natalia. You can't hold yourself accountable for every evil thing your father does."

"Maybe you're right," she says. "Sometimes I wonder if I could try harder to reach him, though. I wonder if my own fear of him gets in the way of trying to help these people."

"Stop. You're beating yourself up over something you have no control over. There isn't a doctor out there who wouldn't diagnose your father as clinically insane. It's okay that you're afraid of him. Even if you did stand up to him, it wouldn't make a difference."

Natalia sits down on the edge of my bed, head hanging low. "I just can't stop thinking that—"

"That's exactly what you *have* to do, otherwise you're going to drive yourself mad."

"They were together, you know. Persephone was here maybe six months before Plato arrived. They became friends immediately. They fell in love some time after that. My father keeps his male and female Servicio separated at night. There are two huge dormitories beneath the house, and they're guarded at all times. They've never slept in the same bed together, never fallen asleep in each other's arms. But they've loved each other for years now. And now my father has even taken that from them."

Sitting down on the bed next to her, I put my arm around her shoulders. "Simon says don't think about it right now," I tell her.

"Simon? Who is Simon?"

"You've never heard of Simon Says?"

She shakes her head. "What is it?"

"If I say, Natalia, take off all your clothes, you don't have to do it. If I say, Simon says taken off your clothes, then you *have* to."

She looks confused. "Why would I obey you just because you say that?"

"I don't know. It's a children's game. It doesn't have to make sense."

"Children get naked?"

I laugh softly. "No, that's definitely the adult version of the game."

"And you can use this Simon Says rule to make the other person do anything?"

"*Anything.*"

Natalia thinks about this. A small frown line appears between her brows as she considers what I've just said. She's so damn beautiful. It hits me every time I look at her. Would I be this attracted to her if I saw her on the street back home? That would be a resounding fuck yes. I'm not drawn to her because of her damsel in distress status. She's stunning. I'll admit, I'm thinking about her mouth wrapped around my dick twenty-four seven, in between fearing for my life and the lives of every one around me. But there's something else about her. Something subtle and at the same time undeniable that draws me to her. It wouldn't matter where in the world I met her. I would still be captivated, regardless.

She smiles as she looks up at me, and a surge of blood rushes to my dick. "I want to play," she says decisively.

"You do?"

She nods. "Anything to stop thinking so much. And...I think this will be fun."

"All right. Well, you asked for it."

She lies back on my bed, exhaling, closing her eyes. I wonder if she has any idea how this is going to end, namely with some hardcore fucking? Because Simon is a sick, perverted motherfucker when I'm talking on his behalf.

"Who goes first?" she asks.

"You can." Instead of lying down next to her, I position myself on the bed, sitting beside her, legs crossed Indian style, watching her as her chest rises and falls. She cracks one eyelid, peering at me out of the corner of her eye.

"Okay. Simon says..." She hesitates. "Tell me why you kissed me the other day."

"Why do you think I kissed you the other day?"

"I don't know. That's why I asked."

"Because..." Man, this is ridiculous. How can she not know the pull she has over men? "I didn't have a choice," I tell her. "It wasn't something I consciously decided to do. You were soaked from the rain, your hair was everywhere. You turned to look at me, and I *had* to kiss you."

She smiles shyly, covering her mouth half-heartedly with one hand. Pressing her fingertips into her lips, she laughs quietly. "Okay. I suppose I will have to accept that as your answer. Do I go again?"

"Yes. Until you trick me into doing something Simon hasn't told me to do."

"I see. Okay." She shifts, getting comfortable. "Now, Simon says, tell me about your life, Cade. I already know where you come from. Do you still live in Alabama? Do you work for your father, like Laura did?"

I look down at my hands, spreading my fingers. I laugh. "No. I don't live in Alabama anymore. I live in New Mexico. And no, I don't work for my father."

"Then what do you do? Are you like my father? Do you sell drugs and guns to the highest bidder?"

"No. I belong to a..." God, this is going to sound ridiculous. How am I going to convince her that I'm not just another violent piece of shit when I explain my life to her? "I belong to a motorcycle club. But the Widow Makers are nothing like the other clubs you've probably met. We don't treat women like shit. We do our best to help people, not hurt them. Most of the time. Jamie and I have spent every day since Laura disappeared using the resources available to us to try and find her. We've been able to help a lot of other women in the process."

"How?"

"By removing them from circumstances of abuse. By finding them work, new names, new homes. New identities, when they've needed them."

"So...this Widow Makers club of yours. You don't fight? You don't kill people?"

I crack my index finger, sighing. "We do fight. We do kill people. The world we're involved in...there's no escaping hatred and fear." I wish I could tell her differently. I wish I could honestly say that the club stood for peace and non-violence. Maybe one day we might be able to. Ever since my sister was taken, both Jamie and myself have been single minded in our goal of bringing her home safely, so people have paid the price. Laws have been broken. Lives have been taken. Now I know for sure that Laura is gone, where will that leave the club? I'm not a violent man by nature. I am a man driven by need. I went to war to protect my country, and to protect my best friend, not because I enjoyed the thrill of pulling the trigger on a gun.

Natalia doesn't seem shocked by my answer. "You're honest, Cade. That's all you can ever be." We're both silent, the seconds stretching out between us, filled with the quiet fervor of our thoughts. After a long time, Natalia reaches out, cautiously running her fingertips against the seam of my jeans. Her touch is light, but it's grounding at the same time. It's a small gesture—the gesture of someone unsure and nervous, yet desperate to make some form of physical contact.

"Were you marked, then?" she asks.

"Marked. Tattooed by your club. To show that you belong to them."

"Oh. Yeah. It's kind of a requirement."

Natalia props herself up on one elbow, looking at me. "Show me."

"You want to see?" Of course, I never turned my back on her the other day when we fucked in her tree house. I know she noticed the parts of my tattoo that were visible over the tops of my shoulders, but she never saw the full piece. Would it have freaked her out then, if she had seen it?

"Yes," she tells me softly. "Please. I'm...*interested*."

She sure as hell looks like she is as well. "All right. If you insist." I take off my shirt in a smooth, fluid movement, grabbing the material behind my head and pulling it off in one go. Natalia's unashamed as she studies my body. She tentatively reaches out and runs her hand over my chest, her lower lip fastened tightly between her teeth. She likes what she sees. She likes the fact that I'm ripped. She likes the fact that I'm strong, and powerful. I don't think this because I'm an asshole, and I'm vain as fuck. I can just see the appreciation on her face, and for the first time it matters to me.

I'm not jacked for the sake of looking good. I work out and I train hard because I need to know I'm going to be the better man in a fight. I always need to know that I'm going to be able to overpower an assailant, and I can't do that if I have a fucking beer gut. But now, with Natalia's eyes roving over my stomach and my chest, her hand skating over my skin, I'm pretty fucking stoked that I look the way I do, because she seems to be into it. *Really* fucking into it.

Slowly, I turn around, so she can see my back. She breathes steadily, apparently calm enough, but I can feel her shock. It's a big tattoo. A really big fucking tattoo. From between my shoulder blades, down to the base of my spine, the black ink spikes and curls, forming the Widow Makers' club badge. A skull, mouth open, with two guns crossed behind it. The top rocker says Widow Makers; the bottom rocker reads New Mexico. Above the bottom rocker, in small, bold lettering: Vice President. My skin feels electrified while Natalia begins to trace her fingers over the lines and shapes of the ink.

"Did it hurt?" she whispers.

"Not really, no." I'm sure she noticed the scars on my chest and on my side. I've taken two bullets before. A knife once, when I was in

Chino. Those hurt way more than being tattooed, but I don't need to emphasize the fact that I lead a dangerous life to her. For some reason, I don't want her to think I'm that kind of guy. I want her to feel safe with me, I want to take her away from nightmares and heartbreak, not introduce her to even more.

"You're lucky," she whispers. "Mine hurt a lot."

I spin around. "You have a tattoo?" I never noticed it before. She was completely naked the other day. How could I have missed something like that on her? Natalia nods. Slowly, she pushes back her sleeve, and there, on the inside of her forearm, is a brand. The exact same brand I noticed on Plato, the very first time I met him: A wolf's head, and underneath it, a large, bold V for Villalobos.

"He had you branded? Like you're his fucking property?" Anger seems to be a constant these days. It pollutes me from the inside out, and I can't seem to get the taste out of my mouth.

"Of course I am his property. I am his most prized possession." Natalia rolls her sleeve back down, holding her hand over the brand like it still hurts her. "He wanted to do it on the inside of my thigh. So any man who dared to try and sleep with me would know he was trespassing. I managed to convince him it would be better to have it here, where it was visible, though."

Jesus. On the inside of her thigh? Sick motherfucker. I'm sure he would have wanted to administer the brand himself. Just the thought of it makes me want to throw up.

"I was only fourteen," she continues. "I was changing. I started to get breasts," she explains miserably. "And my father decided a deterrent was in order."

"God *damn* it."

"It's okay. It was a long time ago."

"I don't care how fucking long ago it was. It was still a shitty thing to do to a child."

Natalia takes my hand. I could easily allow myself to get lost in the cruelty of her father's treatment, but what would be the point here, in this moment? This time is sacred, no one watching, no one primed and ready to report us to Fernando. I won't spoil it by raging over something I can't go back in time and change. I lift our intertwined hands, and I kiss her wrist, drinking in the soft, subtly sweet smell of her as I inhale.

"Simon says take all of your clothes off, Natalia Villalobos," I say quietly, grinning at her.

"What? It's still my turn," she says. Her laughter is hushed, but the ease with which she smiles makes me happy. "I'm not done asking my questions yet."

"Save your questions for another time, when we both have to be fully dressed. Right now, we're alone, and I want to eat that pretty pussy of yours." I half expect her to deny my request. It would be understandable, given the fact that we're under her father's roof, and therefore not entirely safe, but she doesn't say a word. She sits up, still watching me as she carefully slides the straps of her silk slip over her shoulders, pushing them down to reveal her perfect fucking breasts. I try to stifle my groan, but it's futile. The frustrated, heated, need-driven sound escapes me, and Natalia shivers.

"We have to be quiet," she whispers.

"I think we've already proven we can do quiet."

She smiles. "True. But I'm more excited this time."

"*More* excited?"

"Yes. I know how good you are now, Cade Preston. I know how good you fuck me, and how amazing it feels to have you inside me. The anticipation of it is almost too much to bear."

I skate my fingers down her cheek, allowing myself to continue down, down, down, over her jaw, over her neck, her collarbone, and then across the swell of her tits. "If you think I gave it everything I had last time, Natalia, you're sorely mistaken. That was just a sample. A teaser. A mere taste of what I'm capable of. Would you like me to show you how good I *really* am?"

Natalia's eyes are half-closed. She has a doped, hazy look to her that makes it seem like she's already halfway to coming. "Yes. I want to know. I want to experience everything with you." Before our time together is over? There's a melancholy catch in her words that makes it sound like she has missed these words off of the end of her sentence. I take hold of her hand and lift it to my mouth, sliding her index finger past my lips and into my mouth.

"I'm going to show you some of those vices we talked about, Natalia. It's gonna be intense, and it might make you nervous, but it'll never be more than I think you can handle. And I will never hurt you. Do you trust me enough to hand yourself over to me?"

This is a seriously big ask. Every day, Natalia has seen men walk into her house. She's seen them use and abuse the people trapped behind that blue door until they're so worn down by their own lives that they'd rather end it all than continue suffering the abuse. I don't want to run the risk of her ever likening me to Fernando's players. It would fucking kill me. I'm fairly sure Natalia knows I'm different, that I would never do anything to her against her will, but I still have to tread lightly, though.

She lies back onto the bed, briefly lifting her hips so she can slide her slip over her ass and kick it from her legs. She's completely naked. Looking at me with those beautiful hazel eyes of hers, she slowly nods her head. "I know what you're thinking," she says in a steady voice. "You're thinking that I am too fragile to cope with whatever you have in store for me. But I'm not. You think I'm not prepared to offer myself up to you in the way that you want me to, but you're wrong. I am ready. And I can handle it. Most important of all, I *want* it."

Well, shit. She really does know what I'm thinking. I suppose it's obvious I'd be thinking these things, but I'm impressed that she has the backbone to come out and speak her mind. Most girls would be too shy, or too nervous to ever voice their thoughts like that.

She wants to know my vices? Fine. I'll show them to her. Starting with vice number one: deep throat.

"Okay. So be it. Move to the edge of the bed," I tell her. She does so without question. Arranging her so that her head is hanging over the edge of the mattress, I rub my fingers over her lips, parting them, excitement already taking over me. "Open your mouth, Natalia. Open it real fucking wide."

She smiles a little as she does what I've asked her to. That smile is wicked, and filled with desire. Her lips are wet, her tongue darting out between them as she lies there, anticipating what I'm going to do next. I slowly undo the fly of my jeans, lowering them down over my hips. I reach inside my boxers and take my dick out. I'm already hard. So fucking hard that it actually hurts. Feels like my body is trying to jam so much blood into my cock that it's going to explode at any second.

Shit, touching myself feels *so* fucking good when I'm looking down at her flawless body, her nipples peaked contracted into small, pink buds that I want to run my tongue over, her legs open just a little, her hands lying beside her on the bed, her fingers twitching like *she* wants to reach up and touch me. I remove my pants and my boxers, getting rid of them entirely, and then I stand over her, thinking about what comes next.

"If you tell me to stop, I'll stop," I say. "But don't say it if you don't mean it. Don't play games, Natalia. I'm going to fuck you so hard, and you're going to enjoy it. I *promise* you."

She nods, her mouth still wide open. Fuck, she's such a good girl. So obedient. I lower myself an inch at a time, and then I tease her mouth with the end of my dick, rubbing the tip across her lips, slowly pushing myself inside.

So warm. So wet. So fucking good. Natalia huffs heavily through her nose as I push myself deep into her mouth. My balls ache almost painfully as I feel her tongue shift in her mouth, stroking against the side of my cock. She swallows, and the pressure is enough to send a shiver of pleasure through my body. It starts in my balls, spreading outward until I have pins and needles across my shoulder blades, my buttocks and the soles of my fucking feet.

Natalia blinks, her back arching a little. She moans, and I have to fight the urge that rushes me to grab hold of her head and thrust myself down her throat. If I do that, I'll be finished. I'll come so quickly, and I don't want that. I'll still be hard. I'll still be able to fuck her again, but I want to make every second of this last.

I lean over her, cupping her left breast in my hand, squeezing and rolling her nipple between my fingers. She makes a sharp gasping sound at the pain, but she doesn't move. My cock throbs in her mouth, and I can tell she can probably taste me by now. My pre-come will be all over her tongue. The very thought is galvanizing. I allow myself to rock my hips forward, just a little, and Natalia whimpers.

"Suck for me, baby. Slowly. Move your tongue and nothing else."

When she obeys me, massaging my dick slowly inside her mouth, heat blasts me in waves. I bend over her and take her nipple into my mouth, biting down onto the swollen bundle of flesh. Natalia rocks her hips, whimpering again. She likes it. She likes the little jolt of pain I've sent spiraling around her body.

Vice number two: teeth.

I fucking love using my teeth on a girl. On her breasts. On her lips. On her neck. *On her clit.* Just the right amount of pressure on a girl's clitoris can send her bucking and screaming into an orgasm in the blink of an eye. I bite Natalia again, this time on her other breast, just below her nipple, and she writhes, breathing frantically down her nose. If her mouth wasn't stuffed full with my cock, she'd probably be hyperventilating. Since her mouth *is* stuffed full with my cock, I take the opportunity to pull back a little and then I drive forward, grinding my teeth together as I feel myself sinking deeper into her, inch by inch.

My cock is above average in length, and thick. Really fucking thick. It isn't easy to suck a dick like mine, especially the way I like it to be sucked, but Natalia's currently blowing both my cock and my mind. She opens that sweet mouth of hers even wider, letting her head fall loose over the side of the bed, and I can tell how fucking amazing this is going to be.

The insides of her legs are glistening, wet with her desire for me, letting me know just how unbelievably turned on she is already. That's a good sign. A seriously good sign. I reach down and stroke my fingers over her pussy, my pulse skipping all over the place when she grinds herself into my hand, searching for more pressure against her clit.

"Damn," I hiss. "Greedy girl. You want me to touch you there? You want me to make you feel good?" I can't see her face, and she's not in a position to speak, but I can tell that the answer is yes. She rolls her hips, her legs shaking as she seeks out her pleasure, and I have to hold myself back.

Not yet. Not yet. Damn it, this is hard.

Natalia's back arches clear off the bed as she moans loudly. Clearly my cock isn't shutting her up sufficiently. I stand up, and I cup the back of her head in my hands, looking down into her eyes. "Take a deep breath, baby," I advise her.

I feel the cold air rushing over my balls as she sucks in a lungful of oxygen through her nose. "I'm going to choke you with my cock now, okay? I'm going to make you gag on me, and you're going to love it."

Natalia doesn't shy away. There's nothing but lust in her eyes. I wait to see if she's going to object, to shake her head or flat out tell me she doesn't want me to, but instead she nods. Her eyes close, and so I do it. I sink myself deep into her throat.

Fuck, it feels so good. I begin to thrust, allowing myself to get just that little bit deeper each time. With her head kicked back, hanging off the edge of the bed, Natalia's able to take all of me, right down to the base of my shaft. The very first time I feel the back of her throat, feel her gag reflex kick in, and her throat spasm, I pull out entirely, grabbing hold of my dick, stroking my hand up and down myself. I'm so wet from her mouth, covered in her saliva. I'm soaked down to my balls. Natalia gasps, her eyes wide. She's so fucking good. I have to stop myself here, or I'm going to be tempted to get rougher, to hold her head in place while I fuck her mouth, and I don't think either of us are ready for that. Not yet.

"Turn around," I grind out. "Show me your pussy."

Natalia moans again, and the sound is filled with need. She spins around on the bed, her cheeks red, the base of her neck the same flushed crimson. I spread her legs as wide as they will go, roughly pulling her toward me so that her pussy is now in alignment with the edge of the bed, instead of her head.

"God, you're amazing," I tell her. I can hardly believe how wet she is right now. How wet, and pink, and delicious. She props herself up on her elbows, watching me as I sink to my knees. She's probably expecting me to go down on her, but I'm not. I'm going to indulge myself in vice number three: ass play.

As soon as my tongue hits her asshole, Natalia lets out a breathless shriek. I immediately stop what I'm doing. "Shhh. Don't make a sound," I command. "I mean it. Not a sound, Natalia."

Her eyes roll back in her head as I take my tongue to her again. She tastes clean and sweet, and I can taste her pussy all over her. The smell of her excitement fills my head as I massage her with my tongue. I'm harder than I've ever been now. Harder than I probably ever will be. Natalia shakes and shivers as I stroke my tongue up and down over her ass. I can't help myself as I probe; she tastes so fucking good that I just have to lick her everywhere. I tend to her in broad, long strokes, sweeping my tongue from her ass all the way up, sucking and licking at her swollen clit, and she shudders, her entire body trembling violently as I bring her close to orgasm. She digs her fingers into my hair, pulling, closing her legs around my head as I gently begin to tease her ass with my finger. Soon, I have my index finger easing its way into her ass, my middle finger inside her pussy, and my tongue still flicking and laving at her clit.

It must be an intense experience for her. It must be an *overwhelming* experience for her. One second she's rocking against my mouth and my hand, the next she's holding her breath and her legs are locked around my head as she comes.

Holy. Fucking. Shit.

I've never been this turned on before. Never. As she locks up, frozen, unable to move as her body reacts to me, I push my tongue inside her pussy, groaning, while I rub the pad of my thumb over her clit in firm, quick circles.

"Shit. Oh shit. Please. *Please!*"

"Please what, Natalia? Please what?" I growl.

"Please fuck me. Please...fuck me...now," she pants.

I'm more than willing to oblige her. I'm on the point of coming myself. I grab hold of the end of my dick, squeezing hard, trying to tamp down the feeling that I'm about to explode, but it doesn't really help. I'm cursing, hissing the most colorful profanities when I slowly guide myself inside her. It feels...it feels like nothing else. She's so fucking tight, for god's sake.

Time to partake in vice number 4: choking.

I hold myself over her as I push myself deeper, and Natalia cried out. Just as I did back at the tree house, I cup my hand over her mouth, preventing her from making a sound. At the same time, I close my other hand around her throat, carefully closing off her windpipe. Her eyes round out, growing wide, and she holds onto my arm as I fuck her, driving myself inside her harder and harder each time.

"Come on my dick, Natalia. That's it. That's a good girl. Soak me. Drench me. I wanna feel you squirting all over my cock."

To all of the women out there who claim they're incapable of squirting, think again. You just haven't had the right guy inside you yet. You haven't had my cock inside you, pressing up against your g-spot, pushing you closer and closer toward an eventuality that simply can't be avoided. My dick can make anyone squirt, and that's a fucking *fact*.

Natalia finds this out as I hold my hands around her throat, slamming myself inside her, no longer holding back. As soon as I feel her muscles tense, her fingernails digging into my forearm, and I see her eyes roll back into her head, I know it's about to happen. I let myself go. I've been warring with myself, holding off my own climax—a nearly fucking impossible task, given how amazing her pussy feels—but now I release control, and a wall of fire and insanity overcomes me. My cock throbs inside her as I come, and I plunge myself inside her as deep and as hard as I can, over and over again, spurred on by how wet Natalia is now that she's done as I commanded and has come all over me.

"Good girl," I tell her, brushing her hair back out of her face. "Such a good girl." I release my hold on her throat, and she sucks in a relieved, frantic gasp of air.

"Oh my god. Oh my god, Cade," she chants.

I kiss her, licking at her lips with my tongue, savoring the taste of sweat and passion on her mouth, knowing she will be able to taste her own pussy on mine. I shake my head, smiling a little as we both recover ourselves. I press my nose to the crook of her neck and I inhale deeply, commemorating the scent of her to my memory forever. Natalia runs her fingers gently up and down my back.

"I don't want to go back to my room," she whispers. "I want to stay here. With you."

"Then stay." It's reckless and so fucking dangerous for her to sleep here, but I can't bring myself to let her go just yet. As I roll over, spinning her over too, so that her head is lying on my chest, I realize something, and it's pretty fucking scary.

I don't *ever* want to let her go.

THIRTEEN

THREE DAYS LATER
CROQUET

Croquet. On the same fucking lawn where Persephone was mauled to death by wolves only a few days ago. Fernando is one sick, sick bastard.

He is red and yellow; I am black and blue. He expertly knocks his first yellow, and it rolls right through his intended hoop, scoring him a point. I've never played croquet in my fucking life. I have no idea what the rules are, even though I briefly Googled them before we came down here. I'm probably going to screw up any second now, but when Fernando Villalobos asks you to come play a game with him, *any* game, you say yes, or you brace for trouble. The lawn is damp underfoot, the ground soft and sticky with mud. The rains have been consistent, showing up around eleven in the morning every day, sticking around for a couple of hours, oversized raindrops hammering into the earth, and then stopping in the most abrupt way, like a showerhead being turned off.

"You have been here for a while now, Kechu," Fernando says. He has a small cigarillo hanging out of his mouth—surprising, since I haven't seen him smoking before, and he doesn't strike me as the sort of man who would conform to such a trite addiction. "Are you happy here? I was wondering, because you seem a little...*tense.*"

Tense is not the right word. Livid is a good substitute. Furious. Consumed by rage. I am all of these things and more, and trying to hide my feelings is growing harder and harder by the day. That's what

Fernando is sensing: my overwhelming need to dash his brains out of his head with my croquet mallet.

"Oh, y'know," I say. "New York's a crazy city. It's a lot quieter here. I'm busy all of the time. I'm adjusting to having more time on my hands here in Orellana."

Fernando leans on the end of his mallet, listening to me intently. He seems to mull over everything I say, pondering deeply. After a while, he stands straight, smiling at me like he's an old friend. "I understand. You need something to do here, and I know just the thing. You must teach Natalia about America. For so long she has wanted to know about the country where her mother was born, and I'm ashamed to say I've discouraged her from her research. I don't like to leave Ecuador, let alone visit the United States. It is my hope that Natalia won't either. But she is a young woman, and young women rebel if they are told not to do something. Perhaps if she learns the good and the bad about America from one of the country's own citizens, she will see how much better life here in Ecuador is."

I take my shot, and I miss the hoop. I'm glad. Jamie would have a goddamn field day if he knew I was whacking a ball around a manicured lawn like this. It's just not right. "So you want me to make the place sound terrible?" I ask.

"No. I simply want you to tell the truth. People here have a very warped idea of what life is like in America. They think it's all sunshine and roses. That the politicians and the police are not corrupt. That the government are all seeing, and all powerful. That there is no poverty. No crime. No homelessness. If you are honest with Natalia about the true state of affairs in your country, she might not be so eager to charge over there, expecting every city to look like Hollywood." Fernando takes his shot. The ball speeds through the hoop again with ease; he must play a lot.

"Well, I can certainly try."

"Thank you, Kechu. You know, despite the hiccups we've encountered since you arrived, I find myself considering you a friend. Does that surprise you?"

"Uh, yeah. It does a little." How about a whole fucking lot? I'm fairly sure he was hunting me in the forest the other day, while Natalia and I were in her hideaway. And he threatens me with death every time we meet. I guess when you're a violent, insane dictator, you have a warped view of what friendship looks like, though.

Fernando nods. "Natalia thinks of you as a brother, and that warms me."

I try not to react to this, but I'm crowing in my head like a madman. *Yeah, she thinks of me as a brother all right. A brother she likes to fuck.* Shit, if only he knew.

I'm about to take my turn, trying to think of something to say that won't sound suspicious whatsoever, when Harrison appears, hurrying across the lawn toward us. He has a phone in his hand, and he looks like he's just discovered the location of the lost city of El Dorado.

"What is it?" Fernando asks.

"One of our guys in the States," he answers.

"And what do they want?"

"He wouldn't say. Just that he has information he thinks you might find interesting." Harrison's gaze flickers to me, and his meaning is clear: he thinks he might have interesting information about *me.* Fernando's eyes roll. He sighs like a frustrated father being pushed to his limit by a persistent son. Taking the phone from Harrison, he walks away slowly, holding the device to his ear. He speaks, but his voice is lulled, low and soft, and I can't make out what he's saying.

"I'm going to sleep so well tonight, motherfucker," Harrison hisses out of the side of his mouth. "Like the dead. Like a baby. Like a stone. It's going to be the most peaceful night's sleep I've had in years, and it's all thanks to you. I owe you, man."

Damn. That sounds worrying. Harrison knows I was in the military. What if he's gone snooping? What if he's discovered I'm not Sam Garrett, but Cade Preston, vice president of a motorcycle club hell bent on bringing down sex trafficking rings and murdering people like his boss? Doubt that would go down well. Then there's the matter of my sister. Julio's men know exactly who I am, and who I'm looking for. If they know *I* am the one who killed Julio, then what's the stop them from spreading the word? Someone already told Fernando a guy on a motorcycle killed the bastard. How many pieces of this puzzle need to be put together before they figure out who I really am?

"The fuck are you talking about?" I snap.

Harrison bounces on the balls of his feet like a live wire, full of energy. "I couldn't possibly say," he tells me. "It's just too fucking good. I'll let Fernando explain, I think."

Fifteen feet away, still with his croquet stick in his hand, Fernando goes still, standing like a life-size statue of someone who just heard something entirely unbelievable. He turns, his eyes fixing on me. He doesn't say anything else. He listens, and then he hangs up the phone.

He holds the cell out to Harrison, who goes to take it from him. Fernando moves quicker than lightning, snatching hold of Harrison by his neck. For such a thin, frail-looking man, Fernando's a hell of a lot stronger than he seems. Or maybe Harrison tolerates him grabbing hold of him. Either way, Fernando maintains a grip on him as he walks in between the metal loops of our croquet game, driven into the ground.

I try not to act surprised as Fernando shoves Harrison away from him, growling under his breath. "My friend in America just told me something interesting, Kechu," he says.

"Oh?"

"He went to pay a visit to your employer in New York. To check in with him on my behalf, to see if his personal matter is almost resolved so that he can come and meet with me. He said that the office assigned to your Louis James Aubertin was unoccupied. Can you explain why this might be, Kechu?"

I shrug. "Sure. His office is a front. He needs an address for tax purposes. A place where he can have certain mail delivered. If you'd told me you wanted to call in on him, I could have arranged a meet in New York, on mutually safe ground. It wouldn't have been a problem." The lie comes quick and easy. I sound so nonchalant that it seems obvious that this would be the case, that Jamie would never keep an official business address where anyone could drop in and see him.

Harrison's cheeks redden. "That is such bullshit, Fernando. *Bullshit!*"

Fernando shoves Harrison away, groaning in disgust. "Why would you come to me with something as insignificant as this? You are grasping at straws. Honestly, I am growing sick of this nonsense."

Harrison looks dumbfounded. "I'm just trying to prove a point. They're keeping secrets. This man is not who he's pretending to be."

"He is not a representative of this businessman?"

"Yes, but—"

"And he did he not give us fifty thousand dollars as a show of good faith?"

"He did."

"Then I'd say he's representing himself fairly accurately."

"Fernando—"

Fernando spins, teeth bared, his hand gripping his croquet mallet tightly in his hand. For a moment I think he's going to use it the way I had envisioned myself only a few minutes ago, bringing it down on Harrison's head. He doesn't, though. He throws it down on the ground, snarling like one of his wolves. "No! No more! I am sick and tired of this conversation. How many times have I told you I do not wish to discuss this with you?"

Harrison doesn't answer. He glares at the ground in front of him, his chest quickly rising and falling as he pants; he's desperate to argue, to talk back, to plead his case further, but Fernando looks like a pot about to boil over. Riling him up was surely Harrison's intention when he came hurrying out here with that cell phone in his hand, but he definitely didn't intend for his boss's anger to be directed at *him*.

"I want no more of this," Fernando spits. "I make a promise to you, Harrison. If you continue down this path, trying to cast aspersions against my Kechu, I will be forced to set you aside. Do you understand?"

What the fuck does *"set him aside"* mean? Kill him? Fire him? Have him escorted out of Ecuador? And *my* Kechu? Since when has he liked me well enough to claim ownership of me, like I'm his goddamn pet?

Harrison pales. "Yes, Fernando. Please...forgive me. I only want what's best. I see now that you have everything under control, though..." He speaks slowly, as though apologizing this way is costing him dearly. "I'll drop the matter. You have my word."

"Good. Now leave. You're giving me a migraine."

Harrison bows his head, gets up, and stalks back to the house. I can tell how furious he is by the set of his shoulders. I don't think the scolding he just received has done anything to distract him from his mission to destroy me, though. If anything, I think it's only made him more determined.

Fernando huffs like a child. "I cannot concentrate on this now," he says, gesturing to our croquet balls, and his mallet, flung halfway across the lawn. "It's *ruined*." He spies a gardener working close to the tree line, where the gardens end and the forest begins, and he sighs. "I swear. These men just want to die. I'm afraid I must leave you now, Kechu. You'll excuse me. Perhaps go and find my daughter. You can start on those lessons we discussed."

FOURTEEN
INTELLECTUAL STIMULATION

"He told you to teach me about America?"

Natalia seems baffled. She stands three feet from me as we walk down the hallway together toward the library that is apparently located on the ground floor. She looks different today. She hasn't been outside, scrambling through the forest, so she's not covered in dirt and a thin sheen of perspiration. Her clothes are not what I would have expected, either: small black skirt that shows off the delicious curve of her ass, coupled with a dark blue strappy shirt made out of some floaty, see-through material that hints at the fact she might not be wearing a bra. Her hair hangs loose around her shoulders in thick, caramel waves, and she smells like flowers.

I prod her in the side, just above her hipbone, winking. "Did you dress up for me, Natalia Villalobos?"

She flushes bright red. Her blush travels down her neck, to the base of her throat, where it burns crimson. "No, of course not. I just wanted..." She's flustered. Embarrassed. She sweeps her hair back behind her ears, looking down at the ground. "So what if I have?" she declares, changing tack. "Why is it so bad for me to want to look nice for you? For you to want me?" She speaks quietly, so she's not heard, but there's a certain amount of defiance in her tone now.

I hold up one hand, grinning as I shake my head. "I'm not complaining."

"Then what are you talking about?" Her lilting accent slays me when she's riled up like this. She's fucking adorable.

"I'm just letting you know that I've noticed," I tell her.

"Then you should tell me I look beautiful or something, not try to make me feel ashamed."

God. If I could take her in my arms and kiss her right now, I would. Since I can literally hear the electronic buzzing of the camera lenses following us as we walk past them, though, I don't. I rub at the back of my neck, trying not to laugh instead. "You *are* beautiful, Natalia. You're possibly the most beautiful thing I've ever seen. But then, I think that every time I see you. Even when your hair is all over the place and you're covered in sweat. Even when you're drenched to the bone, and you have mud all over your face."

She slows, blinking at me, a tiny smile twitching at the corners of her mouth. "Are all men in America like you? Do you all know how to say the right thing at the right time?"

I can't hold back the laughter now. I just can't. "I don't think many American women would agree with that statement, no."

"So it's just you, then?" She seems so innocent sometimes, like a child. In some ways, she is. She's led such a sheltered life here, cut off from all social media, television, and other external influences. Then again, she has also been subjected to scenes of violence and death so horrific that it seems she should be aged well beyond her years.

"Yes. Just me," I say softly.

Natalia guides me down the long corridor. The library is small, nowhere near as grand as I thought it would be. As soon as we walk through the door, I'm scanning the ceiling and the corners of the room, searching for surveillance. Natalia shakes her head imperceptibly as I go to sit down at a table close to one of the windows. "I don't know where it is, but there is definitely a camera in here somewhere," she says. Instead, she points me to a small table in the back of the room,

"Damn. I was going to bend you over the table and fuck you senseless," I whisper. "Something about books makes my dick hard."

Natalia looks scandalized. She sits down at the table, fidgeting in her seat, trying to get comfortable, but I can tell she's thinking about what I just said and she can't get the thought out of her mind. "My grandfather used to bring me to the library all the time," she says. "He taught me French and Portuguese here. Among other things."

I sit down opposite her. I have to fidget a little myself in order to get comfortable. I wasn't lying; there's something about libraries that turns me on. I have no idea why, but my cock is getting harder by the second and there's literally nothing I can do to prevent it. The cameras won't pick up a bulge in my pants, though. It's dark here, at the back of the room, thank god. Maybe that's exactly why Natalia picked this spot instead of one of the other tables by the huge picture window on the far side of the room.

Natalia's legs are tangled up in mine, her right leg in between my own, her kneecap dangerously close to brushing up against my hard-on. I give her thigh a squeeze under the table. Fuck, her skin is so warm and smooth. It feels like silk beneath my fingertips. She tenses when I touch her, and looks around, as if she expects someone to be lurking behind one of the book stacks.

"So what do you want to know about America?" I ask.

"I don't know. Have you ever been to Philadelphia?"

"No, I haven't."

She's disappointed. I can tell from the look on her face. "Okay. Well, then. What can you tell me about the people from your country?"

"You meet Americans every day," I say quietly, angling my head in the direction of the party room. "I think you know as much as you need to there."

"Are you saying that all Ecuadorian people are the same as my father?"

She has a point. The people in the village of Orellana itself seemed like simple, happy people who lived clean, uncomplicated lives. I can't imagine any of those happy-faced children I saw when I arrived growing up to be psychotic murderers, but then again you never know. "Fair point," I concede. I think for a moment, and then say, "Americans are just like citizens from other countries. There are good people, and bad. Smart people, and not so smart people. It's just that the bad, not so smart people seem to have a way of ending up in power, or in the spotlight for some reason. Those are often the people representing the country. It can look like we're *all* bad and *all* not so smart."

"You're good," Natalia tells me. "You've stayed here way too long, so I can't comment on how smart you are, but I can see that you are a good man, Cade Preston."

I just look at her. "I have no idea why you would think that. I've done plenty of dark, fucked-up stuff that I'm not proud of."

"And why did you do them? For joy? For pleasure? Entertainment, perhaps? A good man will do necessary, evil things in order to help others, but he will not revel in his actions. A bad man will do the same necessary, evil things, and his heart will sing as he holds the knife, or pulls the trigger. See what I'm saying?"

It's not as simple as that, it never is, but I smile at her anyway. "Open your legs, Natalia."

"Pardon?"

"You heard me. Open your legs."

"Why?"

"Because I asked you to."

"Cade, we can't. What if the camera is—"

"Under the table? You think it's under the table?"

She shakes her head. "No, of course not."

"Then it won't be able to see what I'm going to do, will it?" I reason.

A second passes. Another three. Natalia is as still as stone while she thinks about my logic, and then she glances around, taking one last look, trying to find the camera she knows to be in here. She's going to tell me no. She's going to tell me not to be so fucking stupid. But then she opens her legs, sliding down in her seat, so that her knee finally does press up against my dick. I grunt, digging my fingers into her thigh. When I make eye contact with her, she looks a little startled.

"You're very hard, Mr. America."

I feign ignorance. "I am?" I still have my hand on her thigh. Moving my way upward, I don't stop until my fingers are brushing the bottom of her skirt. She gasps as I slide them underneath the material, up, up, up, until I'm as far as I can go. To an outsider, it must look like I'm simply leaning across the table. Natalia's the only one that knows I'm brushing the tip of my middle finger up and down the soft, silky material of her panties.

"Do it," I whisper. "Open your legs all the way for me, Natalia. I need to make you come." A shiver runs through her—one I can plainly see. The bare skin on her arms breaks out in goose bumps, despite the heat of the library.

"It's a bad idea," she says breathlessly. "What if someone finds us?"

"Then they'll see that we're talking and hopefully leave us the fuck alone."

"*Cade.*" Her willpower is dissolving, though. I can feel the muscles in her thighs relaxing ever so slightly, every time I rub my finger over her clit through her panties.

"It'll be worth it. I want to make you lose your fucking mind," I whisper.

"I'm already losing my fucking mind." She closes her eyes, her breath catching in her throat. Slowly, her head begins to tip back.

"Stay with me. Look at me. You need to keep your eyes on me, Natalia. If someone does come in and you look like that, they're definitely going to know what's going on."

She rolls her head back around, opening her eyes, but they have a glazed over quality to them, filled with lust, and I don't think she's focusing on much. "God, I..." She trails off, and I can feel how wet she's getting through her underwear. Beyond wet. I know that when she finally gives in, allowing her legs to fall open, I'll be able to slide her panties to one side and feel the warm, slick heat of her all over my fingers, and it's going to drive me fucking crazy.

Applying a little more pressure, I rub my finger in a small circle, knowing exactly what she likes. Every woman is different, and Natalia prefers a firm touch. I know by the way her hips angle upward as I sweep my finger from left to right. I don't have to wait much longer for her to give me what I want. Her knees part, and I push forward, hooking my finger beneath her underwear, and then I'm swearing under my breath as I find out exactly how turned on she is.

"Fuck, Natalia. Tell me not to fuck you right here," I growl.

"I want you to," she whispers. "I need you inside me so badly. *Please*."

This is just her desire talking, though. We both know it's impossible for me to take what I want...to give her what she just told me she needs. "Grind against me," I command. "I want to feel your pussy on my fingers."

Her lips part, and her back arches as she angles her hips again, rocking her pelvis so that she's working with me to create a delicious friction between my hand and her clit.

"Shit," she hisses, trying to close her eyes again. I was raised in a household, where, for right or wrong, a woman does not curse. I've spent many years with women in the military and in the club, and I've heard plenty of them swear like sailors, language colorful enough to make the air turn blue, but when Natalia utters this exclamation, a thrill of excitement powers through me. Her accent makes it hotter somehow, and her choice of word makes it seem as though she's out of control. So hot. So intense. So fucking wild.

I want a repeat of our last encounter. I want to get her so wet, to free her from her inhibitions, and I want to be the one to claim her during that moment when the world falls away and nothing remains for her but her climax and the sound of her own heart slamming in her ears. Here, though, in this library, with its book stacks, and its deserted tables, and the tall, sweeping windows, overlooking Fernando's prize fucking garden? It would be all the hotter in here, where we have no lock on the door and there's a risk we might get caught.

This is a perilous thought. It's not fucking a girl without a rubber and hoping she doesn't get pregnant. Or that your dick doesn't fall off afterwards. The consequences of getting caught here, with my fingers inside Natalia Villalobos, are beyond any of that. It would be the difference between life and death. But what a way to fucking go...

She rocks against my hand, working her hips, and I have to stop myself from sliding down from my seat and disappearing underneath the table, to use my tongue on her. It would be too much to taste her right now. Way, way, *way* too much. I'd lose my shit, and that would be it. Natalia would be laid out, flat on her back, in less than a heartbeat, and I'd be thrusting my dick inside her harder than she could probably bear.

She'd pant. She'd beg. She'd moan. Most importantly, she would scream, and I just can't allow that to happen. She whimpers now, as I apply a little more pressure to her clit as I rub, and I give her a warning with my eyes.

"You can't do that," I tell her. "You've got to be a good girl. You've got to behave."

"Easy for you to say," she pants. "Would you be able to keep quiet if I had your dick in my mouth?"

I almost groan at the mere thought of it. She was so good the other night, letting me push myself all the way to the back of her throat. She's right; I wouldn't be able to keep quiet, either.

"Come closer to me." I shift around the table, sitting at the shorter end, and Natalia moves, too, drawing closer. "Lay your head on me. Bite down on my shoulder. Bite as hard as you need to. It'll help when I make you come."

"Oh, you think you're going to?" she asks, smiling wickedly.

"You're about three minutes away, beautiful. One hundred and eighty seconds away from total oblivion. Do you want it?"

She closes her eyes, turning her face into me, leaning her forehead against my shoulder. She seems embarrassed to even admit to such a thing.

"Natalia? *Do you want it?*"

"Yes," she whispers. "God, Cade. Please. I want it."

Yeah. That's what I thought. I roll her clit under my fingers a little faster, using the pads of my index and my middle finger now. I'm stimulating her, rubbing more of her, causing her to shudder against me. She does as I told her to, and she bites down on my shoulder, her breath coming out in jagged, tense blasts.

"God...three minutes is too long," she pants. "Please, Cade... Please, please..." She begs me over and over again. I could stretch this out, make it last longer and give myself more of a show. It's so fucking hot to see and hear her this turned on, her tits straining against the material of her shirt, her nipples obviously budded and swollen underneath her clothes. It would be far too cruel to do that to her, though. Not when she's this pent up and ready to explode.

"Okay, beautiful," I tell her. "Okay. I've got what you want. Shhh." Sitting forward, I roughly shove her legs even wider still underneath the table. Her skirt is up around her waist now, exposing her pussy, and it's the sexiest, hottest thing I have ever fucking seen. I have to finish this now, before it gets any further out of control. I pull her as far back into her seat as I can, and then I rub my fingers quickly from side to side, making sure I'm firm enough to make her claw at me, hands grabbing at my arm, her teeth cutting into my skin though the material of my shirt, but not hard enough to hurt her.

I've found the right rhythm and motion for her. Natalia is a ball of pent up energy as I drive her closer and closer toward the edge.

It's not long before her back is arching, her eyes screwing shut, and my fingers are suddenly soaking with her pleasure. She jolts every time I flick her clit, jumping and moaning, clearly very sensitive.

I am one proud motherfucker. I've made plenty of girls come with my hands, my mouth, my dick, and any other body part you'd care to mention, but this time is different. When Natalia opens her eyes, looking up at me, dazed, her lips bruised-looking and swollen from her desire, her cheeks flushed bright red, I'm so fucking pleased with myself. I'm elated that I've made her feel this way.

"I can't feel my legs," she whispers, grinning from ear to ear.

I run my hand up and down the smooth skin of her thigh, grinning back at her. "Well I can. And they feel pretty fucking amazing." Slowly, I raise my hand from underneath the table, and I slide my index finger into my mouth. Natalia watches me with a look of confusion on her face, until she suddenly realizes it's one of the fingers I've been fucking her with, and she looks mortified.

190

"Cade! Don't!" She tries to stop me from sucking her come from my fingers, but I take hold of her wrist restraining her with my other hand.

"I'm not apologizing for this," I tell her. "I'll never fucking apologize for wanting to taste your pussy all over my hands. It's the hottest thing ever." I move onto my middle finger, savoring the moment, savoring the way my dick is throbbing, aching so badly now that I have her on my tongue.

"You just wait, beautiful," I say. "You just fucking wait. It won't be long before we can enjoy each other's bodies without holding back. It won't be long before we can scream the fucking house down, I promise you that.

FIFTEEN
IN MOTION

The last thing I want to do right now is get ready for a party. I didn't bring smart clothes with me, and most of what I did bring was torn to shit by Harrison and his men. So a suit and tie? I highly doubt they have a tailor down on Orellana village, and I'm not all that great at producing designer clothes out of thin fucking air. I should have kept the suit I wore when I flew here from Mexico, but I didn't know I'd be needing it again, and carrying it around in a backpack would have fucked it up anyway.

I've made peace with the idea that I'm going to have to wear the casual clothes I've been wandering around the forest in for the past month, when I come back to my room and find a black garment bag laid out on my bed for me. I stand there and look at it for a while. I shouldn't be surprised that Fernando thought of this. He asked me to help Harrison with security for the event, so he wants me looking my best, no doubt. I'd rail against this, make a point of wearing my ripped jeans and stained t-shirt just to be an asshole, but I need to blend in. If my plans are going to come to fruition, I need to disappear in a crowd. The rich bastards who have flocked to the Villalobos estate from far and wide are going to notice a guy in fucked-up civvies way more than they'll notice another tall dude with designer stubble, in a designer suit, gliding around with a glass of champagne in his hand.

I open the garment bag, and the smell of freshly woven and cut fabric hits me. No hand-me-downs here; this is a brand new suit, and it's fucking beautiful. It's black as pitch, and the material is the finest money can buy. Shame it's going to be covered in blood by the time the night is over.

••••

Music floods the vast hallways and reception rooms of the Villalobos mansion, subtle notes resonating against delicate glass ornaments and cut crystal chandeliers, making them sing. There were so many "guests" at the house already, but as the night draws in the place grows busier and busier, people arriving by the carload. Ocho shuttles back and forth in the Patriot or the Humvee, driving down the mountain to collect more visitors, opening doors and escorting both men and women into the house. He's still wearing his headphones, the sound of Jurassic 5 thumping out of the tinny speakers loud enough that it can be heard over the chatter and bubble of conversation that fills the front foyer. I'm surprised Fernando hasn't told Ocho to make himself scarce. He cuts a fairly ragged figure in his sweat stained khaki shirt and faded gray combat pants, his boots battered and worn almost to the point of destruction, but Fernando has him running around all over the place in preparation for the party's commencement, apparently unfazed by his man's appearance.

I stand at the foot of the stairs, observing everyone, watching, committing the face of each new person to memory. I'm shocked by how normal everyone looks. How young and attractive. And the women are just point blank confusing to me. They seem kind-natured and soft spoken. In some cases, they're downright sweet and retiring. It makes no sense that they would come here all the way from another country (most of them are American or even European), knowing what kind of party this is. It makes my skin crawl.

The earpiece Fernando gave me when I came downstairs an hour ago has made me invisible. People take one look at me, see the coiled wire running from my ear down the back of my shirt, along with the small radio attached to my hip, and it's as though I suddenly don't exist. I'm a piece of the furniture, off limits and therefore of no interest. Great news for me. Harrison's fuming that I'm included as a part of his staff this evening. He made it clear I should stay the fuck away from him and just mind my own damned business when I asked him where he would like me, which is also good for me. If the guests aren't paying attention to me, and Harrison wants me to steer clear of him and his men, then this should be a fucking cakewalk. My plans should go off without a hitch, and boy are they spectacular fucking plans.

First: I need to get my gun back from Harrison. I spent a long time stewing on this, and then I realized that I *don't really* need to get my gun back from Harrison. I just need to procure *a* gun, it doesn't matter who it belongs to, and I already have my sights set on a prize. Art, one of the guys who helped hold me down in my room the first night I arrived at the estate has been positioned by the kitchen door, making sure people don't accidentally wander out of bounds into sections of the house they shouldn't be in. I have a score to settle with the motherfucker. I aim on making him hurt for the part he played in attacking me in my fucking sleep like a coward.

Once I have his gun, I can then implement the second stage of my plan: creating a diversion. I've already figured out that part; it's going to be too fucking easy, not to mention ironic, and I can't wait to see the look on Fernando's face when shit begins to go sideways. It's going to be goddamn perfect.

I haven't told Natalia what's going to happen. She needs to be just as surprised, if not a little panicked, just like everyone else. She knows to be ready, though, and she's carrying her serrated knife with her, just in case anyone gives her any trouble.

Waiters walk around with trays, overloaded with glasses of wine and tiny vol-au-vents, and everyone seems to be getting a little buzzed. It's not until almost eight when Fernando signals to one of the waiters, who then proceeds to sound a small, polished copper gong that sits on a tiny table by the foot of the stairs. A silence falls over the crowd, and they all look up expectantly, awaiting what comes next.

Limping slightly from the hammer blow Fernando dealt him the other night, Plato leads the group of men and women down the stairs, and a small sigh of anticipation runs through the crowd. Fernando's Servicio are all dressed in white, from head to toe. The men wear pristine white suits, complete with white shirts and white ties, their hair either shaved close to their heads or slicked back with styling products. The women are all in white dresses or short white skirts, with revealing, low cut tops, their cleavages spilling over the tops of the material. Their makeup is immaculate, not a hair out of place. Strangely, they all look very calm. Flat, even. Their eyes are a little glassy as they follow each other down the stairs toward the awaiting crowd, and I get the sneaking suspicion that they're all dosed and high as fuck right now. Seems like something Fernando would do—have his workforce drugged to be compliant and docile.

I curl my hands into fists, growling under my breath. Next to me, a tall guy leans against the wall with a dark-haired woman on his arm, both of them scanning over the Servicio, whispering to each other when they see someone they like.

Him: *"The woman with the wavy blonde hair. Her tits are amazing."*

Her: *"Oh god, yes. Her lips are to die for. I can't wait to see your cock in her mouth."*

Him: *"Fuck. This is crazy. I'm already hard."*

Her: *"What about her? The girl with the white ribbon around her neck? Her ass is incredible. Picture me between her legs, eating her pussy, baby. Would you like that?"*

Him: (Groaning) *"Shit. I want to see that right now. Give me your hand. You have to see what this is doing to me."*

The woman smiles seductively, holding out her hand. The guy takes it and casually places it over his cock, squeezing so she can feel how hard he is. I have to look away.

Her: Baby…What about the guy at the front? He's very handsome, don't you think? Would you like to watch him fuck me? Would you like to be in my ass while he is fucking my pussy?

Him: Is he the one you want, my love?

Of course, they're talking about Plato. He's almost a head taller than everyone else. And I'm a dude, but I'm not fucking blind. I can see that he's a handsome guy. Why else would Fernando have gone to the trouble of snatching him otherwise?

Plato's gaze slips over me like he doesn't even see me when he walks by. He's holding hands with a slim dark-haired woman I haven't seen before, and the two of them together, so perfectly manicured and turned out, look like Ken and Barbie dolls come to life.

"Welcome everyone!" A cry goes up from the other side of the foyer, and then Fernando is standing on a chair, tapping a fork against the side of his champagne glass. "Welcome, welcome. I am so glad you all could make it to this celebration at such short notice."

I hadn't even thought about that. Fernando announced the party three days ago, and all of these people have somehow managed to get here in time. These are the top one percent, though, the richest of the rich. They don't have jobs to attend, and it's unlikely they have families to care for, either. They probably all have private jets they can fuel up and fly off in whenever the fuck they want.

"I am pleased to see some familiar faces here this evening. I'm equally as pleased to be meeting many of you for the very first time. For those of you who are new to my household, please note, you are welcome to participate in any kind of sexual activity with my friends in white. All that I ask is that you are respectful and make sure you are not jumping the line ahead of another of my guests. We are all gentlemen and gentlewomen here at the Villalobos estate, and my friends are happy to accommodate all of you. They will be taking regular showers as the night progresses in order to maintain the height of cleanliness. All of the women in white are on birth control, so please feel free to ejaculate where you wish. Similarly, all of the men in white have had surgical procedures to ensure they are not capable of fathering children. If you would like for them to complete inside you, all you have to do is ask."

I feel like I have razor blades underneath my fucking skin. He has to be fucking joking. He's not only doping the Servicio, but he's got the women on birth control? I suppose they're no good to him if they get knocked up. And the guys have all had vasectomies? I'm itching to lose my shit. I've never been so furious in my entire life. This, from the man who happily discards dead bodies in open graves for the animals to pick over, though. Should I have expected anything more? Bile rises up the back of my throat, leaving a sour, acidic, bitter taste in my mouth.

This will all be over soon.

This will all be over soon.

This will all be over soon.

I have to repeat it over and over in my head, otherwise I'm not going to be able to keep a lid on my temper. I try to tune out, then. Try not to see anything, or hear anything, but it's pretty impossible. The crowd is swarming around the bottom of the stairs now that the Servicio have arrived, and it's like a fucking meat market, people dressed in black, arguing passive aggressively over the people dressed in white. Plato smiles blandly as three people try to talk to him at once, trying to get him to go with them. The girl he was holding hands with laughs strangely as a guy with full sleeve tattoos and a nose piercing picks her up and throws her over his shoulder, like she's a sack of potatoes. Three other men join him as he carries her through one of the reception room doorways off of the foyer.

There's no screaming. There are no objections. There is only mild indifference, and the empty, vacant eyes of the Servicio as they are led off one by one by excited, assertive guests.

The couple who were discussing who they would like to play with a moment ago has secured the woman they were admiring, and the guy is making out with her, jamming his tongue into her mouth, cupping the back of her head in his hand as his partner in crime helps herself to a ridiculous amount of cocaine from a shiny metal bowl being held by one of the regular servants. She must deal about ten thousand dollars' worth of blow out onto a large, flat mirrored tray. The servant hands her two metallic looking straws, bows, and then he walks away, handing someone else a similar mirrored tray, and similar metal straws.

To my right, two men are caressing and stroking another of the women in white. One licks and bites at her neck, while the other undoes the ties at her shoulders that are keeping her dress up, folding down the material to expose her breasts. Both of her nipples are pierced, which seems to excite the guy undressing her. He undoes the top button of his shirt, and then ducks down, taking one of her pink, peaked nipples into his mouth, running his tongue around her areola while kneading and squeezing her other breast.

In front of me, through the ever-shifting sea of people milling around, simply talking, I can see a guy sitting on one of the plush white couches, with a woman on her knees, blowing him while another guy watches. He has his dick in his hand, and he's slowly stroking it up and down. None of them are part of the Servicio this time. They are all willing participants in what they're doing. The girl on her knees blowing the first guy pauses in her attentions, grinning up at the guy. She takes his hand, and slowly, cautiously moves it so that he's touching the other guy's cock. I can read this moment like a book. The guys know each other. Maybe they're friends. This is the first time either one of them has had any interaction with another guy, and neither one of them knows how the fuck to react. The girl strokes one of the guy's faces, and then the other, guiding them together so that their mouths meet in front of her.

They don't kiss at first. They both freeze, chests rising and falling, but slowly they begin to come to life. The girl sits back on her heels as the two men begin to tentatively make out. It's not long before the first guy is running his hand up and down the other guy's hard cock, and his friend is rocking his hips upward, thrusting into his hand.

The scene is like something from Dante's Inferno. People are exposed everywhere, men and women alike. As the minutes pass by, barely anyone is wearing any clothes and it's not so easy to pick out the Servicio from the guests. Only when they open their eyes can I tell them apart.

I see Plato through an open doorway, leading through to what looks like a Bedouin tent—there are white silks hanging from the ceiling, and huge, white satin cushions scattered all over the floor—and a group of people are lounging around, watching him. His hands are all over a naked woman, who appears to be a guest. He touches her everywhere, his fingers teasing lightly over her breasts, her stomach, down her sides, between her legs. She's gripped in ecstasy, though Plato doesn't seem to be sharing her enjoyment. His dick is rigid, rubbing up against her pussy as he leans up, stroking the woman's body. I doubt his cock is that way because he's into what he's doing. The cocktail in his system must be considerable—he's definitely been dosed with Viagra, heroin, and god knows what else. Once again our eyes meet across the bustling space, and he doesn't react. It's as though he's looking right through me.

"Dios mio," someone mutters. "This girl, she is stunning. We should have her, my love." I glance around, trying to see who spoke, but the crush of Fernando's guests is pure chaos. I see who they're talking about, though: Natalia is walking hesitantly down the staircase, her hands pressed flat against her sides, and she looks like she wants to about-face and run back to her room. She's so incredibly beautiful. Instead of being dressed in white or black, she's wearing a sheer green silk dress that hits the floor, cut low so that her breasts are almost on display. It's backless, and hugs her slender figure, accentuating her curves. Her hair has been curled and shimmers as she moves, caramel shot through with spun gold. Her lips are a shock of crimson, complimenting the tan of her skin perfectly. She is the only splash of color in a monochrome world, and she is breathtaking. Men stop what they're doing as she descends the stairs. Women, too. Her arrival is enough to bring the party to a screeching halt.

"My beautiful daughter, everybody," Fernando says loudly, making sure everyone hears him. "Natalia, come and stand with me, child. I have someone I would like you to meet."

Her eyes flicker to me as she passes me by, and I see how uncomfortable she is. I want to reach out and take her hand, to try and reassure her, but with so many people watching her it's just not possible. She crosses the room, weaving her way through the mass of bodies, until she reaches her father. Fernando laces an arm around her waist, turning back to talk to the tall, slightly overweight man beside him.

I have had enough. Tolerating this bullshit before was difficult, but now that Natalia is here, it's just unbearable. I have to act, and *now*. Scanning the room, I search for Harrison. He's by the front door, talking to a beautiful red headed woman who just so happens to be naked. With his back turned, this is the perfect opportunity for me to slip away. Quickly, before anyone can notice, I head for the kitchen entrance, and toward my target. I place my hand to my ear, making a show of frowning as I pretend to listen to something in the earpiece. When I arrive in front of Art, Harrison's guard, I tap the device, shrugging at him.

"Fuck. Harrison's super pissed at you, man. Damn, I wouldn't want to be in your shoes right now."

His eyes grow wide. "Why? I'm doing what he asked me to do."

"He's been trying to get you on the radio for the last ten minutes. Someone's snooping around near Fernando's office. He wants you to go check it out, make sure it's nothing we should be worried about. Says he's going to report you to Fernando if you don't get a handle on the situation right now."

Art looks panicked. "Shit. I swear no one's passed through this way. I've been here the whole time."

"I'm only telling you what he said, man. Don't shoot the messenger."

"My headset must be broken. Can I borrow yours for a second?"

This clown must have a really short fucking memory. He must have forgotten all about the night he busted down my bedroom door, and grabbed me when I was wearing nothing more than a towel. I give him a sickly-sweet smile, pushing the kitchen door open behind him.

"Yeah dude. In the kitchen, though. My radio's on the fritz as well. Can hardly hear a thing."

Art doesn't even look worried. He goes ahead of me, disappearing into the hallway that leads to the kitchen, and I'm filled with a sense of euphoria. A little premature, I'll admit, but it's about fucking time I let loose on these assholes. Now the time has come and the moment is upon me, I almost don't want it to end. The anticipation is addictive, but it's nothing to what I'm about to feel.

The hallway is deserted. It won't be for long, though. I grab the guy by the back of the collar, spinning him around, and I smash my fist into his face, sending him crashing to the ground. Blood splatters up the wall, and the guy yelps, surprise transforming his face. He scrambles, trying to get hold of his gun, but it's too fucking late because I already have it in my hand, and I'm ripping it from his belt.

"What the hell?" he yells. "You're insane!"

I can't count how many times I've been told this recently. Natalia's told me enough times to make me think it might actually be true. Whether I'm sane or not isn't something I have time to ponder right now, though. I spin the gun around in my hand and bring the butt down on Art's head, and his eyes roll back into their sockets. A weird, gurgling noise comes out of his mouth, and his body starts to shake. Ooops. Maybe I hit him too hard. Head wounds can easily kill, depending on where you land them. I didn't necessarily want the guy dead, per se, but I'm hardly going to hang around and make sure he doesn't swallow his own tongue or anything. He forfeited any right he might have to my sympathy the moment he decided a paycheck was more important to him than common human decency or morals.

I grab him by the ankles and drag him down the hallway, leaving a long streak of blood on the tiles behind us. Not very subtle, but screw it. The whole world is about to come crashing down around these motherfuckers. They're not going to be paying attention to a blood streak in a hallway. The kitchen is far from empty. A chef stands at the cook top, focusing on the pans in front of him, and three waiters and a sous chef stand to one side, talking. They look at me when I enter, their mouths falling open, though none of them say a word as I drag the unconscious guy into the room and drop his limp body onto the ground. Slowly, I raise my finger to my lips—*ssssshhh.*

I leave, running down the hallway, back toward the party. When I open the door, slipping back into the foyer, I'm calm and composed. There's blood on the cuff of my shirt, though no one will notice. Not with so many groups of people now writhing and grinding on top of each other. I keep my head down as I cross the room. I can hear Fernando talking somewhere loudly behind me, but I don't turn to find him. I move quickly and efficiently, taking the exit closest to the Bedouin tent room, where Plato is now balls deep inside the woman laid out on the floor. He watches me as I fast walk by the doorway, and then he is gone.

Fernando's office is easy to find. I've sat in there enough times to know how to get there with ease. Surprise, surprise, when I try the handle, the door is locked. There's a camera above the door, but I'm beyond caring about being seen at this point. I raise my leg and smash my foot into the wood, just below the lock, and the doorframe shatters, sending splinters of wood everywhere.

Inside the office, my goal is mounted to the wall above Fernando's desk: a small, innocuous looking button, black with a small white circle on it. How many times has Fernando hit that thing in his rage? How many times has he hit it out of sheer boredom? Too many fucking times. I cross the room, my heart hammering away in my chest like a pneumatic drill, and I slam my palm down on the button.

For one terrible second I expect nothing to happen, but then a wall of sound blasts through the house, deafening, rattling the window-panes in their frames. I've only heard the alarm once, when I was out in the forest with Natalia, and it was ear-splittingly loud then. Now, it feels as though the sound is alive, shaking the house with its bare hands, determined to raze it to the motherfucking ground.

This is not a practical alarm. It's designed to strike the fear of god into the inhabitants of the house, Fernando's Servicio, to warn them of what will happen if they step out of line. I'd say that it probably works.

I pick up a heavy cut glass ashtray sitting on the edge of Fernando's desk, and I use it to smash the button off the wall. I have no idea if you disable the alarm by hitting the button again, but better safe than sorry.

Then, I'm running.

I don't go back the way I've come. That way leads to too many people, and also to Harrison and his men. I race in the opposite direction, running as fast as I can until I reach the side entrance with the keypad Natalia led me to when we came down the mountain the other day. Thankfully I don't need a key code to get out. The door smashes into the wall as I rip it open, and the heavy steel vibrates, making a jarring, warped, popping sound. Behind me, I hear screaming.

Outside, the night air is cool and smells of smoke. I don't know what's burning, but the air is thick with the acrid twist of something on fire. I carry on running, skirting the perimeter of the house until I reach the patio, where Fernando's precious lawn begins. Hoards of people have spilled out of the house and are rushing about on the grass, mostly naked, trying to find their clothes or each other. Harrison is out there, too, squinting into the dark, presumably trying to figure out what the fuck is going on.

I stay hidden in the shadows. I need to find Fernando. If Harrison sees me now, he's gonna be right on top of me, fucking up my plans. Side stepping, I duck low, holding my breath, waiting.

A sound slices through the night air, sending a ripple of panic through the crowd on the front lawn—a single solitary howl. A number of people begin to rally, holding each other's hands, dashing back toward the house, as if they're running for cover—the Servicio. They may be out of their minds on black tar heroin, but they're conscious enough to recognize the low, blasting bass of the wolves' alarm sounding from multiple speakers mounted onto the outside of the house, and they're not sticking around to wait for the monsters to arrive.

Everyone is scattered, clueless, running into each other in their haste to escape the unknown threat.

Fernando's in front of the house, then, head shaking from side to side as he tries to comprehend what's happening. He looks furious, his brow pinched as he takes in the madness. "Please, everybody, be calm.

We will have this under control shortly. Head back inside."

Aside from the Servicio, who know better, no one else looks like they plan on heading back inside. It goes against their nature. They've been trained for as long as they can remember that an alarm as shocking and aggressive as this means evacuation. The smoke, wherever it's coming from, isn't helping matters as far as their panic levels are concerned. I'm sure they must think the house is on fire or something, which isn't going to persuade them back indoors any time soon.

I need to separate Fernando from Harrison and his men. I need to somehow get him on his own. I've been patient thus far, so I'm just going to have to be wait a little longer. In the forefront of my mind, as I'm crouched down in the dark, I'm freaking the fuck out. Where is Natalia? I don't see her outside anywhere. Would Fernando have left her on her own? If he had, would he have left her with someone surely? She's a capable woman, but I can't help myself. I'm worried about her.

The wolves howl again, and this time there are many voices joining the song. They are on their way. I shiver a little as I picture what's about to go down—the violence and the bloodshed that will be unavoidable once the animals arrive.

I don't feel bad. I've been pushed too far here, in this fucking evil place. I won't help Fernando's guests as they're mauled to death. I will step over the shredded remains of their bodies as I walk away. Not a scrap of guilt will plague me as I go.

It won't be long before it begins.

Overhead, somewhere on the second floor, a window breaks, sending shattered glass raining down to the ground. I can hear the tinkling, smashing sound as people scream. Looking back over my shoulder, I finally see the source of the smoke in the air: flames rushing out of one of the bedroom windows, angry red and orange tongues of light licking up the façade of the building. What remains of the curtain material billows out of the yawning window frame, being consumed by the roaring blaze.

"Fuck!" Harrison screams. "That's my room."

Fernando graces him with a disgusted look. "Just find Garrett. Do your job."

Harrison runs out into the dark, gun raised, talking into his earpiece. Apart from the fact that his bedroom is on fire, he must be feeling pretty vindicated right now. If Fernando had listened to him in the first place, I'd already be dead. I wouldn't be running around out here in the dark, ruining their party and generally making trouble for them.

Now that Fernando's on his own, I'm in a prime position to make my move. I get ready, preparing to race around the front of the house, take the steps three at a time and grab the motherfucker. But just as I'm about to go, I hear something that has me hugging the wall again, attempting to vanish into the darkness:

Jurassic 5.

I spin around, and there he is, Ocho, headphones blasting music louder than ever, and I don't have time to react. I've been so focused on Harrison and Fernando's whereabouts that I forgot about the weathered old mute man. He lifts his arm, and a jolt of ice-cold adrenalin slaps me hard. I'm expecting him to have a gun, for him to shoot me dead, but he doesn't. The object he's holding in his hand is much larger than that, and unmistakable in its shape—a garden shovel.

As he brings the flat blade if the shovel down, swinging it through the air, I kick myself. I should have really been more observant. I should have seen this coming.

••••

I don't know how long I'm out for. My head is throbbing as I crack my eyelids open, and the sound of people screaming fills my ears. The night sky overhead looks orange, great clouds of dirty gray smoke funnelling upwards, and I think I'm about to throw up. I am no longer by the side of the house. I'm laid out on a small patch of dirt, surrounded by trees, maybe only twenty feet away. I can see the grand white building in snatches through the forest, people running, the flash of fur and teeth as something lithe and limber runs by. God, my head is killing me. It hurts to fucking *blink*.

"You didn't need to hit him so hard," a voice whispers in the dark. "He probably won't be able to walk now."

My stomach rolls. I'm having fucking hallucinations. Ocho is looming over me like a paunchy, sour-faced statue, his face cast in highlight and shadow, making him look even sterner than normal. And next to him, my sister is pulling a knife out of a cracked leather sheath, turning the blade this way and that in the dim light. She looks down at me, shaking her head. There are dark circles under her eyes, and her blonde hair is dirty, knotted in a snarled tangle around her head. She looks like she's just gone five rounds in a cage fight.

"Ha!" I laugh, then wincing at the sharp bolt of pain that needles me in the head. "I thought the dead would look a little more glamorous in the afterlife."

Ocho makes a loud gurgling sound, stabbing a finger toward the forest, twisting his left hand around in a series of strange gestures that my dead sister seems to understand. "I know, I know," she hisses. "But he's completely out of it. Look at him."

Ocho does look down at me, and he doesn't seem too impressed. More gurgling, and more hand gestures follow. His headphones are looped around his neck, silenced, and I realize that this bizarre, out of body hallucination I'm having is the first time I've ever seen the man try to communicate with anyone. He makes a growling sound, pretending to gnash his teeth together. My sister shakes her head, sighing. "They're not going to attack us," she says. "Not when there are so many people out there to pick off."

Ocho grimaces, rolling his eyes. He glances down at me again, nudging me with the toe of his boot, then makes a gesture that I do understand; he extends his index finger and stabs it repeatedly toward the sky.

Up.

And not just up.

Get the fuck up. *Now.*

He digs his boot into my ribs again, and a blast of pain shoots through me, ricocheting around the inside of my head like a pinball. I try to sit up, but the ground beneath me pitches sideways, threatening to tip me right off the very surface of the earth.

"Wait, damn it. Give him a second to figure out what the fuck is going on," Laura whispers. She touches her hand to the side of my head, grimacing when her fingers come away bloody, and suddenly I'm not breathing. Not blinking. Not moving. Not able to make my brain function in any way whatsoever. My sister? My sister in front of me, dressed in a dirty black shirt and dirty black jeans, giving me the same look she always used to give me when we were fighting as children? What the *fuck*?

My lungs are screaming. I need to take a breath, but I'm too goddamn scared. If I move a single muscle, take my eyes off her for even a second, I fear she'll disappear. How is this happening? How the hell on earth can this possibly be real?

A weak, sad smile slowly spreads across Laura's face. She looks older than I remember. Tired. Different, in so many ways, and yet still...*her*. She takes hold of my hand and squeezes tightly.

"Hey, brother of mine."

I couldn't make a sound, even if I wanted to. I just stare at her, aware of how real and solid her hand feels in mine.

"I assume you came here for me," she asks, "and not because you wanted to attend one of Fernando Villalobos's top secret parties?"

"I—fuck, this can't be happening," I rasp. Reaching up with my free hand, I move my fingertips over her face, scanning her features, searching for some dissimilarity between this woman and my sister, trying to prove to myself that it can't possibly be her. But it is. It fucking *is*. "Natalia told me you were dead," I whisper. "I thought you were gone."

Laura's eyes are full of hurt. She looks like she's trying her best not to cry and doing a horrific job. She always did find it hard to hide her tears, even as an adult. "She couldn't know," she says. "She had to believe I was dead. Everyone had to. Ocho helped me escape."

I turn my head to look at the short, aging Ecuadorian man, immediately regretting the movement when my vision begins to swim. "*You?* How could *you*...?" Ocho is Fernando's right-hand man. He's been watching me since I showed up in Orellana, always there, loitering in the background, observing everything with those dark, unfathomable eyes of his. How can *he* have helped Laura escape?

Laura smiles up at the old man like he's an old friend. "Ocho's been hiding me in the forest for a long time, Cade. I told him about you, of course. When you showed up here, he brought me to the outskirts of the estate to show you to me. He said you were here to buy drugs, but I knew the truth. I've been waiting for you to leave the estate so I could come to you, but you've never been alone. Always with Natalia, or with Fernando."

I screw my eyes shut, trying to process all of this, but it feels like an uphill climb that I'm not cut out for just now.

"You think you can get to your feet?" she asks. "We have to move. It's only a matter of time before the wolves are finished with the guests. Once they're in a frenzy like this, they don't stop killing when their stomachs are full. They only stop once everyone is dead."

"I can't leave. I have to go back. Natalia's still inside."

"I know, but we're out of time. If we don't get down the mountain before Fernando has a chance to rally his men, then we're all dead."

Taking a deep, agonizing breath, I push myself up into a sitting position, bracing against the throbbing inside my skull. I'm numb everywhere else. I still can't believe it. She's alive. Laura is *alive*, and Ocho has been helping her. I have so many questions. Too many. If I start asking them now, I don't think I'll be able to stop, though. Getting to my feet is seriously fucking shitty. If I could, I'd lie down in the dirt for the foreseeable future, until everything quits spinning like a merry-go-round, but I can see the worry on Laura's face and her fear is all too real.

Once I'm upright, Ocho's grabbing at the sleeve of my suit jacket, trying to hurry me off, deeper into the forest. I jerk myself free, and then I'm taking hold of Laura, pulling her to me, crushing her in my arms. I remember the last time I cried. It was two days after Laura disappeared, when I realized that she wasn't coming back. When I realized that she was gone, and that someone had clearly taken her.

Now, holding her in my arms, I cry again. "Fuck, Laura. Seven years. *Seven fucking years.*" I want to tell her about the countries I visited, the people I've killed, the thousands and thousands of miles I've traveled while I've been looking for her, trying to bring her back home. Instead, all I can do is squeeze her tightly, stroking my hand over the back of her tousled hair.

"I know," she whispers. She's crying too, now, allowing her tears to spill; I can hear how choked up she is in her voice. "It feels like half a lifetime."

I don't want to let her go. I can't. Ocho doesn't appear to be willing to sit through our emotional family reunion, though. He yanks on my sleeve again, making yet another anxious gurgling noise. Laura releases me, sniffing.

"We have to leave now," she insists.

She's right. I came to find her, and here she is, found. I shouldn't risk another moment standing around on the side of this mountain where Fernando could capture us again any second. But when I think about slipping off in the dark and leaving, I know I just can't do it. I turn to Ocho, steeling myself for what I'm about to say. "Take her. Get her out of here. Look after her. I'll be right behind you guys, I promise."

Laura grabs my hand again, her grip almost painful. "Please, Cade. I—" She's about to beg me not to remain behind, but her eyes settle on mine and something hardens in them. A kind of resolve she never possessed back in Alabama. "No. You're right. No one should have to stay here against their will. Go and find her, Cade. Find her, and get her out."

SIXTEEN
REVELATION

I took a shit load of drugs in my youth, but I never took acid. I think this is probably what it feels like to trip balls, as I sneak back onto the estate. Nothing feels, looks, or smells real anymore. I'm trying to focus on the nightmare scene in front of me, but all I can think about is the fact that Laura wasn't buried in one of those mass graves. She wasn't buried at all. I have no idea how Ocho managed to convince not only Fernando that she was dead, but Natalia, too. However he did it, it obviously worked. If Fernando suspected for even one second she was alive, he would have turned over every stone, and chopped down every single tree in the forest in order to find her.

As I predicted, there are dozens of dead bodies on the lawn. I don't see their faces, don't recognize who they are. I hurry past them, my focus directed toward the house and the people who still remain inside. Fernando is nowhere to be seen. I enter through the open doorway, straining to hear or see anything, but the entire lower floor is choked with smoke, and the only sound to reach my ears is the crackling roar of the fire that's taken hold.

Where would she be? Not on the second floor. The fire must have started early on, before I hit the alarm, so it's unlikely she would have gone up there. Not when the smoke was obvious. So downstairs, then. Not Fernando's office. Not the kitchens. Not the—

It hits me all of a sudden. The library. Of *course.* She said that's where she used to go when she was little to escape her father. It makes sense that she would go there to hide from him now, when everything is disintegrating into madness. I cover my mouth with my arm as I run down the hallway, heading in the direction of the library at the other end of the house. Left. Right. I have no idea where the fuck I'm going. I know I'm heading north, though, and the library over-looked the northern most aspect of the lawn, so I have to be getting close. People rush by me in the hallway, nothing more than dark shapes headed in the opposite direction, out, toward the main entrance, choking and coughing as the smoke settles on their lungs. I ignore every single one of them as I continue to hunt.

"Natalia!" My shout is deadened as soon as it leaves my mouth. *"NATALIA!"*

Shit. Please let her be safe. Please *let her be safe.*

I open door after door, not finding what I'm looking for, only smoke and more smoke. I can't breathe. My eyes are stinging, running like crazy, and my lungs are on fire themselves. My body is telling me that I need to leave immediately, but I can't. I refuse. Until I find her, I will not leave this house. I should have told her what I was going to do, but really what good would it have done? I didn't plan on there being a fucking fire. I didn't know I was going to be running blind through the house, screaming her name, unable to find her.

I try three more doors.

Nothing.

And then, as I'm really beginning to lose my shit, I try to open a door and it won't budge. I throw my weight against it, and still it remains firmly closed. It's not locked, though. I can feel a little give before it jams, which means it's probably been blocked with something.

"Natalia?" I holler as loud as I can.

A muffled cry comes from the other side of the door. There's a scraping sound, and then the door opens. She's there, in that beautiful green dress, though it's ripped now, and she's tied her hair back into a ponytail, out of the way. A dark smudge of soot marks her cheek. She looks wild and panicked. She rushes me, throwing her arms around my neck. "I thought they'd killed you," she sobs. "I thought my father found you or something. I didn't know where you were."

"Shhh, it's okay, it's okay. I'm right here." She feels so small in my arms. So vulnerable. She would have found her way out if I hadn't come for her, I'm sure of it, she's capable of fending for herself, but damn. Knowing that I have her in my arms is the sweetest fucking relief. I kiss her temple, pressing my lips against her skin, and then I set her down. "Come on. There's no time." I sound like my sister, but it's the truth. Somehow, the fire is contained upstairs right now, but it won't be forever. And once the ceilings start to collapse...

I take her by the hand, dragging her out of the room.

"I thought I'd find you two together."

Ahead, hidden by the smoke, a figure stands, blocking the hallway. He's taller than Fernando. Broader than him, too.

Harrison.

He stalks forward, and the first thing I notice is the gun in his hand, which is pointed directly at my head.

"You're a piece of work," he snarls. "I knew you were full of shit. I fucking *knew* it."

I step in front of Natalia, holding up my own gun. "Get out of the way, Harrison."

"What the fuck, man? You seriously think *asking* me to move is gonna do the trick?"

"Actually, no." I lunge forward, ducking as I grab for his gun. Maybe he thought there'd be further preamble to this fight, but I'm not one to hang around. He seems surprised that I've just flown at him. He reacts quickly, but I've already got hold of his wrist, and I'm forcing his arm upward, so the gun is aimed at the ceiling.

Harrison lashes out with his free hand, striking me in the throat. For all the shit I've given him about being hired help instead of military, the bastard knows how to hit. It feels like my windpipe has been crushed. Pain blinds me for a second, but that's all it is...a second. I don't release his wrist. He's expecting me to back off, to let him go so I can recover myself, but this isn't my first time at the rodeo. I've had practice at this, and I'm pretty fucking good at it.

I headbutt him, smashing my forehead against the bridge of his nose—the strongest part of my head against the most sensitive part of his. I know I've broken bone when he yells out. He grits his teeth together, but he doesn't release his gun, either.

Natalia's somewhere behind us. I clench my hand into a fist, driving it into Harrison's ribs as hard as I can, trying to move him out of the way. I'm successful. He staggers to the right, his body slamming into the wall.

"Natalia, go! Wait outside for me!" I shout.

She hesitates, but not for long. She runs past me, and then she's enveloped in the thick gray-white smoke, vanishing like an apparition.

"You think he's going to let her live after this?" Harrison spits. "He's gonna fucking destroy her. He'll take whatever he wants from her. He'll make her beg for his forgiveness, then he'll dump her body off the closest cliff face. Not even the wolves will be allowed to have her after he's finished with her."

Harrison is right. Fernando's such a selfish guy; he probably would rather Natalia was dashed to pieces on the rocks rather than hand her over, even to his pets.

"You did this to her," Harrison says. "When he's done punishing her, and there's nothing left of her, you'll know that it was all your fault. You should have listened to him. You should have done as you were told!"

Such bullshit. I grab hold of him by the hair, yanking his head back so I can smash his face into the wall. The impact is so satisfying. The plaster crumbles, small cracks appearing like a spider web in the paintwork. Harrison sags a little, but it's only a moment before he's back up and swinging. I'm so fucking dizzy, my head swimming from the smoke inhalation, that my response time is delayed. He clips me on the jaw, and lights dance in my eyes. Again, he hits me—the stomach this time—and I double over, trying to recover myself. Oxygen is already thin on the ground right now. I don't need a slug to the gut to make breathing even harder.

"But you never know," Harrison says, leaning down to whisper into my ear. "Maybe I'll kill Fernando myself. Maybe I'll shoot the psycho in the back while he's distracted. Then I can have Natalia all to myself."

If Harrison wants to pour gasoline on this fire, he just made the right call. He shouldn't talk about her. He shouldn't have even *thought* such a thing. I gather what little strength I have left in my body and I right myself, drawing up to my full height. Harrison knows he's pushed the right button; he points his gun at me again, smiling like the asshole he is.

"You'll never best me, motherfucker. You keep throwing the fact that you were military and I was private security in my face, but it's precisely why I will survive this and you won't. All those rules and regulations. Always doing things by the book. *We* didn't have to adhere to any bullshit rules when I was in the desert. There ain't no Geneva Convention in this kind of war, my friend."

I can see it in his eyes. He's going to shoot me, and he's going to take great pleasure in watching me die. I don't plan on giving in that easily, though. His finger hovers over the trigger, twitching restlessly.

Any second now.

Any second...

Just as he moves into action, I drop to the ground, though. He fires, the loud snap and zip of the bullet rushing past my head. I roll onto my back, aiming my gun upward, and I fire. His shot missed me by a mile, whereas my shot hits home, driving deep into his shoulder. Harrison rocks sideways, his body hitting the wall, and his gun falls from his hand, landing on the floor at his feet. A stream of blood begins pumping down the front of his white shirt. The surprise on his face is classic; he really did believe that was going to be his defining moment of victory. Well, too bad so sad, motherfucker. Sorry to disappoint.

His shoulder wound won't kill him. He'll lose a lot of blood if he leaves it long enough, but he's not going to drop down dead immediately. He falls on me, strong hands clawing and pulling at me as he tries to overpower me. I'm done fucking around, though. Time for Harrison to learn a real lesson.

I plan on shooting him in the temple, but he knocks my gun away in the struggle. It goes skittering off into the smoke and darkness, and I have no idea where it ends up as we wrestle. Harrison's gun is down on the ground somewhere, but in the confusion of limbs and flying fists, it must get knocked away, too.

I can feel my body starting to lag. I need fresh air and I need it badly. The synapses in my brain are firing in slow motion, and every single cell in my body is screaming for oxygen. I don't give up, though. I can't. My arm hits something, sharp and hard. I scramble for it, closing my hand around...

...a handle.

A knife handle. I can't see what kind of knife it is, and to be honest I don't really care. So long as it has a sharp edge to it, it will suffice. Harrison's trying to get on top of me, to pin me to the ground so he can pummel the shit out of me, but I have other ideas. I drive the knife upward, slamming it into his torso, grinding the blade in between his ribs. This is a high damage zone. The lungs, the heart, the liver. The kidneys, depending on how big the blade is. I could hit any of these major internal organs, and it's the long goodnight for Harrison.

He goes still.

Blood bubbles from his lips, trickling out of his mouth as he releases a strange, relieved sounding sigh. "Fuck...you..." he whispers.

I lean toward him, shoving my face into his. "No, Harrison. Seriously. Fuck *you*." I twist the knife, yanking it around, feeling the sharpened edge of the metal scraping against his ribs. More blood spews from his mouth. He begins to shake, his eyes rolling back into his head. I shove him away from me, pushing him off me, and I get to my feet. Harrison lies in a sprawled-out mess on the floor, hands resting gingerly on either side of the knife, which is still sticking out of his body. I leave it in there, not because I pity him. Not because I regret what I've done. I leave it there because I know he'll bleed out if I remove it. He'll lose too much blood too quickly and die, and where is the justice in that?

I turn around, and I walk away. Harrison remains behind, choking on his own blood. The smoke will get him. If not, the fire or his injuries will. Either way, he is no longer my concern.

SEVENTEEN

CARNAGE

Outside, the place is laid to waste, bodies everywhere. The wolves are nowhere to be seen, though I can hear them yelping to one another excitedly in the distance. They won't need to eat for days now.

I scan the area, looking for Natalia. At first, I don't see her, but then there she is, hunkered down, hugging her knees on the ground by one of the parked Patriots in the driveway. She sees me and comes to life. "Thank god!" She runs, barrelling into me, throwing her arms around my neck, and I catch her, laughing under my breath.

"I'm okay," I tell her. "Are you?"

"I'm fine. It hurts to breathe, but I'll be okay."

She's right—it really *does* hurt to breathe. I wonder how many years being stuck inside the building, inhaling all of that shit has shaved off our lives. More than is fair. Less than I would have gladly traded to make sure she was safe.

"Did you see anyone else in there?" she asks.

"No. Not a soul." I know what she's thinking. *Fernando.* I haven't seen him since before Ocho knocked me out. I have no idea where the fucker is, and to be honest I don't want to know. We've taken too many risks. I hate the man, and he deserves to die, but waiting around here for him to show his face is a bad idea. It's time to get the fuck out of here.

"Where are the keys to this thing?" I nod to the Patriot.

"In the maintenance shed," Natalia tells me. "There's a lock box on the wall where they keep the keys to all of the vehicles."

"Show me."

She leads me to the maintenance shed. I've noticed the building before, a decent-sized barn-like thing with a corrugated metal roof, painted green, presumably so it blends in with the surrounding rainforest. Inside, the open space is packed with all of Fernando's gardening equipment: hedge clippers mounted on the walls; a wood chipper; three expensive looking John Deere lawn mowers; a small tractor, of all things, and a plethora of other random machines that are concealed in the dark. Along the back wall of the shed, a huge pile of chopped wood has been stacked; it almost reaches all the way to the ceiling.

Natalia beelines for a metal box on the wall, which appears to be locked. She steps up onto a block of wood, reaching on top of the box, though, finding the key to open it up, and then she's rifling through a multitude of labelled vehicle keys, searching for one in particular.

"It's not here."

"What about the key for the Humvee?"

"Yes." She selects the correct set and tosses them to me. "Ocho moved the Humvee, though. I don't know where he left it."

"All good. I know where it is." Or rather, Ocho knows where it is. Once I've found him and my sister, all four of us will be able to pile into the vehicle and burn it down the mountain. God knows where they are, though. I'm sure they've been watching the house. They've probably seen Natalia and me come in here.

We're about to leave the shed, when a loud metal clanging sound stops us dead. There, in the doorway, a figure stands in silhouette, just as Harrison did in the hallway outside the library. At first I think it's Ocho, come to find us, but then I notice how tall the figure is. And the hammer in his hands. Looks like I won't be leaving this mountain without fighting Fernando after all.

"Oh, god." Natalia sounds petrified. "He' going to kill you," she hisses.

"No, he's not." My gun is gone. I left that knife behind, stuck in Harrison's gut. I'm standing in a shed full of chainsaws and hedge trimmers, though. I think I'm going to be okay. Stooping down, I take hold of the closest object I can find: an axe. The handle is worn and smooth, obviously well used, and the edge glints in the darkness, wickedly sharp.

"You were a guest in my house," Fernando says darkly. "You betrayed my hospitality."

"Are we playing who's more pissed at who right now? Because guarantee I'll win that game." My voice sounds as cold and empty as Fernando's does. He takes a step forward, casting his eyes around the inside of the shed. He looks like he's searching for something—his men, maybe? Or an extra weapon?

"Why would you win, Kechu? I welcomed you with open arms here, when I was told to skin you alive and have you killed by so many people?"

"Does the name Laura Preston mean anything to you?"

Fernando frowns. "No, it does not."

"Well it should. You kidnapped her and kept her here against her will for years. *And she was my sister.*"

"I'm afraid I don't know what you're talking about," Fernando says, smiling. "The women that come here do so willing—"

"Daddy. *Don't.*" Natalia looks alarmed. "How can you lie so easily? None of the Servicio are here willingly."

Fernando shrugs. "Don't they enjoy the free drugs I give to them? The free food? The free bed? The free clothes?"

The man is fucking certifiable if he thinks he's doing those poor bastards a favor. Natalia grinds her teeth together, pinning her father in a furious glare. "None of it is free. None of them asked for it, or wants it. They want to go home to their families. They would never have come here voluntarily. I know the truth, I always have. There's no point trying to hide it from me anymore."

Fernando considers this. His expression is stormy, his eyes full of madness and anger. "All right. You are an adult now. Perhaps it's time you knew the ways of the world."

"I'm twenty-six years old! I've been an adult for a long time, Daddy. And this is *not* the way of the world. It's the way of your fucked-up, evil world, and I want no part in it."

"How do you think you would have survived without the money I make from my businesses here? Do you think you would have had such fine things if I were a fisherman, or a carpenter?"

"I don't care about fine things. I care about honor, and kindness. And I would gladly have starved to death before exploiting another human being for my own gain!" She's crying, a river of tears rolling down her cheeks. Her backbone is straight, though, her chin held high. She's finally facing him, and I am so damned proud. She needs this. No matter what happens next, even if we both die, she will die in the knowledge that she spoke her mind and stood up to him. Fernando doesn't seem to like his daughter's new attitude, however.

"You're an ungrateful, spoiled little bitch," he hisses. "I have given you everything, and you're tossing it away for what? A man? He is no good for you, Natalia. He is the dirt beneath your feet. *This* is why I must protect you. *This* is why I must prevent you from making mistakes."

"*You* are the dirt beneath my feet. *You* are the black taint that marks my soul! You're a murderer and a psychopath. You're going to hell for what you've done."

The prospect of hell doesn't seem to bother Fernando. Or the fact that his daughter has turned against him. He must have expected it at the end of the day; he must have known that eventually it would come to this. "Hell is of no concern to me," he says. "My only concern is you."

"Bullshit! You sold your soul for power."

Fernando steps forward, a look of pure fury in his eyes. "Don't you raise your voice to me, child. I will cut your tongue out of your head." This, given what he did to Ocho, is no threat. Natalia pales.

"You won't. This is it for you, Father. This is the night you die. Don't you see that?"

He jerks back, confusion on his face. "Why? Because my house is in ruins? My guests are all dead, or gone? Or..." His eyes flicker to me. "Do you propose this man will kill me?"

"Of course I'm going to kill you," I say wearily. "You're a grade A cunt. I'm actually really looking forward to it."

"And you think she will still love you if you murder her father? You think she won't see my death every time she looks into your eyes?"

"You don't know your daughter, Fernando. You don't know her at all."

I run at him. I'm not going to wait for him to make the first move. Fuck that. It takes all of a second for me to reach him, but it's a second that Fernando has time to prepare. I'm waiting for him to raise his hammer, but he doesn't. He reaches behind himself, and suddenly there's a gun in his hand.

I'm sure there's an old adage about this. Never bring a knife to a gunfight? Well, in this instance, the adage still holds up; an axe in a gunfight is just as useless. Fernando doesn't waste any more time. He fires the gun, and an explosion of sound rings around the inside of the shed. He misses me, but only just.

Natalia screams as he aims again. This time I'm so close that he can't miss. Still I heft the axe upward, swinging it over my head. He'll have to kill me with this bullet, otherwise I'll keep coming. Nothing but a headshot will prevent me from planting this honed slice of metal into his body.

The steel sings as it cuts through the air. Fernando leaps back, dodging the first cut. He shoots at the same time, and the bullet hits me in the shoulder. The impact nearly knocks me off my feet. It feels like a drop of molten lava has landed on my skin, and the liquid metal and rock is burning its way through me, tearing me apart from the inside out. It hurts like a motherfucker, but I know what to expect. This is not the first time I've been shot. I'm sure it won't be the last either. My left arm is going numb. Thankfully my right arm is still in perfect working order, though. I lift the axe, determined to finish this.

Fernando grins savagely, raising his eyebrows. "You're a brave man, Cade Preston. But I told you what I do to dogs who attack my family, did I not?" He shrugs almost apologetically. "I gave you Kechu's name. I suppose we both should have known how this story ends."

I brace to take the next shot, but it never comes. One second Fernando is standing there, right in front of me, and then the next a loud shout fills the air, and Fernando is off his feet, toppling to the ground. The gun goes off, a bright flash of light illuminating the inside of the shed, but the bullet lands in the rafters somewhere overhead.

And Plato... *Plato* is on top of Fernando, striking him over and over again. He's wearing his white suit pants and a pair of white, patent leather shoes, but it seems as though he didn't have time to find a shirt. His face is bloody, and he's sporting a black eye, but other than that he looks uninjured. He screams, his face a rictus of rage as he continues to hit Fernando with every ounce of strength he possesses. When I last saw him, he looked half out of his mind, his eyes glossed over and vacant, as he fucked a naked brunette. Now he is *completely* out of his mind. He's far from vacant, though. He attacks with the ferocity of one of Fernando's wolves, teeth bared, eyes flashing with hatred.

I want to help him, to lash out with the axe, but it's too fucking dangerous. They're both struggling so wildly that I could easily hit Plato instead of Fernando, and that would be disastrous. I can do nothing but watch as Plato beats the shit out of his master. With each strike he lands, I can see the victory in his eyes. He's been waiting to do this for years.

Fernando drops both the gun and his hammer as he tries to defend himself. This is a big mistake on his part. Plato snatches for one of the weapons—I'm sure he'll go for the gun, but instead he takes up the ball hammer, spinning it menacingly in front of Fernando's face.

"This is for Persephone," he growls. The hammer comes down, making contact with the side of Fernando's head, and a shower of blood explodes everywhere, so much of it that it looks like some kind of Hollywood special effect. He hits him again and again, and Fernando makes a sickening, voiceless cry each time. It reminds me of a French film I saw once, where a man had his head caved in with a fire extinguisher. The camera didn't pan away. Not even when the guy's head cracked open, and pieces of skull and brains were flying everywhere. Unlike that camera, I could easily look away now, but I don't. I watch with grim satisfaction as Fernando's face is reduced to a bloody, meaty pulp.

It's all over for the Villalobos cartel boss. It will be any second, anyway. But then out of nowhere Fernando's rallying, thrusting his hips up and unseating Plato, who falls sideways onto his back. It all happens so quickly. Fernando leaps on him, fingernails scratching at his face as he tries to claw Plato's eyes out.

I race forward, grabbing hold of Fernando, restraining him. He's fighting with the strength of a man possessed, though. He's hard to keep hold of. I stagger backward, and I am lost in the moment. The shed fades away. There is only the adrenalin firing through my veins, and my heart beating like a piston.

A loud, whirring, grinding noise cuts through the madness, and then Plato is in front of me, grabbing hold of Fernando by his shirt.

"You can't kill me," he howls. "I am the head of this family. I am your master!"

Plato spits in his face. "Not anymore, motherfucker. Now, you're red dust in the wind." He drags him out of my arms, and then he's trying to lift the other man off the ground. Plato's strong, but not strong enough to heft a grown man directly over his head. I rush to his side, grabbing hold of Fernando's thrashing feet, and then we're lifting him, carrying him, throwing him…

…into the wood chipper.

This is the source of the loud whirring, grinding noise. Plato must have turned the thing on while I was grappling with Fernando. As Fernando's body feeds into the machine, the grinding noise takes on a new, urgent high-pitched whine.

This. This is the moment. A few days ago, I couldn't decide what the most violent, awful thing I'd ever seen was. But it's this. This is it.

Fernando screams as he is consumed by the machine. Blood and pieces of flesh shoot into the air as he disappears, inch by inch. Plato's prediction is proved right when the chipper begins to dispense with Fernando's body parts out of the chute at the other end, sending gusts of red mist and blood cascading into the air.

"*Holy...fucking...shit.*" This is a vision I'll never be able to forget. *Ever.* I turn away as the machine draws close to finishing its task. Fernando has stopped screaming—he died a while ago—so there's no point in seeing him fully consumed. Natalia is standing with her back against the wall, her eyes unfocused, her mouth hanging open. She's covered in blood, soaked in the stuff, and her hair is hanging loose down past her shoulders again.

She's in shock. She must be. No matter how much she hated him and wanted him to die, seeing her father being fed into a fucking wood chipper is still going to fuck up her head beyond belief. It's fucked up mine, and I know the bastard deserved it.

I take her into my arms, holding her close, stroking my hand up and down her back. "I have you, baby," I tell her. "It's okay. He can't hurt you anymore. He can't hurt you ever again."

In the middle of the shed, Plato stands with his hands clenched into fists, staring at the wood chipper. He's frozen to the spot, his chest rising and falling like an injured animal.

"Hey, man. Are you okay?" He doesn't even seem to hear me. "Plato?"

Slowly, he turns around, the tension in his shoulders easing fractionally. He has that look to him now, that look I've seen on so many guys before: a shadow of darkness and pain lurking behind his eyes, that says he's done something so messed up and so dark that he'll never be the same again.

"Don't call me that," he says, looking me square in the eye. "I'm not Plato. My name is Freddie Arcane."

EIGHTEEN
THE ROAD OUT OF HELL

"**It can't be true. It *can't* be.**" **Natalia bursts into tears the** second she sees Laura. During the violence and chaos of the past hour, I haven't had chance to tell her about my sister. When Ocho and Laura walk out of the rainforest, cautiously creeping toward us, both Natalia and Plato look up disbelievingly. Plato sinks to the ground, simply unable to process what he's seeing. Natalia runs to Laura, and the two women cling to each other for dear life. They're both crying, sobbing, in fact, and neither one of them seems like they're planning on ever letting go. I have no idea what trauma Laura went through here at the estate, but I know Natalia helped her through it. Or she tried as best she could. Their friendship is an obvious, tangible thing.

Ocho hovers off to one side, clasping hold of his Walkman headphones in one hand, a rifle in the other. Plato studies him warily, looking like he's about to hurl himself at the man any moment.

"It's okay," Laura says. "He's one of us."

One of us. One of the broken. One of the wounded. Plato grunts, struggling to his feet. He approaches my sister, slowly taking both her and Natalia in his arms. They stand like that for a long time, while Ocho and I simply watch them.

An hour later, we're on the road. Ocho drives, while I sit beside him in the passenger seat of the Humvee, which he had stashed three hundred meters down the mountain, already waiting for us. None of us have a cell phone. God knows where the fuck mine went, lost at some point while we were all fighting for our lives. Ocho takes us to a small, run-down shack in the village as soon as we reach the foot of the mountain, and through a series of grunts and gestures manages to persuade the owner of the only landline in Orellana to let us use it.

"Hello?" Jamie's voice is on edge. He already knows it's me calling, and he's bracing for the worst.

"We're out," I say simply. "Any chance you might be able to organize a ride?"

"How many seats?"

I look at the faces of the stunned, exhausted, blood-covered people surrounding me, and I say, "Five."

We drive through the night, and into the next day. Around two in the afternoon, Laura insists that we stop off somewhere to buy medical supplies. She says I look like dog shit, and I can believe it. I *feel* like dog shit. I've lost a lot of blood. Just because I've taken bullets in the past doesn't mean the experience of being shot is any more pleasant. Natalia argues with an old man in a pharmacy just outside of a small settlement called La Frontera, The Border, aptly named considering it's proximity to the crossing into Peru.

The old guy in the pharmacy doesn't ask any questions as he inspects my shoulder. He says it's a through-and-through, that the bullet traveled straight out the other side of my body, and then he cleans the wound, stitching me up and handing over a couple of antibiotics. The wound is almost one hundred percent going to get infected, but I'll be able to receive more comprehensive medical treatment once I'm back in New Mexico. The painkillers the guy gives me are legit, and soon I feel like I'm fucking flying as Ocho drives us through an unmanned checkpoint into Peru.

Colombia would have been closer, but planes entering the States from Bogota or any other port out of there are monitored so rigorously, we would never make it back into the States. Jamie decided departing from a tiny airstrip in Peru would be safer, so we head south instead of north.

We're on the road for forty-eight hours. A heavy, tense silence settles over the car, no one really feeling the desire to discuss what we all just went through. Occasionally, I feel Natalia's cool touch on the back of my neck, and I can't help but wonder what the fuck is going on in her head. The life she knew is now over. Nothing can ever be the same again. Is she happy to be running from Ecuador, ducking off highways every time we see a cop car, sleeping in snatches whenever we can? Is she happy that Fernando's dead? I'm too fucked up on pain meds and pain itself to ask her right now, in front of others, where she might be too upset, worried or ashamed to admit otherwise.

We arrive at the tiny airfield Jamie picked out just as the sun is going down. It's not really even an airfield. It's a flight school, of all things, and the place looks like it's been closed for years. Full-blown trees are growing out of the cracked blacktop, and the control building looks like it's about to fall down. If it weren't for the single, pristine white single prop Cessna sitting at the far end of the runway, I'd think we'd come to the wrong place.

There's no one to stop us from driving out onto the blacktop. No one to ask us for passports, or confirm our visas. Ocho guns the Humvee's engine, and then we're pulling up alongside the small aircraft, and Carnie, one of the Widow Makers' recently promoted members, is hopping down out of the plane.

"Took you long enough, motherfucker," he says, punching my arm. I wince, trying to hide how painful the light tap is, but Carnie notices.

"Another war wound, man?"

"You could say that."

"Oh well. Chicks dig scars. And speaking of chicks..." His eyes are all over Laura, appraising her, devouring her hungrily from the ground up. Such a fucking asshole. I give him a warning glance so caustic it could strip paint.

"Don't even think about it, shithead. That's my sister."

Carnie's eyebrows hit his hairline. "No fucking way! You're Laura? You're *alive*?"

She nods.

Carnie can't stop looking between the two of us, shaking his head, grinning like he just won the lottery. "That is bad ass, man. *Bad. Ass.*"

NINETEEN

REUNION

Since the Cessna's such a small plane, we have to refuel in Mexico. Only Carnie gets out of the plane, though, and the airport officials don't ask questions. Pick the right town in Mexico, and a ten-thousand-dollar bribe can buy you anything.

Soon, we're flying over New Mexico. The wheels touch down, and the Cessna bounces once as Carnie aims the plane's nose directly toward the Widow Makers' compound in the distance. In the back of the plane, Laura's forehead is pressed up against the seatback in front of her, and she's white as a sheet. Anxious, by the looks of things.

Natalia seems less fragile. She hasn't slept at all. I feel her eyes on me, burning holes into the side of my head as I talk with Carnie, but I make a point of pretending that I don't notice. She needs time to figure out what she wants to do, and I think her intense study of me is a part of that problem solving. She has options open to her now. She's entered the States illegally, but that can be fixed. Jamie has enough dirt to bury a number of politicians in the state of New Mexico; a green card shouldn't be too hard to drum up once a few phone calls have been made. So she can either stay here in New Mexico, here with me, or she can go somewhere else, explore the rest of the country, see what there is to be seen. It's her call. I won't ask anything of her.

At the very back of the plane, Freddie buries his face in his hands, taking ragged, uneven, bottomless breaths. When he uncovers his face, sitting back in his chair, his eyes are bloodshot and his cheeks are bright red, his hands trembling like crazy.

"I can't believe it," he says. "I seriously can't fucking believe it. I never thought I'd step foot on American soil again. I thought for sure I was going to die on that godforsaken mountainside." He's wearing a t-shirt Carnie had in his backpack, plain white, now spackled with flecks of blood, and I get the feeling the poor bastard's spent a lot of time either naked or dressed in a full suit over the last three years. I can tell by the way he keeps running his fingers over the hem of the t-shirt that it's a novelty to him.

"What do *you* plan on doing now?" I ask him. He looks stunned at the very thought of having a say in the matter.

"I don't know. I hadn't gotten that far. I've been so focused on getting out that I never really considered what would come after that."

"Where are you from?" Carnie asks.

"Texas. Not far from the border of Mexico. I'm not going back there, though. No way."

There's a story there. Has to be. From the anger and the pain in his eyes, the idea of going back to his hometown fills Freddie with the same horror and panic as the idea of staying in Orellana probably would. There will be time for questions later, though. Right now, I just want to get Laura and Natalia into the Widow Makers compound. I won't feel that they're one hundred percent safe until those gates have closed behind us, and the outside world can no longer reach us.

Carnie navigates the plane toward the fenced-in structure ahead of us, and I can make out a line of people already waiting at the gate for us. I asked Carnie not to say anything to Jamie about Laura. My friend has spent just as long looking for her as I have, he has every right to know she's alive, but telling him over the radio just seemed wrong somehow. The plane stops a hundred feet from the compound—protocol in case there's trouble at the clubhouse, or equally any trouble on board the plane—and we begin to disembark.

A huge plume of dust kicks up in the air, spiralling up toward the sky as a masked rider burns toward us on a motorcycle. It's Jamie, of course. I know from the sound of his bike's engine. I also know it's him because he would never allow anyone else to ride out here. He's always the first to face any potential danger, before the other members of the club. That's why sending me alone without him to Ecuador was so damned hard for him.

Both Natalia and Freddie look worried, while Laura, leaning against me for support, looks a little apprehensive herself. "Is that—" she whispers.

"Yeah," I answer. "He's going to shit the bed."

"I can't believe it. A motorcycle club." She shakes her head. And then, "He's going to be mad at me," she says quietly.

"What? Why the hell would he be mad at you?" I hug her holding her to me, and I can feel her trembling.

"We fought the last time we saw each other. I was angry with him. I said things I shouldn't have."

"Do you really think he's been clinging onto a handful of angry words for the past seven years? God, you're crazy, girl. You're fucking *crazy*."

She clings to me, burying her face into my chest as Jamie gets closer. The grunt and snarl of his engine fills the air, drowning out the thrum of the plane's engine when he arrives. Suddenly all is quiet as both machines are powered down. Jamie hops off his motorcycle, ice blue eyes roving over our party, studying each person in turn, assessing the situation, until finally his gaze falls on me...and the woman in my arms.

"Cade?" he says. "*What...?*" He's confused, and I don't blame him. Fuck. I'm still confused, myself. It's a lot to take in, even though I was there to witness everything unfold myself. Jamie steps forward, and then stops again, raising his hands, threading his fingers into his hair, interlocking them behind his head. "What the *fuck?*" he whispers. "I thought..."

Laura hasn't turned to face him yet. She's still hiding in my shirt, but her identity must be obvious to my best friend, who has known my sister since before any of us could walk.

"What happened?" he asks me.

"It's a long, weird story," I reply. "I'll fill you in once we're inside." From the very brief conversation we had on the plane, I know that Ocho turned against Fernando when he cut out his tongue. That he has been like a protective father figure to my sister ever since he helped her fake her death at the Villalobos estate. I'll explain all of this to him and more. For the time being, Jamie just nods. He looks like he's in shock.

"Laura?"

She goes still in my arms.

"Laura, look at me," he says.

Slowly, she releases her death grip on my shirt and lifts her head. Her eyes are swimming with tears. I give her a quick squeeze before I let her go. "It's going to be okay. It's all going to be okay now. I promise."

She nods, giving me a weak smile. "I just feel like I'm in a dream."

She moves like her limbs are made of lead as she turns to face Jamie. His expression is a mixture of joy and concern as he takes in her appearance. Just like the rest of us, she's covered in blood and dirt. She's still Laura, though. She's still my blood.

"Hey," she says softly. "Good to see you."

Jamie swallows, looking from Laura to me, as if he doesn't quite know how to conduct himself in this unexpected, surprising situation. "Good to see me?" he says, repeating her words. "Are you fucking kidding me?" In a heartbeat he's striding toward her, throwing his arms around her, pulling her fiercely to his chest. "You have *no* idea," he says. "We turned the world upside down looking for you," he rasps.

"I'm sorry. I'm so sorry." Laura's crying, her shoulders shaking as she weeps. She must be running on fumes, but she somehow manages to stand upright as Jamie rubs his hand up and down her back, whispering soothingly to her.

"God, don't apologize," he tells her. "Do *not* fucking apologize. None of this is your fault."

"If I hadn't left the house that night, sulking like a fucking child, none of this would have ever happened."

"And if I hadn't given you cause to go running? There are too many ifs, Laura. You are *not* to blame."

She's heard this from me already, more than once, but I think she will believe it now. Only Jamie can relieve her of her absurd guilt. It's as though she visibly relaxes as he holds her, the weight of her remorse finally falling from her shoulders, and I know it: she's going to be okay. She's really going to be okay.

EPILOGUE

The Widow Makers have their fingers in many pies. In order to fund the work we've been doing to find Laura, alongside helping other victims of sex trafficking, we've had to become resourceful. We *do* run guns occasionally. We *do* transport weed every once in a while, though we don't sell it ourselves. And we also have a tattoo shop in New Mexico—the Dead Man's Ink Bar. Above the tattoo shop is an apartment I've been using as a base for a while now. Separate, away from the compound, I've always found I can think better here. Breathe better.

As I show Natalia into the apartment, I'm wondering what she's thinking. She's used to luxury. She's used to having people around her, twenty-four seven, to wait on her hand and foot. And now, she's going to be living in a two-bedroom apartment full of guy stuff. Old plastic tubs filled with my military gear. Toolboxes, grease-covered towels, and a small mountain of shoes discarded in a heap beside the front door. At least there aren't dirty plates and cooking utensils all over the place. She walks around the apartment, lifting up random items—a photo of Jamie and me out in the desert, arms slung around each other's shoulders; the scratched and scuffed silver pocket watch that belonged to my grandfather; my cut—Widow Makers Vice President, New Mexico emblazoned on the back.

I've never thought what another person might think of the place where I live. I'm barely here, really. I often end up sleeping at the clubhouse when shit is going down, so my bed remains unslept-in a lot of the time.

"It smells like you," Natalia says.

"Ha. Sorry."

She shakes her head. "You smell good, Cade. You *always* smell good. I like it."

"Well I guess that's okay then."

She smiles, her eyes curving into half crescents. "So what do I do here?" she asks matter of factly. "What is my role here, Cade? How do I fit into this life of yours, here in New Mexico?"

This is the conversation I've been dreading. "I don't know. I guess the first question we need to answer is, do you want to fit in here? Do you want to have a life in New Mexico?"

"Are *you* staying here?" She hangs my cut over the back of the sofa, turning to face me. Her expression is open, her eyes inquisitive and clear.

"Yes. I'm going to stay. My parents still live in Alabama, but my real family is here. Jamie. The club. I don't want to move on any time soon."

"Then yes, I do want to stay here, too. I want to be where you are, Cade. I want to be with you, wherever that is. Is that all right with you?"

I try not to smile too wide. I don't want her thinking I'm fucking soft in the head or something. "Yeah, Natalia. That's all right with me." It's more than all right. It's fucking perfect. It's exactly what I hoped she would decide. She smiles too, and for a moment we just watch each other—two grinning idiots, happy for the first time in a long time.

"You can always help out in the shop," I tell her. Her expression falters. "I mean, I know it's not the most glamorous work. Not the most mentally challenging. But the pay is decent, and it would mean you'd be close by all the time. I know booking in appointments and doing admin stuff probably sounds really fucking boring, but it's not too bad." From the look on her face, I think she's going to tell me to go fuck myself. But then she rushes me, throwing her arms around her neck.

"A job? A real job?" she asks.

"Haha, yeah a real job. You'd like that?"

She beams, planting a kiss on my mouth. "I'm going to love it! My father would never have let me leave the estate to get a job. *Never.*"

I kiss her on the side of her head, laughing under my breath. "There will be lots of things you can do around the compound, too, if you want that."

"I do. I am looking forward to staying here and being with you. But I'm also looking forward to building my own life. I want to figure out what I like and what I don't like. I want to experience so many new things. I want to go to a bar! Will you take me to a bar, Cade?"

She seems so excited that it seems cruel to burst her bubble by describing the dive establishments in town. They're certainly nothing to write home about—sticky floors, peanut husks and sports on the old school TVs mounted on the walls—but she will probably love them. "Of course I will, beautiful."

"Good." She crushes her tits up against my chest as she hugs me, and I'm sure she can feel the effect it has on me. My cock is getting harder by the second.

"What about Laura?" she asks, leaning back. My dick mourns the loss of her pressed up against my body, but that can wait. I'm going to fuck her all night long, and Natalia knows it. She keeps eyeing the door to the bedroom, like she already knows what's about to go down and she can't wait.

"Laura's going to stay, too," I tell her. I honestly had no idea what to expect from Laura. She was a high-powered lawyer before Fernando's men took her. She'd just been made partner at Dad's firm. She was making a healthy six-figure salary, and she was kicking ass, winning all of her cases. In my head, it seemed reasonable that she would want to go back to that, to resume her old life, pick up where she left off. I was surprised when she said that she couldn't. Didn't want that life anymore. Too much has happened to her. She's changed so much that she said she wouldn't even know how to insert herself back into her old life. Besides, she hasn't even told Mom and Dad she's alive and well yet. We're going to do that together later, and boy is there going to be fireworks. Dad's going to be pissed that I didn't take her straight home.

"She's going to be our on-site legal rep," I tell Natalia. "And, just like you, hopefully she can have a fresh start here, too."

"What about your friend? She was in love with him once. Are they going to be together now?"

I've thought about this. Once upon a time it would have made sense if my best friend and my sister ended up together. Now, it makes no sense at all. I shake my head, tracing my fingers down Natalia's cheek, studying the perfect symmetry of her face as I talk. "Jamie's heart belongs to someone else now. He doesn't belong with my sister. He never did. He belongs with Sophia. Laura's got a long way to go before she's ready to be with anybody, anyway. It's going to take a lot of time and work before she'll want that, I'm sure."

Natalia nods. "You're right. She's been through so much."

I don't think I'll ever know exactly how much Laura's been through. She refuses to talk about what happened to her at Fernando's estate, and I haven't been pushing her for information. Her nightmares are her own. If she needs to talk them out with anyone, I'll be the first person to listen. But until that time, I aim on being the best brother I can be. Whatever she needs from me, she's going to have.

"So," Natalia says. "Are you going to mind if we don't have a half-built motorcycle in the living room from here on out?"

"If it's a choice between you and the bike, then it's really no contest."

"I am happy to hear it." She tucks her hair back behind her ear with one hand and shoots me a seductive, very suggestive look. "Now all of that's out of the way, what are you waiting for, Mr. America? Don't you have any more of those wicked vices of yours you'd like to show me?"

I have plenty more. Countless deviancies and kinks that I think she's going to love. Her eyes glint, and I find myself thinking that perhaps she might have one or two of her own that she might like to show me. Or at least I hope she does.

I stoop down and pick her up in my arms, making her squeal. "If you insist," I growl, biting roughly at her neck. I'm about to show the new head of the House of Wolves what a real animal can do with his teeth.

FAQ WITH THE AUTHOR

1)   Why doesn't Vice feature more from the other characters in the Dead Man's Ink Series, or the Blood & Roses/Chaos & Ruin Series?

While Cade Preston's character has been featured heavily in both of the aforementioned series, I wanted to make sure new readers would be able to enjoy this story without having prior knowledge of the other books. Also, both Zeth and Sloane's, and Rebel and Sophia's storylines are very important to me. I didn't want to compromise or detract from the arcs of their adventures by continuing them as B-stories in Vice. Yes, there will be new books in both of the other series. I don't have confirmed dates or titles for those books, however both will be released in 2017.

2)   When Cade and Julio spoke in the beginning of Vice, Julio mentioned that his private escort, Alaska, was taken by the Villalobos family. Why was she never seen at the Villalobos estate?

Alaska is an intriguing character to me. I wanted to be able to tell her story separately, and as such I have avoided featuring her in this novel.

3)   Cade left his motorcycle in Mexico! How's he gonna get it back??

Sadly, he's not. In his mind, the loss of his new scrambler is a price worth paying to ensure both Natalia and his sister are safe. He's also VP of a motorcycle club, as well. He'll have another badass bike in no time.

4)   Is there going to be more from Cade and Natalia?

Yes! They will definitely either have cameo appearances in future books, or they will have their own stories.

5)   When is Michael getting his own book?

Definitely in 2017! I have no confirmed dates just yet, but please keep an eye on my website and my social media platforms, and I will make sure I post updates as and when I have them.

6)   What about Tribeca and Bleeker Street, the books after Hells Kitchen? When can we expect those?

Lili Saint Germain and I have been very busy bees over the past 12 months, so it's been tough to schedule a time when we're both free to complete these books. Fear not, though. We have both locked in time to complete the stories, and we'll be working on more Theo and Sal Barbieri madness in the new year. Rest assured, we haven't forgotten about the books, and we're SO excited to be working on them together soon.

7)   Why wasn't Vice cover-to-cover with sex??

Cade's story is more than just a physical attraction between him and Natalia. Cade's sister has been missing for an awfully long time, and I felt it would be very remiss of me to not make Laura his primary focus in the first part of Vice. Also, Cade and Natalia have just met, and insta-love is a pet peeve of mine. While my books are obviously always works of fiction, where unimaginably dangerous and thrilling things occur on every other page, I do think that romantic connections between characters have to be built and nurtured, not fabricated out of nothing. I thought it better to build a connection with them in the first instance, and then allow their physical relationship to develop.

8)   Wolves don't behave in the way you have described. What gives?

I love wolves. They are one of my favorite animals, and the complex pack relationships they share with one another are truly beautiful. Fernando's wolves are not wild, natural animals, however. He trained them to be vicious, cruel and unforgiving beasts with voracious appetites, and that's exactly how they remain in the novel. Thankfully, in real life, wolves are much more placid, inquisitive, calm creatures that only kill for sustenance and never really for sport.

CALLIE'S NEWSLETTER

As a token of her appreciation for reading and supporting her work, at the end of every month, Callie and her team will be hosting a HUGE giveaway with a mass of goodies up for grabs, including vouchers, e-readers, signed books, signed swag, author event tickets and exclusive paperback copies of stories no one else in the world will have access to!

All you need to do to automatically enter each month is be signed up to her newsletter, which you can do right here:
http://eepurl.com/IzhzL

The monthly giveaway is international. Prizes will be subject to change each month. First draw will be taking place on Nov 30 2015, and continue at the end of each month thereafter!!

ABOUT THE AUTHOR

Callie Hart is the international bestselling author of the Blood & Roses and Dead Man's Ink series.
If you are yet to dive into either series, book one, Deviant, is **FREE** right now!

If you want to know the second one of Callie's books goes live, all you need to do is sign up at: http://eepurl.com/IzhzL

In the meantime, Callie wants to hear from you!

Visit Callie's website:
http://calliehart.com

Find Callie on her Facebook Page:
http://www.facebook.com/calliehartauthor

or her Facebook Profile:
http://www.facebook.com/callie.hart.777

Blog:
http://calliehart.blogspot.com.au

Twitter:
http://www.twitter.com/_callie_hart

Goodreads:
http://www.goodreads.com/author/show/7771953.Callie_Hart

Sign up for her newsletter:
http://eepurl.com/IzhzL

TELL ME
YOUR FAVORITE BITS!

Don't forget! If you purchased **VICE** and enjoyed it, then please do stop over to your online retailer of choice and let me know which were your favorite parts!

Reading reviews is the highlight of any author's day.

Made in the USA
Middletown, DE
15 March 2017